Child of Sorrow

Child of Sorrow

Una Horne

PIATKUS

Copyright © 2003 by Una Horne

First published in Great Britain in 2003 by
Judy Piatkus (Publishers) Ltd of
5 Windmill Street, London W1T 2JA
email:info@piatkus.co.uk

The moral right of the author has been asserted

A catalogue record for this book is available from the British Library

ISBN 0 7499 0649 9

Set in Times by
Action Publishing Technology Ltd, Gloucester

Printed and bound in Great Britain by
Butler and Tanner, Frome, Somerset

To
Tot and Cilla

Prologue

1962

'They should never have got permission,' said Mrs Morrison and Edie Wright, in front of her at the store counter, nodded glumly. The noise outside the shop became louder so that both assistants and customers had to shout to make themselves heard. An enormous digging machine was rumbling past, on its way to the opencast mining site, halfway between Winton Colliery and Eden Hope Colliery. Flurries of dust came through the open door and an old miner, waiting to buy cigarettes, coughed.

'The Coal Board can do whatever it wants to do,' Jane, the girl behind the counter said. She went over to the cheese slicer and expertly cut half a pound of Cheddar and wrapped it.

'One and sixpence ha'penny, please,' she said. 'Anything else?'

'No thanks, pet,' said Edie and turned back to Joan Morrison. 'My Don's seen the plans, you know. He reckons they're going right up to Old Pit.'

Joan sighed. 'I hope not. It's a piece of history that place. They should leave it alone.'

The women nodded. All of them had played 'House' in the old village, in their imaginations the ruined houses becoming a proper row, like the ones in Winton Colliery. The lads had played Cowboys and Indians and lately,

1

British and Germans in and out of the buildings, pretending they were falling down because they'd been bombed. They'd had no thought for danger then. And now the Coal Board had the area fenced off with high banks of topsoil reinforcing the fences.

They'd said they would put it all back when they were finished and perhaps they would. At the moment the NCB was bent on winning the last ounce of coal from the seams once worked by underground miners by extracting it more efficiently from the surface. And they would put the old slag heaps in the hole too and the valley would be green again.

It was the following week when Big Geordie, the giant digger that pulled a dragline behind it over long stretches of ground going deeper and deeper into the earth as it created its own valley, came across an old gallery a couple of hundred feet down. There were wicker corves in one place, which disintegrated as the air got to them and an old shaft with broken ladders leading up to the surface.

'By heck, I wouldn't have liked to live in them days,' a burly worker said as they broke off to eat their bait. 'They had a bloody awful life them old pitmen. Fancy doing a shift underground and then having to climb up ladders to the top.'

The other men nodded and chewed on their sandwiches as they thought about it. The buzzer went and they got to their feet. Four more hours and they could go home to their dinners. A cold wind blew down the valley.

'That was one thing that was better,' Jack Morrison said. 'It was always warm in the pit.'

'Aye,' one replied. 'Sometimes too blooming warm.' He climbed into the driver's cabin of Big Geordie and started the engine.

The great machine worked on and on trundling along the bottom of the man-made valley, broadening it out. Until they uncovered something which made them all down tools for a day.

2

A tunnel, or gallery actually, following the line of the coal seam they were ripping from the earth had been found. In the tunnel there were the remains of men and, heartbreakingly, boys who could have been no more than eight or nine, together with pit ponies still attached to small waggons with bits of leather harness. Both ends of the gallery had been sealed with falls of stone and coal to a width of fifty or more yards.

'It's a mark of respect,' said Jack Morrison, facing the site manager in his portable cabin. He stared at Ben Atkinson across the desk. Ben shook his head.

'It happened a long time ago, man,' he protested. 'In those days there were no proper plans for the mines, let alone detailed maps. We wouldn't have exposed it on purpose, would we?'

'No, mebbe not. But we have. And now we have to do something about it,' said Jack.

'Well, we are doing something. The authorities have been notified, haven't they? There'll be an inquest. But there's nothing to stop us extending at the other side, is there?'

'I'm the union representative here and I say we'll stop work as a mark of respect,' said Jack, taking on a stubborn look.

'Well, I'll get on to the Area Office again, that's all I can do,' said the manager.

The site lay idle that day and the next. There was a report in the local paper.

Are these the remains of the men caught in the explosion in Jane Pit way back in the 1870s or was it 1880s? There is an old stone memorial, battered and worn in the deserted mining village that lies fairly near the site. Maybe the site should be covered in again, the dead left in peace. Or should the bones be removed

3

and buried in consecrated ground? Readers are invited to give their opinions on the matter.

'There's one person who ought to be asked,' Mr James, the Methodist minister wrote in. 'Merry Gallagher was born in one of the cottages of Old Pit and she insists it happened on the very day of the disaster. Of course she is very old and frail but she is in full possession of her faculties. I understand she lost her grandfather, father and brother in the disaster.'

'Mother, there's a bit about you in the paper today,' said Marian Gallagher. 'It's in connection with that curious story of the entombed miners that was in a few days ago. Would you like me to read it out to you?' Taking the answer for granted, Marian settled down on the chair beside her mother's and read out the minister's letter. 'What do you think of that?' she asked when she had finished. Sitting back she removed her spectacles and rubbed her nose where they had rested.

Merry said nothing for a moment and Marian felt a twinge of concern. Had she better call the doctor? After all, her mother was so very frail now and this finding of the entombed miners might have stirred her feelings too much. But suddenly Merry began to speak.

'Tell Mr James I want to speak to him,' she said. 'And he can bring that newfangled tape recorder with him. I had the whole story of the disaster from my gran. And what happened to the families that were left. I reckon it's time it was told.'

Chapter One

Vera Trent moved heavily from the table to the fire. As she carefully lifted the lid of the pan steam gushed out so that she had to jerk her face back out of range. The potatoes were boiling a little too fast, she thought, and pulled the pan back on to the bar a little, next to the kettle. Still holding the piece of sacking she used as a pan holder she sat down on the rocking chair and closed her eyes. Just for a minute, she told herself. She laid her hand across her belly, feeling the baby within her. Only one more month to go, she thought.

There was an ache in the bottom of her back and she leaned forward and rubbed at it. Catching sight of her feet she sighed. She couldn't get her boots on now – her feet were too swollen so she was wearing a pair of Lance's thick pit stockings to protect herself from the cold shooting up from the flagged floor.

She gazed around her, noting with pleasure the gleaming press and the floor, scrubbed only yesterday. Maybe she had worked too hard yesterday but she had been filled with energy and determined the house should be clean from top to bottom.

The pit hooter blew and she rose to her feet and picked up the pie she had ready on the table and opened the oven door to put it in. And then it happened. The whole house shook and the pie was jerked out of her hands by a force that terrified her. Losing her balance she fell heavily against the steel fender, catching her head a glancing blow from the poker that was jerked out of its stand.

Dazed, she lay on the clippie mat as pain shot through her belly.

'Lance!' she cried but of course Lance wasn't there, he hadn't come in yet. She felt the poker by her side and grasped it. If she could hit the iron fireback with it she could get help from May Morrison. If only she could stand up.

Suddenly there was a loud rumbling, the ground trembled again and the iron kettle that had been teetering on the bar fell onto the fender, spilling boiling water over her shoulder and splattering her face. Vera screamed once before she lost consciousness.

May Morrison ran out of the house into the back yard when the earth tremor came. She was standing, unsure what to do, when a rumbling, thundering crash shook the houses again. A few slates came sliding from the roof into the yard and she ran to the gate.

'What the hell's going on?' Albert, May's husband, who had been in bed as he had worked the fore shift, pushed the sash window up and stuck his head out of the window. A slate came down and narrowly missed him so he hastily drew back inside. And then Vera screamed and at that moment the pit hooter blew, a long continuous blast that made terror spring up in every person in the village. The children who had not been crying began now, sobbing and wailing.

'It's the pit,' said May, rather obviously for everyone was out of the houses now and they all knew what it was. 'My God, there's been an explosion.' She looked over her neighbour's gate; there was no sign of Vera yet her house had been shaken too and her man was down the pit. She ran up the yard and into the kitchen, followed by her daughter, Dora, and stood in horror at what she saw.

'What is it, Mam, what's wrong with Mrs Trent?'

May started. 'Never you mind! Go on and fetch old Ma Trent, will you? Tell her the babby's started.'

Half an hour earlier, Lance Trent had been working underground in the Low Main Seam putting the coal to the shaft bottom, driving the pony that was pulling the tub along a narrow railroad. He was desperate to get this last tub of coal to the shaft bottom before the buzzer signalling the end of the shift blew but all his efforts were frustrated by the pony.

'Howay now, Bonny, nearly finished,' he said trying to keep the irritation out of his voice. Ponies knew when they were winning. Bonnie was a small Shetland pony with intelligent eyes and he had been sluggish all through the shift. Now he wedged himself at an awkward bend in the tunnel and stood, four-square. Lance knew that the pony knew he couldn't get at him there, force him to move on. The ponies soon find out these places, he thought savagely.

'By, I could have done with old Peter,' said Lance to himself. Peter was his usual pony but he had had a stone fall on his shoulder, cutting it, so he was away recuperating. Bonny had a reputation among the miners he was too clever by half.

'Go on, lad,' Lance said again. 'I need the money, man.' He was forcing himself to keep his voice low, reassuring. 'Nearly home now.'

The buzzer sounded and suddenly Lance erupted with rage. He had not made enough money this fortnight to keep himself and Vera, let alone pay for the lying-in woman. What was more, the rest of the men on his cavil blamed him for not managing the pony better. Suddenly his frustration got the better of him and he kicked out at the only bit of pony he could reach – his steel toecap connected with a hock and the skin broke.

Bonny squealed and jumped causing the coal tub to overturn and hit a pit prop, one that should have been replaced days earlier but the gaffer had said the maintenance could be done at the weekend. The pit prop bent and broke, and then the next one to it and the one after that. Lance, crouching against the fallen tub heard a great rumbling and began to cough as coal and stone dust started to fall.

Bonny's bucking was ever wilder, his eyes rolling in terror, but Lance couldn't get to him even if he'd wanted to. He wouldn't have been able to calm him anyway so he tried to move backwards between the tramlines but the roof started to fall as more props broke. It was close to the junction with the main way and pit props were going down like ninepins. Bonny's screaming stopped abruptly as man and pony went down, both hit by great chunks of stone.

At the top of the shaft the engine house that worked the winding wheel bringing up the cage for both men and coal shuddered and strained, then the engine stopped altogether as below ground there was a great explosion. Coal dust had been disturbed, the air was thick with it and lurking firedamp – methane – had been ignited by a falling miner's lamp. Fire raged.

'Oh God, oh God,' whispered Tommy Trent, 'it couldn't be worse. Our poor Lance.'

'Do you think me dad is dead, Grandda?' asked Johnny. The group of miners clustered together. Johnny had just joined the men working the cavil, the part of the coal seam allocated to the group of marras. He had been looking forward to the pie his mother had promised she would bake.

When the noises came even Johnny knew exactly what they meant, as the roof caved in, cutting them off from the way out. They crouched together, heads down as stone dust swirled in the air, choking them.

'Grandda!' he croaked and Tommy managed to reach him and put an arm around him.

'They'll get us out, lad,' said Tommy, for Johnny was only just coming up twelve. But Tommy knew there was

8

next to no hope. Behind them the roadway had been cut off, so they couldn't even try for the old shaft. And already the air they were breathing was becoming foul.

'Howay, lass, see if you can push,' said Peggy Trent, though Vera's eyes were closed and her face blue white. Vera gave no sign of hearing. Indeed, May thought, she looked as though it was already too late for her. But the baby's head was crowned – it would surely come. Almost imperceptibly the girl lying on the clippie mat let out a tiny breath.

'If we could just get her up on the settee,' said May.

'Well, we cannot move her,' Peggy answered. 'Not 'til the bairn comes.' She slid her hand over Vera's belly, found the right place and kneaded. Vera moved slightly and the baby's head came out, the little face red and screwed up with effort. After that it was only minutes before Peggy had her out.

'It's a bit lass,' said May. 'By, she's a fighter an' all.' For the baby's fist waved in the air and from her open mouth came a loud wail of rage.

'Tak' her,' said Peggy, and May pulled a piece of worn blanket from the line over the fireplace and wrapped the child in it. Peggy was bending over Vera, looking in dismay as blood gushed suddenly and then stopped.

'I'll give you a hand getting her up,' said May as she laid the baby in the bottom drawer from the press, in lieu of a cradle.

'There's no hurry now,' said Peggy sadly. 'She's gone. Will you get a blanket to cover her, May? And can you stay for a bit? I have to go up to the pit yard to find out what's happening.'

'Eeh!' May looked stricken, for in the urgencies of the last half-hour the fact that something had happened at the pit had slipped her mind. How could that have happened? Just because her own Albert was safely off shift. 'You go on, Peggy, I'll attend to things,' she said. All of Peggy's menfolk were on shift. In spite of herself May couldn't help a profound though guilty thankfulness that it wasn't her own.

Peggy picked up her shawl from the back of the chair where she had dropped it when she came in and wrapped it round her thin shoulders. She could do nothing for Vera now. All her instincts were drawing her to the pithead.

Albert came in just after Peggy left, dressed in his pit clothes, his leather and tin hat on his head, his knee protectors strapped on.

'I didn't like to come in before,' he said. 'Oh no, the lass isn't dead, is she?'

'Aye, she is,' May replied. 'You can lift her onto the settee for me if you like.'

Albert picked up Vera, still with the blanket covering her and laid her as carefully as he could on the horsehair settee. Then he turned back to his wife.

'I have to go, lass,' he said. 'I might be needed at the pit.'

'Aye,' said May. 'Hadaway, lad, I know. Mind, be careful.'

'I will.'

After he'd gone, May filled an enamel bowl with the water left in the kettle, and some cold from the bucket in the pantry. Then she laid the baby on her knee and washed her. Peggy had tied off the cord with cotton thread, which May inspected and it seemed all right. She dressed the baby in one of the flannelette nightgowns she had found in the drawer and tied a rag on for a nappy. The baby didn't cry, just made sucking motions with her mouth. May mixed up a little sugar and water and tried to feed her but the baby would have nothing of it. In the end she carried her up the street to the yard of a woman who had birthed a baby only a few days before, Eliza Wearmouth. She didn't go in, for it would bring bad luck on the house to take a baby inside before it had been christened. Eliza's man was one of Albert's marras so he must have escaped the explosion too, which meant that Eliza would not be among the women waiting at the pithead.

By this time, the baby was screaming and Eliza came straight out. Thank God, thought May, she had been right.

'It's Vera's babby,' she said and told Eliza what had happened.

'Eeh, poor bairn,' said Eliza, and thought for a minute. 'I tell you what, you go back and I'll come, give her a bit tittie.' She banked the fire and wrapped her own sleeping infant, John Henry, in the corner of her shawl, then followed May down the street to the end house.

'Eeh, man!' she said when she saw Vera's body lying on the settee covered in a thin, old sheet. 'They've got their troubles in this house the day, haven't they?'

'They have that,' May agreed. 'Peggy's away up to the pit yard now, waiting to see what's happened. Aye, but I doubt it was a bad accident. My Albert's up there an' all. With the rescue workers I should think.'

'Aye, Big John an' all,' said Eliza. She bent over the press drawer and clucked in sympathy at the baby who was sniffling quietly by now. Eliza laid her own John Henry at the other end of the drawer and picked the new baby up. The baby nuzzled at her bare arm, making sucking noises. Eliza opened her blouse and offered her the breast and the baby clung to it. 'She seems strong enough, any road,' Eliza commented as she settled herself in the rocking chair by the fire. 'It's a good job I have plenty of milk for the both of them.'

'Aye. The first bit of luck in this house the day.'

May glanced over at the settee. 'I don't know whether to wash the lass or wait for the doctor. The authorities get funny these days, you know, if you do anything without a death certificate.'

'Daft, I call it,' said Eliza. 'Doctor Brown will have enough on his hands up at the pit. And it doesn't take a doctor to tell that one's gone, poor soul.' She lifted the baby and changed her to the other breast. 'I tell you what

11

though, you'd best let the fire die down. An' pull the settee as far away from the range as it'll go. It might be the night before he gets here.' She looked down at the baby in her arms. Sated now, she had let go of the nipple and was dropping off to sleep. Her little fists were bunched up tight as a prize fighter's and there was a furrow between her brows.

May came over and looked down at her, wiped a bubble of milk from the corner of her mouth. 'Mind,' she said softly, 'she looks like a fighter, an' she'll need to be an' all, poor motherless bairn. I reckon she'll have a hard row to hoe, this one.'

She took the baby from Eliza and laid her back in the makeshift cradle. Then she sat down in the chair opposite her friend. 'We'll have two minutes while we can,' she said. 'By, they're a long time at the pit. I doubt, I doubt.' What she doubted she didn't say.

Both women gazed into the dying fire as the burnt-out crust of it collapsed in a shower of ash, the red coals dying to grey.

Chapter Two

'Will you stand up for the babby at chapel?' asked Peggy. 'I'm going to call her Miranda after me own mother. Merry for short.'

'I'd love to be godmother,' replied Eliza. 'But what about May?'

'Aye well,' said Peggy, 'May and Albert are away at the weekend. He's got work at Thornley, over past Durham. I'm away to see the minister now.'

She wrapped Merry in the end of her shawl and held her close for the wind was biting as it was channelled down the row. Peggy had lost weight since the disaster, she just couldn't eat anyroad, she told May when she tried to persuade her to.

Eliza watched as Peggy went out of the door and took the black path along the line. There was no chapel at Jane Pit, as the colliery was too small for that, so Peggy had to go up through the fields and along the path to the road and down to Winton Colliery, a distance of two miles.

'Peggy looks blooming awful,' Eliza told Big John when she went round to see to his tea. 'She's that thin.'

'Well, what do you expect, woman?' asked John. 'She lost her man, her son and her grandson in the explosion, didn't she? And then to lose the bairn's mam an' all ...'

'Aye, I know, John,' Eliza replied. 'That babby's all she's got in the world. But if she doesn't look after herself

Merry'll have no one. Then it'll be the workhouse for the poor mite, won't it?'

'Merry? Is that what she's calling it? Bloody fancy names at a time like this an' all.'

'It's after her own mother,' said Eliza. 'I like it. Any road, I'm going to stand up for her. Sunday likely.'

'I expect so. If I get this job at East Howle we'll be leaving. They reckon there's some fine two-bedroomed houses an' all, with a proper staircase.'

Eliza stared out of the window at the house opposite. It was empty now for already the people were beginning to go looking for work elsewhere. Some of them had only stayed for the funeral service that had taken place the week before. Oh God, she thought, I hope the young lads didn't suffer. The men an' all, of course. There was no way of telling for they were entombed in the pit. The gaffer had explained there was no way they could be reached, what with the shaft being blocked off at the bottom and water seeping through. So the pit was abandoned, the shaft capped with a wooden cover nailed over it. The whole of the village, those who were left, that is, had watched as it was done.

Eliza turned round and faced Big John. 'I'm staying a few weeks more,' she said. 'I have to give that bairn a chance and it's too early for her to have to suck pap.'

'Eliza pet, your heart's too big for your own good,' said John. 'What do you think we're going to live on if we stay here? You have your own bairns to think about.' He didn't sound angry, just weary.

The whole community was weary and bitter. The company had just left them here. The gaffer didn't even care if they stayed in the houses or not. They were no good to him now, houses or men. There had been no compensation for the widows and orphans, no extra for the men left when the pit closed down. Though the union were fighting for that now it was too late for the folk of Jane Pit. Aye well, thought Big John, bitterness got a man nowhere.

'Just another week then?' asked Eliza. She had picked up

14

her own baby and now she began to change the clout on his bottom. She knew it was hopeless, they had to look after their own. And if she starved, her milk would go anyroad.

'We're moving on the morn,' she said to Peggy a couple of days later as she held little Merry to the breast. 'I'm that sorry, Peggy. How will you manage?'

'The Lord only knows,' said Peggy. She sat down heavily on the cracket that had belonged to Merry's father. Lance had been so proud of the stool he had made when he first started at the pit. But she couldn't think about Lance now, not now. She had the living to think of.

'Eeh, Peggy, I don't know what to say,' said Eliza. 'I've got fond of the little lass an' all.'

'You have to think of your own,' said Peggy. She roused herself, forced herself to be pleasant. 'There's one thing for sure, we're not going to the workhouse, not while I have breath in my body. I'll find work, never you think I won't. And at least we have a roof over our heads, me and the babby. I was just thinking, anyroad – I could take in washing couldn't I? With all the empty houses there's plenty of space to dry it here. No, no, I reckon I'll go round the houses, see what I can pick up.'

As soon as Eliza had gone Peggy slung the baby in her shawl and went down to the other end of the rows where Jim Hawthorne had a nanny goat. It was tethered along the track and she'd seen it often – why hadn't she thought of it before?

'You just caught me, missus,' Jim said. He was loading a handcart with his furniture, his young sons struggling to help. His wife sat at the door, looking bewildered, her baby in her arms. Poor Bessie Hawthorne had been a bit strange since the disaster when all of her five brothers had been killed.

'Where are we going, Jim?' she kept repeating, and when he patiently told her, 'but why, Jim?'

Peggy's heart dropped to her scuffed black boots. 'I was

15

hoping for goat's milk for the bairn,' she said. 'But if you're going—'

'I tell you what missus,' said Jim. 'You can have the old nanny goat. I doubt she'll have another kid and I can't trek her halfway across the county. She's nearly past it, man.'

'I can't pay for her,' said Peggy. 'I'm sorry, lad.'

'No, you tak' her, it's all right. At least I have the family left to me. You need the milk any road. I'm off over to the east of the county, and like I said, old Nannie wouldn't stand the journey. You'll soon get the hang of milking her. Howay now, I'll show you.' He took a pan from a box on the handcart and strolled over to the goat, Peggy following him with Merry.

'See now, she's as gentle as a baby hersel'. Just grab her dugs firmly and squeeze gently like this, you'll manage.'

Peggy laid the baby down on the grass and did as she was told. It took a few tries but in the end she had a satisfying half-full pan of warm, frothy milk. At the same time she had milk spattered all over her blouse and down her skirt but that was matterless, clothes would wash.

'I'll fetch her along to your end for you,' said Jim. 'I can spare a few minutes.'

'Eeh, thanks, Jim, I'll never forget you,' said Peggy.

'Getaway, it was nowt,' he declared and strode off with a wave of the hand.

Peggy looked about her. Already half the folk had gone, she thought sadly. Whoever would have thought it – a few short weeks ago? She went in and changed the baby's nappy and laid her in the drawer. The milk she took through to the pantry at the back of the house where it was cool. Outside she could hear the goat bleating so she went out and drew water in a bucket from the pump standing on the end of the rows. The agent had had the pump put in when the union had petitioned for one. After all it was a wet pit and the water, after percolating through the rocky ground, was pure and sweet as spring water.

Outside it was very quiet. A few more families had

moved off and some of the windows already looked dark and desolate without their dolly-dyed net curtains, the doorsteps not yellow-stoned for more than a week.

'I doubt I'll be on me own,' she said softly to herself. But where could she go? She put the bucket of water down where Nannie could reach it and watched as the animal drank. It was no good thinking like that, she thought. Anyroad, she wasn't on her own, was she? She had Merry and now she had the animal, Nannie. She'd best try to gather some fodder for the beast with winter coming on. She could start that tonight and then tomorrow she would go about outside the village and see if she could get any washing to do.

The afternoon was turning cooler, so she'd best make herself a bite of dinner, she reckoned. Not that she felt hungry but she had to keep her strength up for the sake of the babby. There were carrots and turnips in the garden, Tommy had made sure of that. And she had the heel end of a bit of cheese to flavour them. And maybe, if she got enough milk from Nannie she'd be able to make some cottage cheese with what Merry didn't want, and flavour it with some of the herbs that grew about the place. There were the gardens of the empty houses an' all, she thought. There might be some foraging there.

Peggy sighed, she couldn't fool herself. It was going to be a tight few years 'til the bairn got up a bit. But she couldn't afford to look further than the winter that was coming on.

Miles Gallagher, agent for a number of collieries in the area, happened to be looking out of the drawing-room window when Peggy, with the baby slung in her shawl from her shoulders, trudged up the drive. She hesitated for a moment and hoisted her bundle a little higher against her breast, then turned to go around the house to the back.

He knew that woman, he thought idly, and racked his brains to remember where he had seen her. Of course, it

17

was at the memorial service for those killed in the explosion at Jane Pit. She was the one who had turned her head and stared levelly at him as he took his place in the front row of the mean little chapel, alongside the manager, Jack Mackay. Jack had been a little uneasy about having the service only a fortnight after the disaster.

'Supposing they're not all dead yet?' he had asked. 'Supposing there's an air getting in to them?'

'Nonsense,' Miles had replied robustly. 'Of course they are all gone. An act of God it was.'

It was then he had felt the old woman's eyes on him; had turned and met the direct stare. A feisty one that, he had thought. But his conscience was clear, he had persuaded the owner to give the widows and orphans an average week's pay to help them get over the first few weeks. What more could anyone do? Mining was a business after all. And the enquiry, such as it was, had not put any blame at the door of the management.

The woman was walking back down the drive now, her head bent, whether over the child or in dejection it was difficult to see. The domestic staff had orders not to give charity to anybody – they couldn't start that or the house would be besieged by mendicants. Still ... on impulse, Miles rang for Polly, the parlour maid.

'Who was that woman with the child, Polly?' he asked when she answered the bell.

'Mrs Trent, sir,' said Polly. 'She was the one—'

'Yes, I know who she is,' said Miles. 'Was she begging?' The one who lost her husband, son and grandson in the accident, he thought.

'No, sir. She's a washerwoman now, sir,' said Polly. 'She wanted to know if we had any work for her.' She kept her voice neutral though she was full of sympathy for Peggy Trent. She had felt terrible when Cook had explained that they did their own washing.

'I'm good with fine linen, embroidery and such,' Peggy had said. 'I used to work in the bishop's laundry.'

18

'A long time ago though, Peggy,' Cook had said. 'Thirty years it must be.'

Peggy had nodded. 'Well, thanks anyway. I'd best be on me way,' she said and walked back round the house and down the drive.

'Mrs Trent used to work in the bishop's laundry,' Polly said now. 'She's good with fine things.'

'Thank you, that will be all,' said Miles dismissively. Polly bobbed a curtsey and went back to the kitchen. She'd tried, she told herself, done her best for the woman. In the old days, when Mrs Gallagher was still alive, things had been different. She always did her best for destitute folk. Mr Gallagher was harder.

Normally Miles would have forgotten all about the incident. After all, miners' widows were ten a penny, weren't they. But it had put him in mind of Jane Pit. He really ought to go there, and check that the joiners had done their job properly in capping the pit; see if there was anything else that could be salvaged and perhaps used elsewhere. He would ride, he decided. There was no proper road anyway and his hunter, Marcus, could do with the exercise.

That woman, Mrs Trent, was climbing over the stile that led from the fields to the footpath alongside the old waggon way. She climbed stiffly, awkward because she was carrying a baby in her shawl. He pulled Marcus up and waited impatiently for her to get out of his way. Marcus snorted and she looked alarmed for a moment and then, safely over the stile, she stood back. The baby cried suddenly, not loudly but a thin wail. Bittersweet memories rushed back at him – his son Thomas in Mary's arms on the day he was born. It had been a difficult and prolonged labour and Mary was exhausted. She had lain back against the pillows, her dark hair spread out around her. Her face had been as white as her nightgown and she hadn't lasted the night through.

'Come on, woman, get out of my way!' he barked and the old woman stumbled but managed to keep on her feet. Miles bent down and unfastened the gate by the stile and went through, turning off for Jane Pit, leaving Peggy gazing after him.

There was not much to salvage, he decided. Though there were slates on the roofs of the houses that could be used again, and doors. Most of the houses were empty but there were still one or two occupied. He would tell the colliery joiners to wait a week or two before stripping them – there was plenty of time, he thought. New rows would have to be built at Eden Hope where they were sinking a shaft to Busty seam, but it wouldn't be working for months yet. Still, they could take the roof slates from the engine house and rip out the iron staircase. Owners liked to see evidence of thrift.

He was mounting his horse to return home, watched by a group of urchins who stared up at him with large eyes and their thumbs deep in their mouths as though they would eat them altogether, when he saw the old woman, Peggy Trent. She came round the top of the rows and trudged down to the end house. She looked careworn; weary to death. The baby had stopped crying and was looking out at its bleak world with large, solemn eyes.

On impulse he trotted up to them.

'Come to the house tomorrow,' he said. 'There will be fine laundry for you to do.'

Now why did he do that? he asked himself as he trotted down the waggon way. He must be going soft. But after all, he hadn't been satisfied with his dress shirts the last time they had been laundered. Poor Mary used to do them herself when she was alive. No one else could do them as she had.

'Eeh, thank you, sir,' said Peggy and her dark eyes lit up as she smiled, and suddenly he realised she wasn't so old. Her hair had a white streak in it and there were lines at the corner of her eyes and mouth, but she stood upright with the baby in her arms and when she moved off she walked with a spring in her step that he hadn't detected earlier.

Miles watched for a moment then went on his way. She

20

was probably younger than he was, he reflected. These miners' wives looked old at forty, it must be the life they led. He forgot about Peggy as he turned his horse and trotted off along the path by the line. He would go to Winton Colliery, he decided. He might as well while he was near. Besides, he wanted a word with the manager there.

She had one customer, Peggy thought as she milked the goat that evening. She leaned her head into Nannie's rough hide squeezing rhythmically and the warm milk squirted into the pan. Thank God for it, she thought. It provided a lifeline until she managed to get more work. When she had finished she pegged the goat out on a fresh patch of weeds and grass and carried the milk into the house.

Merry was still asleep in her drawer, her thumb stuck firmly in her mouth. Peggy gazed at her for a moment. There was a furrow between the baby's eyebrows and she smoothed it with her forefinger. Poor little mite, she mused. Poor little orphan. Peggy prayed she would be spared long enough to raise her. God save her from the workhouse.

Moving away, she stirred the fire and put on a small shovelful of coal. Tomorrow she would have to find time to scour the pit heap for pieces. She broke up a crust of bread into a bowl and added a sprinkling of sugar. There was the end of a cinnamon stick in the pantry, she remembered, left over from last Christmas. She would grate a bit on the broily as a treat. Warming a little of the milk she poured it over the bread and the smell of cinnamon rose from it. Peggy closed her eyes for a moment, dwelling on the memories the aroma evoked.

Christmas last, when the family had been all around her, Tommy had brought in holly and ivy and they had garlanded the house. She had made a plum pudding and they had eaten it after the chicken she had got from the farmer up by Coundon in exchange for a day's turnip snagging. They had potatoes from the garden and sprouts, and a turnip from the farmer's field; Vera had confided that she had fallen for another baby after all this time.

Suddenly her memories were interrupted by the sound of the baby crying and Peggy was brought back to the present. Her face was wet, she realised, as she put the bowl of broily to keep warm on the hearth and went to attend to Vera's baby.

'Aye, well,' she told the child as she lifted her out of the drawer. 'You'll learn, pet. Crying gets you nowt in this life.' She wiped her eyes with the corner of her apron and brought a clean clout to change the baby's dripping nappy. Merry had stopped crying almost as though she understood her and was gazing at her grandmother with eyes that were already turning brown.

Peggy rocked her gently. 'Aye, you're a bonny bairn,' she sang softly and with the baby on one arm warmed more milk for her feed. Tomorrow she would have to go to a chemist's and see if she could get a rubber teat – she already had a medicine bottle that would do. She'd scoured it well under the pump, but for now she would have to spoon the milk into the baby's mouth.

Chapter Three

Peggy opened the door of the little house on the end of the row and the wind howled in. Snow had piled against the door in a solid block but now bits fell inside. She would have to dig a path to where she had Nannie stabled in an empty house opposite. Well, she might as well get started. Bringing the fire shovel from the back kitchen she set to shovelling snow, closing the door behind her as soon as she had enough room. Methodically she worked her way past the frozen pump to the house and finally was able to open the door.

Nannie was lying on the thin pile of straw she had managed to get the animal for bedding. She didn't move as Peggy went in. Bending, she felt the goat – she was cold, very cold but she was alive. Peggy brought some wisps of hay for her to eat and Nannie chomped on them weakly.

She had to face the fact that she could no longer feed the old goat, Peggy realised. Besides, Nannie had stopped giving milk. The blizzards that had raged for the last few days had cut off the tiny village from the world. In the old days there had been other people and they had helped each other. The boys and young men had made rough snow shoes and clambered up the hill to Coundon or along the line to Winton Colliery. But Peggy and Merry were on their own now, their last neighbours having gone in the autumn.

'To Auckland, Mrs Trent,' John Blackburn had told her. 'I've work at Toronto pit. The promise of a house soon an' all.' The Blackburns had been the last to go, so now all the houses were empty except for hers.

Well, thank goodness she had bought a stone of flour the last time she had earned two shillings for working as a washerwoman. And she had a little yeast growing in the pantry. She looked at Nannie now, and the old goat looked back at her with trusting eyes before nuzzling in her bedding straw, looking for bits she could eat.

Peggy went back into the house. Merry was sitting up on the bed Peggy had brought into the living room so they could take full advantage of the fire. Not that the fire was very big, she had to use the coal sparingly to spin it out. There was no picking on the slag heap in this weather. The heap was covered in hard snow and the coal beneath was frozen solid too.

'I'll get you a bite of breakfast, pet,' said Peggy. She went into the pantry and inspected the food shelf. There was a small quantity of oatmeal and a tin of condensed milk, already opened and half gone. No meat, no cheese. Of course she knew there wasn't, but still she stared at the shelves in the forlorn hope she had overlooked something. Peggy's shoulders sagged and for a moment she felt complete and utter despair. Dear God, the two of them could starve alone in this deserted village. Behind her, she could hear Merry talking and singing to herself as she played with her peg dolly.

Peggy came to a decision. She broke the ice in the water bucket and dipped a small pan in, taking enough water to make gruel for the child. She cooked it on the smoky fire and added condensed milk until it was at least sweet and more palatable. Then she put some on a plate and picked up Merry to feed her. The rest she put back on the hob to keep warm. She would have a spoonful or two herself and the rest would feed the baby later on.

When she had finished feeding the child she made a sort

of playpen on the clippie mat with the aid of chairs and the washing line. 'Sit there, petal,' she said. 'Be a good bairn now.' Merry played happily, banging a spoon on a pan. Thank the Lord she's a contented bairn, thought Peggy as she took the carving knife from the kitchen drawer and went outside.

Twenty minutes late and she was back. There was blood on her apron and in her hair and on her face but she had done it. Merry had fallen asleep, lying face downwards on the mat with her bottom stuck in the air. Gently, Peggy lifted her and laid her on the bed, careful not to get any blood on the baby. Then she took off her apron, boiled a pan of water and washed her face and hair.

Next door Nannie's carcase dripped blood from its gaping throat into a battered tin dish.

Miles Gallagher stood at the dining-room window and watched the snow as it came floating down onto the trees and bushes outside. He was restless; fed up with the weather which had kept him from his work for the last three days. He drained his coffee cup and turned to where Edna, the housemaid, was clearing the breakfast table.

'I'm going out,' he said. 'Tell Cook I won't be in to lunch.'

'Yes sir,' said Edna, glancing involuntarily at the snow through the window and looking surprised.

Miles was soon riding his horse down the drive and out on to the Durham road before taking a small farm road that lay in the lee of a stand of trees and so was sheltered. The farmer had been along here during the morning and some of the snow was trampled down making progress easier. As he went he looked down into the valley, seeing the pithead of Winton Colliery a hazy dark grey through the snow.

The chimney was smoking and a row of coal trucks were going along the waggon way. The work went on unaffected by the weather, he thought. On impulse he turned aside and urged his horse through a field gate and down in the lee of the hedge to Winton.

25

The fore shift were coming up, the wheel buzzing round as the cage disgorged miners into the yard, their eyes showing white on their black eyes. They shivered as the cold air hit them after the warm temperatures underground and hurried along not speaking for the main part in their rush to get home.

Miles went into the office where the manager sat with a roaring fire behind him. He got to his feet hastily.

'By, Mr Gallagher, I didn't expect to see you,' he said. 'Were you wanting anything in particular? I sent the figures up—'

'Morning to you, Watson,' Miles replied. 'Sit down, man, I've just called in for a minute.'

They discussed a few items of the business over cups of strong tea the manager's secretary kept hot on the hearth, but Miles soon rose to his feet for he couldn't leave Marcus too long in this weather, even though he was partially under cover in the overhang of the engine house.

On another impulse he took the path along by the waggon way that led along to Jane Pit, which was already being called Old Pit, thinking he might as well visit Eden Hope while he was about it. Near Winton the path was sparsely covered with snow as it was protected by the huge slag heap to one side, but as he approached Jane Pit Marcus had to stumble through huge drifts that stretched down from the exposed hillside, and on past the waggon way. In the end Miles had to dismount and lead the horse.

He almost turned round and went back but he was close to the deserted village by this time and the snow had begun to come down thick and fast. Marcus could do with a rest, he reckoned. There would be shelter in one of the houses, for the men had not yet begun to strip the roofs of slates, though some of the doors had been removed.

Grateful to get out of the weather, he led Marcus into what had once been a kitchen. It had an iron range that was now red with rust, while the flagged floor was wet and struck cold even through the stout leather of his boots.

'Godforsaken place,' he muttered. What on earth had possessed him to ride here anyway? In the back of his mind there had been the thought he could strike out up the field for the Coundon road but that was bloody stupid. And in any case, the ride hadn't settled the restlessness that bestirred him lately. He carried it with him.

Miles went to the doorway and watched the snow. He glanced back along the line – the trail he and the horse had made was almost obliterated; they would have to go soon. He'd just give Marcus a few more minutes. The horse had found a straggle of weed that had pushed its way up between the flags by the window and was nibbling delicately.

He glanced the other way to where the top of the old water pump stuck out of the snow, the tap with a long icicle hanging from it. It was all a bit eerie he thought, the empty houses with their blank windows looking out onto the snow, some of them with glass in them and some without.

Then he noticed the thin wisp of smoke coming from the end house on the opposite side. Someone was there, someone still living in the house. Even as he realised it, a baby's cry echoed above the soughing of the wind. Good God, how could anyone survive here?

Miles glanced back at Marcus. He wasn't going anywhere, he decided, there was nowhere for the horse to go. Pulling his collar up around his ears he set off, picking his way along the track, stumbling through snow that was almost to the top of his knee-high boots. As he approached the door he could hear a woman's voice singing.

'Clap your hands for daddy coming down the waggon way,
A pocket full of money and a cart load of hay.'

Looking through the window he could see the woman with a child on her knee and the little one was laughing now and clapping her hands to the old tune.

Peggy's hair hung down her back. It had taken all morning to dry for there was a fairly small fire in the grate and that was covered by a large iron pan in which stew was cooking. There was a rich smell filling the house, which Peggy reckoned smelled like mutton, old ewe in fact. She had found an onion to flavour the stew and added salt.

Poor old Nannie, she thought. 'But needs must when the devil drives,' she said aloud. She often found herself talking aloud to herself these days – after all, there was no one else to talk to except the babby.

The knock on the door made her jump, her heart beating wildly. How could anyone be out there when everyone had left and the place was snowed in? For a second or two superstitious fears filled her but then common sense prevailed and she put the baby in the makeshift pen and went to the door. Nevertheless she shouted through it before lifting the sneck.

'Who's there?'

'Let me in, woman! I'm not going to hurt you!'

Peggy opened the door and peered out, amazed to see the gaffer standing there. She stood and gaped. Had he come to throw her out of the house? He had the right but oh, where would she go, she and the bairn?

Miles moved impatiently. 'Let me in, woman, I said. The weather's enough to freeze a man to death, standing here.'

Peggy stood back and he strode past her to the fire. Without asking he raked coal down from the back shelf into the grate; coal that Peggy had reckoned would last all day.

'Can't you keep a decent fire?' he demanded.

'I've no more coal,' said Peggy evenly. She was seething and didn't add 'sir' or 'Mr Gallagher'. Who the hell did she think he was? But of course he was the mining agent, the gaffer, and he could do what he wanted. The roof over her head was his to take away.

Miles looked at the baby in the makeshift playpen. Merry had pulled herself to her feet and was holding on to the back of a chair, staring solemnly at him. Suddenly her face puckered and she looked at Peggy.

28

'Ganma!'

'It's all right, flower, the man won't hurt you,' said Peggy. She bent and picked the child up again and held her close.

'Her grandmother, are you? Where's her mother and father?'

'Dead. Her father and her grandfather and her brother, killed in the disaster. And her mother from childbirth.'

Peggy said it so prosaically that Miles was speechless for a moment. He had been going to ask what the woman was doing, still living here – it was stupid when everyone else had gone. If she had nowhere to go there was the workhouse, wasn't there? He himself was on the Board of Guardians, and the inmates were treated as fairly as in any other workhouse – he knew that for a fact.

'You shouldn't be here,' he said looking down into the fire.

Peggy sat down heavily on the rocking chair by the range. Oh God, he was going to hoy her out, the rotten sod.

'We have nowhere else to go,' she said. 'Me and the bairn, we're all that's left. Besides, our men are here, in the pit.'

'It's no good talking like that!' said Miles. 'You've to look to the future. You're not so old, you know.' Uncharacteristically, he didn't know what else to say.

'The food's ready,' said Peggy after a pause. 'Will you have some?' The tradition of hospitality was too hard to go against, though she was full of resentment towards him. Resentment and despair.

Miles glanced at the window; outside it was a whiteout, the snow piling up on the window ledge as great flakes came down from a slate-grey sky. He should refuse, his better instincts told him, but he was hungry. Anyway, he could always pay her.

'I'll have a little,' he said. After all, she couldn't be in such financial straits if she could afford lamb stew.

He watched as she ladled out two plates of stew and they

29

sat down to the table. The day had darkened until the main light was coming from the fire now that the pan had been removed. It was true, she wasn't so old, he realised, no older than he was himself, even if she was the baby's grandmother, and in the half-light she looked almost pretty, with her hair hanging down her back like that – dark hair, almost black and with only the occasional glint of silver. Her mouth was soft and a good shape and her teeth good, unusually good for a woman of her class.

Peggy looked up and saw him watching her. 'Eat,' she said. She picked up the baby and began spooning gravy into her mouth. The baby dribbled and Peggy went back to the range and took a cloth from the rail above the grate. She had to reach for it and he watched surreptitiously as her breast strained against the thin stuff of her dress. Damn it, it was a long time since he'd had a woman, he thought. Not since long before his wife died and after all, he was only thirty-eight, a young man, wasn't he?

'It's good,' he said. 'The lamb stew I mean.' It was too, though probably lamb was a misnomer. The meat was a bit stringy and strong tasting, but satisfying nevertheless.

Peggy put the baby down and began to eat her own meal before she replied.

'It's not lamb,' she said.

'No, well I know it's mutton really.'

Peggy took another spoonful into her mouth, chewed and swallowed. 'It's not mutton,' she said.

'No? What is it then?'

'It's the old nanny goat. She stopped giving milk and I had nothing else.'

Miles gagged. He took a handkerchief out of his pocket and dabbed at his lips.

'The first time you've eaten goat, is it?' Peggy asked and smiled, her eyes twinkling in amusement. 'You're not going to waste that, are you?' For Miles had put down his spoon.

'I'm damn well not going to eat it!'

30

'No? Well, isn't it nice that you have a choice? You can go back to your own grand house an' no doubt you will have chicken for dinner an' . . . strawberries an' . . . fresh cream an'—'

'For God's sake, woman, shut up!'

Miles had risen from his chair and Peggy did too, though she still had to look up at him.

'Meantime you are turning us out of our home; what I want to know is how can you sleep at nights?'

Suddenly she lifted her arms, bunched her fists and began to hit him on the chest for that was as far as she could reach. Miles took a step backwards before catching hold of her wrists and holding them tight. Unable to hit him Peggy started to kick out and succeeded in catching him a hefty blow on the shin. Miles swore and pulled her closer, pinioning her arms. She still struggled so he flung her down on the clippie mat and fell on top of her – suddenly his anger turned to something else, he could feel his desire rising.

Peggy could too and she lay for a moment in disbelief before renewing her struggles. But he had her arms pinned down as with the other he flung her skirt over her head and forced one leg between hers. Peggy screamed but of course there was no one to hear her. Except the baby.

Behind her barrier of chairs, Merry began to wail, as Peggy stopped screaming and lay still.

31

Chapter Four

1893

Peggy emptied her bucket down the sluice and stayed for a moment, leaning against the cold ironstone slab. She had the pain in her chest again, the tight, gripping pain. She leaned forward and surrendered to it, closing her eyes. Gradually the pain lessened, faded into the distance where it remained threatening.

She was getting too old for this job, she told herself. The laundry was hot and steamy so that sometimes she was hard put to breathe and the buckets of water and baskets of dirty bedding were heavier by the week. But if she could just hang on for a few more months she could keep Ben at school until he was fourteen at least. A lad who was lettered could get a job at the Co-operative Society, the store, maybe even work in the office. By, it would be grand! And Ben was a clever lad, everyone said so. Didn't he bring in a bob or two now, doing odd jobs and working as a delivery boy on Saturdays?

By, she thought, his beginnings had been terrible. She had tried all she could think of to get rid of him when he was in the womb. Once she had stood on the edge of the quarry and jumped, but the bairn had been a strong 'un, and had held on. All she had done was twist her ankle and bang her elbow so that walking had been painful for a fortnight.

It had been pretty gormless of her, she knew that now. Suppose she'd killed herself? What would Merry have done? She was nobbut a babby at the time. And how could she have done without her lovely Ben? He was a grand lad, whatever his beginnings.

'What's the matter, Granma?'

Merry had come into the sluice and seen her leaning over the brownstone slab. 'Come and sit down,' she said. 'You look as white as a sheet. Is it the pain in your chest again? Will I get something from the doctor?'

'No, don't tell . . .'

But Peggy was too late, Merry had already gone into the ward where Dr Gallagher was doing a round with Sister Harrison. Seconds later she was back, followed by both Sister and doctor.

'What's all this then, Mrs Trent?' Sister Harrison asked. If there was one thing she couldn't abide it was the cleaning staff or indeed, any junior staff, interrupting a ward round for whatever reason. But Peggy didn't care what Sister thought by this time. The pain was gripping her chest like a vice and was getting worse. She was slipping down onto the floor when Dr Gallagher caught her and picked her up as though she was a bairn. He strode into the ward and laid her – horror of horrors – on the clean bedspread of an empty bed.

'Nurse!' Sister called up the ward and a junior nurse came running. 'Help me remove the bedspread at least,' she ordered.

'And make Mrs Trent comfortable,' the doctor said quietly. He gazed searchingly at Peggy. 'How are you feeling now?'

'Better, Doctor, thank you.' Peggy looked up at him anxiously. 'I'd best get on with my work.'

'Now then, I think you'd better stay where you are for today.' He replied. 'Even if you are feeling better.'

'Merry shouldn't have got you, I'm fine,' said Peggy. And even Merry could see she was looking better. 'It was just a turn, I'm over it now.'

33

'There you are, no need to waste the doctor's time then, is there?' said Sister Harrison. She had one eye on the ward door for she was expecting Matron's round and Matron was a stickler for the rules which stated that the beds were for the pauper inmates. Of course, if the woman was really ill it would be different but she said herself she was all right now.

'My granddaughter can take me home, sir,' said Peggy. Merry was standing at the bottom of the bed, watching anxiously. Dr Gallagher glanced at her – she was little more than a child, he thought. But he knew the rules as well as they did. He was well aware too that if the old woman lost her job she could easily be replaced by one of the workhouse inmates, some of whom were able-bodied.

Sister looked at the wall clock hanging over the entrance to the ward. It was close to finishing time for both Peggy and her granddaughter.

'Go then, I'll tell Matron you were unwell,' she said. She pulled a face at the young doctor, which was intended to convey her dissatisfaction with the help brought in from outside Oaklands, the workhouse. But Dr Gallagher wasn't looking at her, he was watching as Peggy climbed slowly off the bed. She stood up straight and had got a little colour back in her cheeks so perhaps she would be all right, he thought.

The ward door opened and Matron sailed in. She stared unsmiling at the group then looked to Sister Harrison who explained the situation.

'You will have to come in half an hour early to make up the time tomorrow, Miranda Trent,' said Matron. 'As for you, Mrs Trent, we have no room for anyone who is not able to do the work. Merry can collect what is owing to you tomorrow. Goodbye.'

Dr Gallagher left the ward before he said anything he might regret. After all, it was the way of it, it was true that the Board of Guardians were hard pressed lately with some of the pits working short time. The men should move away and get jobs in a more prosperous part of the country but they were attached to the area. Goodness only knew why. He found it very depressing. His years in Edinburgh training had been very different.

He walked down the stairs and round to where his pony and trap were waiting, the pony chewing contentedly inside his nosebag. He gave the pauper lad watching it a ha'penny, even though it was strictly against the rules, but hell, he'd had enough of the rules.

He was just going out of the gates when he came across Mrs Trent and her granddaughter again – they were standing by the gates, looking lost and unsure. Both appeared to have been crying; the little girl, for that was all she was – she couldn't have been more than thirteen or fourteen – was supporting her grandmother with an arm around her and the old lady was leaning heavily on her.

'Where are you going?' asked Tom, pulling the pony to a halt. 'Perhaps I can give you a lift.'

Peggy would have refused if she had only had the breath to do so. He was the son of that man; she hated the lot of them. But Merry looked suddenly hopeful.

'We're going to Old Jane Pit,' she said. 'If you can give us a lift as far as the end of the lane where the path goes down that would be grand. I don't know what to do else.'

Tom jumped down from the cart. 'Right then,' he said. 'Come on, I'll help you up.' He lifted them both on to the cart then clucked at the pony and set off.

'Bless you, sir,' said Merry. Peggy said nothing.

'I didn't know anyone still lived down there,' said Tom over his shoulder.

'No, Doctor. Not many do,' said Merry. She glanced at Peggy. Her grandmother was so quiet she was beginning to worry again. But Peggy was all right, holding her head high and gazing out at the fields as they left the town and headed along the country road.

'We will manage from here,' said Merry as they reached the stile on the back road from Coundon. 'I'm sorry we've brought you out of your way.'

35

'I'll help you down to old pit,' said Tom. He had jumped down from the cart to help them alight and now he was tying the reins to the fence.

'No!' said Peggy and the two younger ones looked at her in surprise.

'Granma?'

It just wasn't like her grandmother to be so rude, especially when someone had done them a favour. Merry was embarrassed.

'I ... I can walk from here, it's all downhill,' said Peggy. 'But thank you, Doctor.' She set off down the field path.

'Well,' said Tom, 'I have to be getting home in any case.' Sometimes these heart cases were excitable, he told himself. In fact there was some medical opinion to the effect that it was their nature that caused the problem. And the woman seemed to be walking all right now.

'Thank you anyway,' said Merry. 'I'd better go after her. Thank you, Doctor.' She hurried after her grandmother.

Well, the little girl seemed to have been taught her manners at least, thought Tom as he turned the cart and went back to the main road. She was a pretty little thing too, even if her hands were already rough and red and the nails broken down to the quick. He forgot about the odd couple as he drove the pony home, for he was hungry as a hunter and hoped Cook had made something tasty for dinner tonight.

Peggy always felt the same pain as she entered the deserted village. It was so full of memories for her. How the women used to talk to each other as they strung their washing across the street or gathered by the pump to fill their water buckets. The blowing of the pit hooter that used to warn them when the men were coming up to bank – coming off shift. The thought always came as she turned the corner and walked down the street with the grass coming up between the stones because no matter how they tried they couldn't keep it down. Her men weren't coming up in the cage ever again. They were going to lie in the pit forever.

Then Peggy would dismiss the thought as morbid, but somehow she couldn't stop it coming. She did not look round to where the pit head buildings had stood, now just heaps of rubble. She never walked past them, taking a short cut to Winton Colliery, instead she took the field path.

'I'll go ahead and put the kettle on,' said Merry, interrupting her dark thoughts. 'Ben will have the fire lit, that's one thing.'

A goat bleated a welcome as they approached, the third successor to Nannie. They had needed a goat when Ben was born and besides, it was nice to have fresh milk instead of the eternal condensed stuff; moreover it was cheaper and better for the bairns.

Ben came round the end of the house grinning a welcome. By, she thought, as she always did, she wished he had looked like her Lance. But he didn't, he was tall and fair haired, with bones that were straight and strong, something the goat's milk had done for him. So many of the miners' children suffered from rickets, especially in the bad times. Now, he gazed at her with his blue eyes fringed with fair lashes.

'I've lit the fire, Granma,' he said. 'An' I've milked Betsy an' all. Look though, I helped Mr Parkin in the hay field and he gave me a dozen eggs. Can we have them for our tea? He said I can help with the tatie picking an' all, later on. Isn't it grand?'

'Have you finished your bookwork? You shouldn't have been helping the farmer if you haven't.'

'I did, Granma, I did. I've done it all!' Ben protested and she softened.

'Aye, well, we'll have boiled eggs for our tea,' she said. 'That's a lovely treat you've got for us.'

Aye, he was a good lad, she thought as she went into the kitchen and sat down on the rocking chair. Only for a minute until she got her breath back.

37

She hadn't wanted the lad, by no, she had not. When she stopped having her curses, she had thought it was the change and she had welcomed it. But time had proved her wrong, though it took her weeks to believe the evidence of her own body. She had been that shamed she wouldn't go into Winton or Eden Hope for fear of meeting anyone she knew. That had been the worst time. Well, it was no good going over it now.

'Are you all right, Granma?' asked Merry.

'I'm fine, lass. Howay now, let's have our teas. Boil two eggs for Ben, he's a growing lad, there's a good lass.'

'I will, Granma.'

It wasn't until Merry and Ben were in bed that Peggy allowed herself to think about what she was going to do now she'd lost her job. She wasn't going to get another one, she realised. No one was going to take on an old woman like her. She looked at herself in the small, square mirror in the door of the press. She looked nearer seventy-five than fifty-five, she thought dismally. She was past hard work. Well then, she would try to get something else. Sewing maybe, she could do plain sewing, couldn't she? Mend sheets and that, patch clothes, she could do that. The problem was, who would give her work like that?

Anybody who wanted patching done wouldn't be able to pay her. Anyone who had the money to pay her wouldn't want mending done. Though mebbe they would, some of the folk in Winton were earning better money at the pit at the minute. And some of them were frugal enough.

The problem was she shrank from going into Winton. Of course they knew there was a young lad living with them now, for it had had to come out when he went to school. But they were unsure who he belonged to and he called her 'Granma', not 'Mam'. There was one thing, few of them would think he was really hers. They would think she was too old. Though the women did have children in their forties, but usually they already had a large family.

Any road, she was tired. She would get ready for bed,

she told herself. Yet she sat on in the light of the dying fire and in the end fell asleep with her head against the cushion Merry had made her for Christmas a year or two back. Her feet were propped up on the steel fender in front of her and she dreamed of the old days, when Tommy was alive.

'Now then, lass,' he said in her dreams. 'No use sitting there like you can't help yourself. Get theesel' bestirred.'

Chapter Five

1880

'I'm sorry, I don't know why I did that,' said Miles. 'You made me mad.'

Peggy stared at him, a bitter, level stare. 'Get out of my house,' she said. He sounded as though he was apologising for standing on her toe or something like that. She was pulling her dress together with shaking fingers. A button had been pulled off in the struggle and she held the gaping place together with tight fingers.

'You're nowt!' she said. 'You're not a man, no man would do that. Force a woman.'

The baby, who was sitting inside the makeshift pen, was watching them, tears rolling down her cheeks, her bottom lip jutting out. She had been screaming the whole time of the assault – loud, terrified screams – but her grandma had not come to comfort her and now she simply sobbed quietly. She pulled herself up by the back of a chair and hiccuped softly.

Peggy pulled her hair behind her head and twisted it deftly into a tight bun, tucking the ends in and sticking in a hairpin. Miles watched her. He was unsure what to do having never raped a woman in his life before, and he couldn't believe he had done so now. And a miner's widow, for God's sake?

He cleared his throat. 'You can stay here if you like,' he said. 'I won't put you out.'

'Very good of you, I'm sure,' said Peggy. 'Being as the place is derelict anyroad.'

She went over to Merry and took her out of the pen, holding her close, kissing her and wiping her wet cheeks with the corner of her apron. Outside, the snow had stopped falling and the sky was lightening.

'You won't tell—'

'Of course I bloody won't! Do you think I want to be shamed in Winton and Eden Hope?'

'Can I get you anything? I can help.'

'I reckon you've done enough helping for one day. Coming in here and eating my food and then . . .'

She couldn't go on. She buried her face in the nape of little Merry's neck.

'I'll go then.'

'What are you waiting for?'

Standing with her back to the room she felt the cold draught as he opened the back door and went out. She sat and rocked the baby.

'Whisht babby, whisht,' she crooned and Merry, worn out with crying, dropped off to sleep. Peggy laid her on the old sofa and covered her with a piece of worn blanket. Then she drew the curtains tight shut; something she had not done for a long while. Once again she brought in the tin bath and boiled water, and added clean snow to cool it. Taking the bar of lye soap she scrubbed at herself in an effort to be clean again. But she didn't feel really satisfied when she was finished, even though the skin of her thighs and belly looked red and angry and stung like fire.

Next day there was a thaw. Water dripped from the broken guttering on the roof and the pump at the end of the street dripped both from the tap and the split in the pipe caused by the ice. A tiny river began to form in the middle of the street, black with coal dust against the white snow.

Peggy decided to try to get to Winton along the old line to bring in some oatmeal and condensed milk. She was

41

wrapping the baby in her old shawl, tying it over her head and across her chest on top of the coat she had bought for her from the second-hand clothes stall on the market in the autumn, when there was a knock at the door.

Peggy stiffened. No one came to Old Pit these days. Indeed hardly anyone realised she was still there. Surely he hadn't had the cheek to come back?

'Hey, missus, are you all right?'

It was Bob, the colliery joiner. Though what he was doing there was a mystery. Peggy went to the door still carrying Merry.

'The gaffer told us to come and fix the pump,' he said. 'An' I brought a few bits of things an' all.'

'I don't want them if they've come from—' Peggy stopped herself in time before mentioning the agent. Bob was not noted for his close mouth and he would wonder aloud why she was talking about the man who even told the manager gaffer what to do. Folk would draw their own conclusions.

'Eeh, thanks, Bob,' she said. 'I was just going into Winton to the store.' She looked into the brown paper bag. There was a quarter of tea and a pound of oatmeal and two tins of milk. 'Come on in,' she said. 'I'll soon boil a drop of water and make a cup of tea. I'll give you the money for the groceries.'

'A cup will be welcome, missus,' said Bob. 'But I don't want anything for the bits from the store, I didn't buy them meself, like.'

Peggy's pleasure at the gift diminished. It must have come from bloody Gallagher. By, she wished she could take them and throw them through the bloody window. But there was the bairn – she had to be fed and kept out of the workhouse. Still, why not take it? To Gallagher it didn't amount to more than a few coppers, any road. Not that she wanted more from him. She wanted nowt. But beggars couldn't be choosers.

*

42

Miles Gallagher was at Winton Colliery, in the office with the manager. Production was down this month and he wanted to be prepared with answers when they asked why. After all, the snow didn't affect the working conditions underground, did it? It didn't cool down the temperature one iota.

'There's been more men taken badly, chest problems mostly,' said Jack Mackay, who had taken over Winton after Jane Pit closed. The previous manager had been getting on a bit.

'If they're not fit enough for the work there is no place for them here,' said Miles.

'It *is* an exceptionally bad winter,' said Jack. Some of the men had the miners' disease from the dust, their lungs easily becoming congested in the sudden changes of temperature going on and off shift. And the pit was a wet one, which meant they were often wet when they came to bank. But he didn't say any of this. If the weather were taking a turn for the better the men would soon be back at work.

Miles seemed a bit absent-minded this morning, though, and went to the door without commenting further. He went out to his horse and mounted, turning the animal for home. Tom was going back to school tomorrow; he would go home and have dinner with him. After all, the boy must still miss his mother.

He'd told the joiner to fix the water pump at Jane Old Pit and take some food over for the woman while he was about it. Not a lot but as much as she was probably used to – it wouldn't do to let her think she was being paid off. His conscience was, if not exactly clear, eased.

Tom was building a snowman in the garden. At eight years old he was tall for his age but thin as a lathe. The old jacket he was wearing was short in the sleeve revealing knobbly wrists, red and angry looking above the wet wool of his gloves. His fair hair flopped over his brow from beneath his cap and the tip of his nose was as red as his wrists. When he saw his father he stopped, dropped the carrot he had been about to stick in the snowman's face for a nose and stood still, watching as Miles dismounted and called to him.

'Come and help me with Marcus, Tom,' he called and Tom trotted over obediently. They led the horse into the stable and Miles unsaddled him while Tom filled the manger with sweet-smelling hay. They worked in silence except for the odd word about the job in hand, for Miles didn't know what to say to his son these days. He rarely came into Barnard Castle to the school and took Tom out. In fact he hadn't done that at all last term.

'Have you everything ready to go back to school, Tom?' Miles asked at last.

'Yes father.'

'Has Edna packed your clean linen? There's nothing extra you need this term, is there?'

Tom agreed that there was nothing. He looked down at the slice of roast leg of mutton on his plate, cut a piece off and put it in his mouth, chewing slowly. He wasn't expected to talk while he was chewing.

Miles added mint sauce to the mutton on his plate. The slice was a little pink in the middle as befitted roast lamb rather than mutton. Suddenly it reminded him of the goat he had eaten the day before so he put down his knife and fork and took a drink of water.

'I don't know why I bother cooking for those two,' grumbled Cook when Polly brought back the plates with the half-eaten food. 'The master usually likes mutton.'

'Never mind, we'll enjoy it later on,' said Polly. She had a very healthy appetite and since she had been working here had changed from a thin, pale little girl to a plump, rosy woman.

Back in the dining room, Miles cleared his throat. 'I'll take some time off tomorrow morning and go to the station with you,' he said. 'If the weather were more clement I

44

might have driven you up to school, but perhaps that wouldn't be wise in the snow.' He had to find a way to get closer to the boy, and was suddenly aware of it.

Chapter Six

1893

Merry woke in the early dawn of the October morning as she usually did. She had chores to do before she went to the hospital to work. She turned her head on the pillow and felt a twinge of alarm as Peggy wasn't there. Merry had shared a bed with Peggy ever since she could remember, whereas Ben had a mattress that was newly filled with straw every harvest time. Shivering, for there was a chill in the air, she sat up, pulled on her shoes over her bare feet and ran downstairs.

'Thank God!' she said aloud. Peggy was there, asleep in the rocking chair by the dead fire, her feet propped on the fender. 'Granma!' cried Merry. 'Wake up, you should be in bed. You'll be as stiff as a crutch sitting there. Have you been there all night?'

Merry shook her grandmother's shoulder, just a little, enough to wake her up. Peggy's hand fell down by the side of her chair. Merry's heart beat fast, almost jumping into her throat. Suddenly filled with dread, she forced herself to look properly at Peggy. Her pallor was unmistakable. In her short time at the workhouse hospital Merry had seen too many dead people not to recognise that fact.

'What's the matter with me granma?' Ben came up behind her. She let out a small scream before she took control of herself, turned to him and put an arm around him.

46

'Gran's dead, Ben,' she said. 'Run and see if Mr Hawthorne is off shift, will you.'

'Aw . . . Merry! No she's not! You're just saying that!'

But Ben knew she was not. He started to cry, tears running down his face as he stared at his granma. 'What did she want to die for, our 'Manda?' he panted out at last, and Merry, who was holding him close now, shook her head.

'She was tired, Ben. She was an old woman.' How old was she? Merry wondered. Not that old. Not as old as some of the women in the workhouse, any road.

'It's not fair,' said Ben. He wiped his nose with the back of his hand and made to wipe his hand on the old shirt he slept in. Merry found a rag in her own sleeve and thrust it at him.

'Howay now, Ben! Don't be such a babby. Get away to Winton and tell Mr Hawthorne, will you? He'll know what to do.'

There was no one else. Merry didn't know why Peggy shunned her old neighbours; those that had straggled back to the pit villages around. 'We'll manage on our own,' Peggy used to say. There was only Mr Hawthorne who had sold them the goat and Merry had only met him once or twice. But they had managed on their own. Most of the gardens of the houses at Old Pit had been cultivated at one time, and Peggy had used the others to graze the goat. (They did not name the goat now as Granma wouldn't have it, though Merry vaguely remembered that one goat had been called Nannie and one called Betsy.)

Ben pulled on the trousers which came down to just below his knees. They hung from his shoulders by an old pair of galluses that had belonged to Grandda, the one that was buried in the pit.

'I'll go then,' he said.

'Put your boots on, Ben.'

'Aw man, they hurt me feet,' he protested, but pulled on the boots anyway.

*

47

Peggy Trent was buried in a pauper's grave in the far corner of the churchyard at Old Winton village. There was a wooden marker that soon rotted away. Merry, Ben and Mr and Mrs Hawthorne were the only mourners. Afterwards the man came from the Board of Guardians and said arrangements would be made for them to go to the workhouse.

'Me brother and me, we're not going,' said Merry. The man looked at them as they stood shoulder to shoulder. 'I've got a job, any road. I'm going to be a nurse.'

'An' I'm going down the pit,' said Ben as Merry gave him a sharp glance.

'No you're not,' she hissed. 'Granma would turn in her grave.'

The man from the Guardians shrugged. 'Well,' he said, 'you're both of an age to work for a living, it's true. Lads younger than you work down the mines, Benjamin. You're twelve, going on thirteen, aren't you? And I understand you work in our infirmary anyway, Miss Trent. I cannot force you to enter the workhouse. How old are you?'

'Fourteen. I'm fourteen and me brother's nearly thirteen. We're old enough to manage now. I'll look after him, any road.'

The man shook his head and got to his feet. He looked around the kitchen. It was reasonably comfortable, in the way of the miners' houses, a table, wooden chairs, a rocking chair and ancient sofa and a press. All shabby but clean. It was the deserted village around it that was strange. Outside the two rows of houses, all empty but for this one, were eerie somehow. But the boy and girl didn't seem to mind. Of course they had been brought up here, he understood.

'We don't pay out relief,' he warned. 'If you stay out you get no help from the Guardians.'

'We don't need it,' said Merry, drawing herself up. 'We have the gardens and like I said, I have a job.'

'The boy is old enough to work,' said the man.

'He has a name, Benjamin, and he is still at school. He's clever,' Merry asserted.

The man snorted. 'Lads in his position cannot afford to be clever,' he said. 'He has his daily bread to earn.'

'We'll manage,' Merry said tightly.

'Aye, we will an' all,' said Ben.

After the man had gone away, the two looked at each other.

'I can get work,' said Ben.

'No you can't,' Merry replied. 'Anyway, you can go to school and still look after the gardens, can't you? Maybe you'll get some more work with Mr Parkin. You can snag turnips and that. When you're not at school that is. Granma wanted you to finish school, Ben, you know that. Now I have to go back to work.'

As Merry walked the three miles into town her thoughts were at last coming out of the turmoil they had been in since Peggy died. She had to plan to get through the winter. She calculated that they would have about twelve 8-stone bags of potatoes when they had completed the harvest and they would be able to keep them dry and free from frost in the upstairs room of the house next door.

If Ben worked for Mr Parkin on Saturdays in return for turnips and eggs, they would manage, for she could buy off-cuts of meat at the market on Saturdays from her own wages. The best time was after dark when the butchers wanted to get rid of what they had left and go home. And when the fishwives came in from Shields they could often get fish for next to nothing – caller herring or black-skinned cod that no one else wanted because the fish was older and more coarse. Granma had taught her how to bake the cod in the oven, though, slowly so as to make it tender.

Granma. She hadn't thought of her granma for ten minutes and now the memory of the old woman had popped into her mind. It took her by surprise and the lump in her throat threatened to explode. She blinked her eyes rapidly and pressed on her top lip to stop herself crying. Crying did no good, she just had to get on with things.

Doctor Gallagher was in the entrance of the workhouse when Merry walked in, standing talking to Matron who was also the workhouse mistress.

'You should come in by the back door, Trent,' Matron said sharply.

'Sorry Matron,' Merry mumbled.

'How is your grandmother, Miss Trent?' the doctor asked and Matron looked disapproving. It was not for a doctor to make conversation with the domestic staff; she would have to have a quiet word with him about it.

The question took Merry by surprise, even shock. She looked properly at him. 'Granma died, Doctor,' she said and, her guard down, her eyes filled with tears.

'I'm sorry,' said Tom and she was further upset by the kindness in his blue eyes.

'Yes, well,' said Matron, 'go to your work now or you will be late.' Merry turned blindly away and hurried off to the ward on Block 3 where the infirm and bedridden were housed.

'It's no good letting these girls get too emotional,' said Matron. She was tired having been got out of bed by the night nurse an hour earlier than usual because one of the patients who was suspected of having typhoid had died. As it happened Dr Gallagher had called in to see the old man in any case and he issued the death certificate. Though what he was doing there at this godforsaken hour of the morning Matron couldn't think. She disapproved of it though. There was no real need for doctors to be cluttering up the wards except at the appointed times for the rounds.

Tom Gallagher went out in to the cold morning air to where his horse and trap were tethered close by. At the other end of the site he could hear the noises made as the men from the workhouse began their stone-breaking work in the stone yard. He felt thoroughly depressed.

That little girl, for she was no more than that, had looked so woebegone. She was so pale and her dark eyes looked enormous, the lids pink where she had wept. Her dark hair was drawn back unbecomingly under the enormous cap the hospital made her wear. In fact he wouldn't have recognised that it was dark but for the small lock that had escaped onto her neck at the back. He wondered if she was left on her own now in that tumbledown huddle of miners' hovels. God help her if she was.

Tom climbed onto the seat of the trap and clicked at the horse to get him going. His thoughts wandered back to the old man he had just seen die. His hands had been gnarled and marked with blue scars from the coal, his lips drawn back in a permanent half-grin from the effort to breathe after a lifetime breathing in coal dust. And he had ended a pauper.

The horse took little direction for he knew his own way home. They turned into the entrance of Tom's father's house and Tom drove round the back to the stable.

It was still very early, only just breakfast time so he washed his hands in the downstairs cloakroom which had a newly installed washbasin decorated with green ivy leaves, and even hot water from the copper boiler in the kitchen. Oh yes, he thought, the agent's house has all the latest conveniences, even a water closet on the upstairs landing.

'Good morning. What on earth were you doing out at this time of the morning?' asked Miles as Tom went into the dining room and began to help himself from the dishes of bacon and eggs kept hot over a candle burner. Tom filled his plate and sat down at the table before replying.

'I wanted to see an old man at the hospital. He was pretty poorly last night.'

'How was he?' asked Miles. At least it was a way of making conversation with Tom, he thought, though he wasn't the least interested in how a pauper in the workhouse

51

infirmary was. Sometimes Tom seemed like a stranger, and he never knew what to say to him.

In fact Miles strongly disapproved of Tom attending the paupers. Goodness knows what he might pick up. He buttered a piece of toast and added marmalade before taking a bite.

'He's dead.'

Miles shrugged. 'Nothing contagious, I hope?' Old men who were paupers usually died.

Tom almost said it was indeed contagious, typhoid perhaps, or cholera. But he didn't. 'No, not contagious. The miner's disease, emphysema. And poverty of course.'

'These pitmen rarely save for their old age; they give no thought for tomorrow. All they are interested in is spending their wages in the nearest ale house.'

Tom frowned but said nothing. He would never succeed in changing his father's opinions, he'd tried before. In any case it was true that the ale houses were full on pay nights. He decided to change the subject.

'That woman who stayed on in the old Jane Pit rows died too. I was surprised she was still living there on her own, but for her granddaughter. I think there is a boy too. He's just a child, still at school.'

Miles, who had been raising his cup to his lips froze, the cup halfway.

'Father?'

Miles realised Tom was waiting for a comment. 'Oh, did she? I seem to remember there was one left there.'

'Yes. I was surprised she was allowed to stay really. She would have been better off in Winton Colliery, surely?'

'The houses in Winton are needed for the pitmen. Anyway she couldn't afford to pay any rent. It was an act of kindness to allow her to remain at Jane Pit.'

Tom almost choked on his coffee at the idea of his father doing an act of kindness to one of the mining community. Perhaps he wasn't so hard as he had thought.

'She was a widow. Her husband and son were killed in

the disaster at Jane Pit,' said Miles almost as though he had to explain himself. 'In any case, it costs nothing. Since then there has been the Employers Liability Act of 1880. Iniquitous it is. Now they're bringing in a Compensation Act. More often than not these miners are killed through their own negligence. And accidents happen in any walk of life.'

Tom stood up abruptly. He was too weary to argue and if he stayed he would be unable to stop himself.

'I think I'll have a bath and a rest before it's time for my surgery,' he said. He had a practice in Winton village that barely covered expenses which was the reason he was living at his father's house.

'Why you don't take a practice in the town I don't know,' grumbled his father. 'I have told you I am willing to help you buy . . .'

But it was too late, Tom was already halfway up the stairs.

Chapter Seven

Miles was once again riding along the old waggon way that ran from Winton Colliery along by the side of the deserted village and old pit. Though nowadays it was more comfortable for him to take the tub trap when he went round the collieries in his charge, a horse could go places a trap could not. Not that he had intended to go to Old Pit for really he was on his way to Eden Hope, and usually he took the newly tarmacked road when he went there.

He was thinking of his future plans. Although he had said nothing as yet to Tom, he had been thinking of remarrying lately. Miss Bertha Porritt was the daughter of a mine owner on the other side of the Wear, a man with three mines all producing good quality coking coal and no sons to inherit. She was a bit long in the tooth perhaps but what did that matter? With his knowledge of the coal trade and the burgeoning iron trade in Middlesbrough, he could go a long way. Miles smiled to himself. Her nose was a trifle long too and the only red patch on her face, but who looked at the chimney when you stoked the fire?

Miss Bertha had looked sideways at him the last time he'd been invited to dine with her father. And he could swear that her pale eyes had softened when she looked at him.

It was just a notion, he told himself when he took the branch of the waggon way that led to Old Pit. After his talk with Tom that morning he might as well see for himself if there was anything left to be salvaged from the houses. The woman had gone now so he didn't have to avoid the deserted village. And the owners, despite their wealth, liked to think he was being frugal.

Marcus, the second horse he had had of that name, slowed to a walk and picked his way carefully between the sleepers. Most of the rails had been taken up and those left were rusted and broken. Grass and weeds grew between the sleepers, hiding places where large stones lay or there were unexpected hollows in the track. Miles moved his horse to the narrow path by the side, barely discernible for dead bracken and weeds.

There was still evidence of Old Pit yard, he noticed as he passed it. The shaft, capped with strong wooden beams, the engine house, roofless and gutted and with jagged pieces of iron jutting from the wall where the staircase had once been. Fancifully it reminded him of Barnard Castle which had suffered a similar fate after the wars of the Roses.

The houses still stood in two straight lines with a road between leading to the pump. Some of them had had the roof slates removed, but most had not. He led Marcus on to the pump, dismounted and drew some water into an old and battered bucket standing there.

The end house was still occupied, he saw. Miles walked over and peered in to the kitchen he remembered so well, though he had tried to put it out of his mind. He had not been along this way for years – thirteen years, in fact. He glanced back at his horse; the animal had finished drinking and was cropping at bits of grass between stones of the road. Miles went around the back of the houses.

The gardens were cultivated, or at least some of them were. Winter cabbage and brussel sprouts stood in rows. Earth had been newly turned in places and there was a boy working in the farthest corner from him. As Miles walked towards him, the boy stood up, breathing heavily and stared at him.

'What do you want, creeping up on me like that?' he demanded. He wiped the back of his hand across his brow, leaving a trail of brown earth over pale eyebrows. 'If you're the school inspector, I'm not going back and you can't make me. I'm thirteen and I can leave school if I want to!'

Miles stared at him, unable to believe his eyes. Apart from the ragged clothes and the rough speech of the lad it could have been Tom standing defiantly there. The lad was sturdy, with no sign of the rickets that plagued so many of the miners' children and he was tall and straight.

'Who the hell are you?' Miles demanded.

'Who are you?' the lad countered. He stared levelly at Miles with blue eyes exactly the same colour as Tom's. Only his hair was slightly darker, Miles saw now.

'I'm the mines agent,' said Miles. In spite of his stunned amazement he was pleased to note his tone was normal – with the same tinge of impatient arrogance he always used with these people.

The lad lifted his chin. 'My name is Benjamin Trent,' he said. 'I live here with my sister. We're not hurting nothing, mister. My gran got leave to live here, she told us.'

His gran? Could it be that this was not the product of that snow-bound night? But the evidence was there before his eyes, the boy the spitting image of Tom.

'Where is your gran now?'

Miles couldn't believe that the boy had been here all these years without him finding out. That old witch must have hidden him away. But no, he had spoken of the school inspector so he must have gone to school. How could he ever have bedded that old biddy? If it ever came up no one would ever believe him if he denied fathering the boy. His thoughts flew round inside his head chaotically and he had to pull himself together.

The wonder was that there hadn't been rumours flying about him and the lad, for these colliery villages were hotbeds of gossip and usually the gossip reached their

56

betters. Oh, he had to get rid of him and as soon as maybe; his luck wouldn't last forever and if it ever got out that would be the end of his dreams of Miss Bertha Porritt.

'Where is your sister?' Miles demanded. Vaguely he remembered a baby crying, watching him over a fence of chairs that night.

'She's at work, mister. Where else would she be at this time of day?'

Ben was uncomfortable and beginning to worry. This fella was a gent and the mines agent an' all. He was a bit hazy about what an agent did or what sort of power he had but Ben could guess it was a pretty strong sort. What would Merry and he do if they were thrown out of the village?

'You're on your own?'

Ben took a step back ready to run if need be – he didn't like the look in this man's eye. 'She'll be back any time now,' he said. 'It's her half day.'

'I'm not going to hurt you, lad,' said Miles, forcing himself to alter his tone to sound more friendly. 'I'm just concerned.'

Ben was mystified. He was thirteen years old, almost a man. Why should the man be concerned for him?

'I can look after meself, mister,' he said, clutching the spade.

'Yes, I'm sure,' said Miles. Just at that moment Marcus snickered and gave him inspiration. 'But my horse needs watering and I am at a loss to know how to work the pump back there. I wonder if you could help me?'

Ben stared his disbelief but Miles was smiling easily now, standing to one side and gesturing for Ben to go in front of him. 'I'll give you a shilling.'

Ben was unsure but in the end he stuck the spade into the earth and went. After all, shillings were usually hard to earn and he couldn't pass up the chance of getting one for such a small job. If he was slightly incredulous that the mining agent didn't know how to use the pump he

57

dismissed the thought. Likely the gent had those new-fangled taps in his house.

'See, there's nowt to it really,' he said as he pumped the handle vigorously up and down and eventually a stream of water ran out. 'But look, there's water in the bucket already.' He looked up at Miles, frowning. 'Did you not see it?'

'Oh, is there?' asked Miles and stepped forward to peer into the battered bucket. 'So there is,' he said smoothly. Marcus had come up behind him and was nuzzling at him. 'He must have had a drink too.' Ben straightened up. Oh well, he probably wouldn't get his shilling now, he thought. Might as well go back to work.

'Would you like to have a ride, lad? You can sit in front of me and ride along to Eden Hope if you wish.' Miles was being his most affable in contrast to his tone of a few minutes ago. But Ben was excited at the thought and suddenly no longer almost a man but a young boy offered a treat.

'Eeh, can I, mister? You're not joshing me, are you?'

'No, I mean it, really.'

Miles mounted the horse and held out his hand to Ben. 'Come on now, just put your foot there and jump up before me, it'll be fine.'

It was the work of a moment to get Ben up before him and Miles stepped out back to the junction where the track led off to Eden Hope colliery.

'I've only ever ridden the pit ponies when they're in't farmer's field,' said Ben. His cheeks were flushed and his blue eyes sparkled.

Have you indeed, thought Miles. I'll have to have a word with that farmer for letting the miners' brats ride the ponies. They came to bank to gain strength for their work, not to provide amusement for young hellions. He led Marcus off the track and through a gate onto the field with the path running down, but he didn't take the path; instead he trotted along beside the hedge and through a gap to a smaller garth and on to an old lonnen.

'This isn't the way to Eden Hope,' said Ben. He was not uneasy about it though; he was too happy to be on the back of a horse for that. The feel of Marcus's muscles rippling beneath him filled him with delight. 'It's the old pack donkey trail over to the coast.'

'Yes, so it is. But I thought you would like to go into the woods here, ride between the trees.'

'Oh aye, mister, I would,' Ben said eagerly.

They went along the pathway through the woods for a while and then Miles headed Marcus off at a tangent, climbing steadily between the trees away from the donkey trail. Ben was loving it but even so he began to get a little worried.

'Eden Hope isn't this far away,' he said, turning the top half of his body to look up at Miles. Maybe it was the way he looked up at him with his expression so like Tom's that finally decided Miles. He had been riding along, unsure what to do as his thoughts strayed to Miss Bertha Porritt and what her reaction would be should she find out he had a by-blow among the pitmen's women. He could see his chances of becoming a mine-owner fading into the distance, most likely disappearing forever.

They were approaching the ridge of the hill and he urged Marcus to turn in a semi-circle and ride along the top. 'It is a long way round, I agree. But I thought you were enjoying it.'

'By, I am that, mister,' was Ben's fervent response. 'But I have work to do, I have to get the tatie ground turned before the frosts.' He found this chap hard to fathom, he told himself. He was being too kind for one of his sort and Ben didn't entirely trust him. Besides, he was feeling guilty about the garden, he'd never finish the potato patch today if he didn't get a move on. Then what would Merry say?

'Are we not going to Eden Hope, mister?'

Ben knew every inch of the area – woods, fields and ancient pit-heaps now grassed over with the years – so he knew they were circling round the colliery and were not all

59

that far from Old Pit. In fact they were now close to a ventilation shaft that had once served Jane Pit. It was walled around with stone to a height of perhaps fifteen feet and forming a chimney, for at one time a bonfire would have been burning at the bottom to draw fresh air from the main shaft.

Miles didn't answer at once. Instead he reined in Marcus and dismounted before saying, 'Jump down, lad.'

'I need to get back,' said Ben. He was feeling strangely reluctant to do what he was told. Besides, Merry would kill him if he spent the whole day out and didn't finish his work.

Miles held up his hand imperatively. 'Give me your hand if you're scared,' he said.

Ben bristled. He was not scared, not in the least. Ignoring the hand he swung his leg over and jumped down to the ground.

'Why did we stop here, mister?' he asked.

'Oh, just to give the horse a rest,' said Miles. 'He's been carrying two, you know.'

Marcus began cropping the thin grass, moving towards the edge of the small clearing. They were surrounded by tall trees and at the edge of the clearing bushes and saplings covered the ground. Brambles were climbing over most of them, the leaves turning brown now though huge berries hung in clusters, their weight bending the branches to the ground.

Ben watched the gent, unsure what he wanted of him. Miles was fingering an old iron ladder, its rungs rusted and thin, although they seemed to be strong enough to take a boy's weight.

'Would you like to have a look down the shaft?' he asked Ben.

Ben looked dubious. The ladder might not be fastened very well to the chimney. Still, it wasn't so very high, was it?

'I'll stand behind you if you like,' said Miles grinning knowingly and Ben knew he was thinking he was scared again. He strode over to the ladder and grasped the sides, dislodging large particles of rust as he did so.

'There'll be nowt to see any road,' he said. 'It'll be too dark. I climbed it before, years ago and I couldn't see a thing.' He had been only nine or ten, he remembered, and as the day was grey and overcast he couldn't see beyond a few feet.

'No, lad,' said Miles. 'The sun is shining directly on it. You might even be able to see the bottom.'

Carefully Ben climbed the ladder. It wasn't so high, only fifteen or sixteen rungs, so there was no danger, though the ladder had almost rusted away since the last time he had climbed it.

Reaching the top, he leaned over the wall, resting most of his weight on that. The gent was right, the sun had penetrated into the shaft and there was a sparkle of water at the bottom. By, it must be hundreds of feet down. There were staging posts at intervals up the sides too, black iron with rusty bits.

'Hey!' The ladder beneath him began to shake alarmingly – the daft fella was coming up behind him! 'It's not strong enough! Get back go—'

His shout was cut off as Miles reached his feet. In a split second Ben saw the man's intentions and pulled his foot out of the way, overbalanced and fell from the ladder which was now leaning away from the stone chimney. He banged his head against a stone as he connected with the ground and was knocked out, sinking into oblivion.

Miles bent over the lad and felt his temple for a pulse; it was there though beating fast and erratically. So Ben was alive. Miles felt a rush of relief. Oh God, what had he been thinking of? He had almost murdered his own son. And all for Bertha Porritt, that ugly – no, not for Bertha Porritt. For the mines that came with her. He looked down at the boy. Ben was very pale, the only colour in his face the blue veins in his eyelids and the nasty bruise that was developing on his temple.

He might not live. What would he do then? He looked up at the chimney of the ventilating shaft. He would never get the lad up there to throw him in. What was he thinking of? He was so mixed up, thinking one way and then another. Rising to his feet he caught hold of Marcus's reins and brought him round by the boy. He lifted Ben and put him over the front of the saddle then mounted himself. He would have to take him somewhere, he couldn't leave him lying on the ground for anyone to find. Anyone who might know him – Miles.

Turning the horse he went along the path to where it branched off for Shildon, pausing at the entrance of an old drift mine that was boarded up and overgrown with bushes.

Chapter Eight

Merry walked down the field path and climbed over the stile. She could see the roofs of Old Pit village along to the left but there was no familiar plume of smoke rising from the furthest end house. She frowned and changed her heavy basket from one hand to the other. She was so tired, the day had been especially busy with new admissions to the ward and one man dying. She had had to help Staff Nurse lay the man out ready for the undertaker. They had washed him and combed his hair, dressed him in the plain paper shroud that was provided by the Board of Guardians.

'We must show respect,' Staff Nurse had said. 'Treat the body properly.' She was busy tying up the man's chin with a thin cotton bandage. There were pennies on his eyes to keep the lids closed until rigor mortis set in properly.

Merry had gazed at him. Mr Watson's skin was waxen now, the two spots of high colour on his cheeks faded. His chest was still, no longer labouring for breath. He had had little respect shown to him when alive, she thought. And the way Staff Nurse had stuffed cotton waste into his orifices didn't seem very respectful either.

'Yes, Staff Nurse,' she had said. After all, Mr Watson was at peace now so it didn't matter much to him.

Merry walked down the uneven surface of the track between the two rows of houses towards the end house. The goat was bleating at her, complaining loudly as she stretched her chain to its fullest extent from the patch of ground at the end where she was tethered. She looked and behaved as though she hadn't been milked today. Cold foreboding struck Merry's heart as she pushed open the door and went into the kitchen. There was no welcoming fire in the grate, no vegetables washed and ready to be prepared on the scrubbed table.

'Ben?' she called. 'Where are you, Ben?'

The only answer was the bleating of the goat. Merry put her basket on the table and went through to the tiny back kitchen. The back door stood open. Relief flooded through her – he must be working in the gardens still and had probably just forgotten the time.

He was not in the gardens, nowhere about. He wasn't in the shed either. The vegetable patch he had planned to dig over today ready for the winter frosts to make the soil friable had not been finished. It had barely been started. Ben must have been gone for a long time.

Perhaps Mr Parkin, the farmer he sometimes worked for had come for him for a job he needed doing. Yes, that was probably it. He must have gone in a hurry though, to leave the spade stuck in the ground as it was. Ben was a tidy worker; he always cleaned his tools and put them away in the shed. Merry took the spade, cleaned it with a tuft of grass and hung it on the hook where it belonged. She pushed the barrow into the shed and closed the door before going back into the house. If Ben was working at Farmer Parkin's he would be back soon and as hungry as a hunter. But first she had to milk the goat and put her inside the house next door for the night. Then she would be free to start a meal.

Merry raked out the ashes in the range and lit the fire, using twists of paper and twigs to get it alight, adding a couple of logs and a small shovel of coal dust. The coal house was empty but Ben had gleaned the coal dust and a few small pieces from the Winton Colliery slag heap. She balanced the old tin blazer that her grandda had made at the pit on the bars and the flames roared up the chimney. When she was satisfied the fire was hot enough she took down the blazer and put the iron pan filled with water on the flames, settling it against the bar.

She peeled potatoes and turnip and cut them up to drop in the pan with leeks and carrots. There was a cooked ham shank from yesterday and she added it to the broth together with a good pinch of salt. There was very little meat on the shank but at least it would provide some flavour. Ben could have what meat there was because she had had a meal at the hospital at midday.

There was a treat tonight too, a couple of cooking apples she had got for a penny on the market just as the stalls were closing down. As the oven heated up she washed and cored them and put a little precious sugar and nutmeg where the core had been. They would bake nicely on the oven shelf and they could have them with a little goat's milk.

Ben was a long time coming home. The broth was ready and a delicious smell of apples came from the oven. She pulled the pan away from the flames and placed it on the hearth. Outside the light was almost gone, so she lit a candle and placed it on the table. One would do for there was a good light from the fire.

It was soon black dark outside, for there was no moon tonight. There was a spatter of rain on the window, which meant it would probably be raining in upstairs as the roof had shed a few slates in the last gale. Merry picked up the candle and went upstairs to check. There was a new dark stain appearing above the foot of her bed. She put the candle on the tiny iron mantelpiece and heaved at the bedstead until she had moved it out of the way. In the tiny offshoot room, Ben's bed looked to be safe from the rain.

Ben would not still be working, not at this time of night and not in this weather. Maybe he was sheltering in the farmer's barn or somewhere? Merry was filled with foreboding. Something was wrong, Ben wouldn't do this to her. He would have left a note saying where he was. She went downstairs and put on her coat, before wrapping a shawl around her head, crossing it over her chest and tying it at the back. She lit the storm lantern that hung behind the back door, thanking God that there was even a little paraffin oil in it. Then she went out, closing the door behind her to keep in the warmth and walked along to the path that led up the field to Farmer Parkin's place.

The wind was rising and howling in the trees and her shawl was soon wet through. But she took little notice of it for she was used to carrying on as normal in good weather or bad.

'Nay, lass, I've not seen your Ben, not since Saturday,' said Vincent Parkin, staring at her. Merry looked like a sodden waif with water streaming down her face and her clothes clinging to her. He stood back from the door. 'Howay in by the fire,' he said. 'The missus'll give you something hot. You'll be lucky not to catch your death.'

Merry went into the bright farmhouse kitchen, hesitating to go in further than a couple of yards as her clothes were literally dripping onto the terra cotta tiles of the floor.

'Never you mind the mess,' said Mrs Parkin who had bustled up behind her husband. 'Howay lass, come to the fire. Do you fancy a cup of tea? There's a fresh brew.'

'No thanks, Mrs Parkin,' Merry replied. 'I'm looking for our Ben. I can't understand where he's got to.'

She looked worried an' all, thought the farmer's wife. There were dark smudges of tiredness beneath her eyes and her skin was tinged with pink only where it had been battered with the rain.

'Take your things off and dry them out on the rail,' she said. 'You'll catch your death if you don't, lass.'

'No, I'd best be getting back. Ben might be home by now and worried about me. If you could just let me have a drop of paraffin oil for the lamp? I've run out.'

In spite of their protestations Merry said goodbye and went to the door, pulling her already dripping shawl further over her head. Mr Parkin filled the lamp and held it out to her. 'Ben'll not be far,' he said, trying to reassure her. 'You know what lads are like, scamps the lot of them.'

Merry thanked them both and went out into the storm. She hurried down the path and along the waggon way to the house, but when she opened the door the kitchen was empty except for the smell of apples and burnt sugar. She took off her outdoor things and hung them by the fire to dry, then opened the oven door and took out the baked apples. The baking tin would need to be scrubbed for the sugar was burnt on, she noted with half her mind. The other half was ranging wildly from one possibility to another of what might have happened to Ben. He would not have left like this, he would not, no. He was a sensible, hard-working lad, not a scamp.

Merry didn't know what to do. It was so dark outside, there was such a storm. She would never find Ben in this. She would have to wait for morning. The Morrisons were living in Winton Colliery now. As soon as it was first light she would go and ask them if he had seen Ben.

First she must have something to eat, try to sleep for a while at least. Merry spooned broth from the pan and forced herself to eat it. Then she ate one of the burnt baked apples; no sense in wasting food. It was too hard to come by. She lay down on the settle, stretched out and closed her eyes, but she found herself watching the flickering of the dying fire on the ceiling, imagining pictures of Ben in the shades of light and dark. Ben fallen and hurt, unable to get back home; out in this storm too, with no shelter.

At five o'clock she got up, brought in water from the pump and sluiced herself all over with it. She rubbed herself dry and put on her clothes. Her coat was still wet from the night before but it would have to do. She did have a dry shawl for her shoulders and head, though. Merry tied it on and went out.

The rain had stopped and a three-quarter moon shone down so there was some light to guide her steps as she picked her way to the waggon way and walked along it, treading from sleeper to sleeper. She stopped at intervals and called.

'Ben? Ben, where are you?'

There was no reply apart from the cry of a vixen far off in the woods. Soon she saw the chimneys and engine house of Winton Colliery looming ahead with the slag heap rising dark alongside. She turned off before she got to the colliery yard and went on down to the miners' rows.

It was still only half-past six and the only person about was the knocker-upper with his long pole to rattle against the bedroom windows of the back shift men.

'Rise and shine!' he called softly and again, 'Rise and shine!' He glanced curiously at Merry as he said, 'Morning, lass, mind, you're up early.' But he didn't pause in his stride as he had to get round all of the rows to rouse the whole shift.

Merry hesitated outside the door of the Morrison house. There was no light there so Mr Morrison must not be on back shift. Besides, she didn't know the family very well. For some reason Gran had kept away from her former neighbours, those that had settled close, and she had not encouraged Merry to go into Winton either. She only knew them because they had had a daughter at school with her. Merry had become friendly with Ethel Morrison and been invited to the house, but her gran wouldn't let her go there.

'And don't you talk to her neither,' Gran had said, inexplicably. 'Don't go telling them all our business.' Ben had been sent to school in Shildon; that was another strange thing. Gran said it was better for him, a bigger school in a thriving railway town.

'What are you doing out on a morning like this, lass?'

The speaker was a miner who had come out of a door further along the street. He was in his pit clothes and his lamp swung at his belt. Even as he spoke others were coming out of the houses, meeting up and making their way to the pithead.

'You're that lass from Old Pit, aren't you?' he went on.

68

'Yes, that's right. I'm looking for my brother, he didn't come home last night,' said Merry. 'He's a lad of thirteen?'

'Well, I've not seen anybody about,' said the miner. 'But I'll ask the others.' He turned to what was now a line of miners walking along in the middle of the road. 'Nobody seen a young lad about, have they?'

There was a general shaking of heads and quiet nays, when suddenly the buzzer sounded at the pithead and the man moved away. 'Go home, lass,' he advised. 'He'll turn up, you'll see.'

Merry thanked him and followed the back shift along to the pit yard, passed the lit-up engine house, skirted a row of coal trucks on the waggon way and set off on the walk back.

Ben was not at home when she got there. The fire was out, the kitchen cold and the goat bleating plaintively next door. Merry didn't know what to do so she took refuge in routine. She milked the goat and put the jug in the cold pantry. She forced herself to eat a slice of bread with a smear of bramble jam on it and drank a cup of water from the pump. It tasted icy cold and slaty but she was thirsty and besides, she had had hardly any sleep and she needed to go to work. She couldn't afford not to. At least it was her fortnightly half day and she only had five hours to endure before she could look for Ben.

The morning seemed more like ten hours than five but at last she was walking, almost running down the drive and through the gates – and it was there that she nearly bumped into Dr Gallagher.

'Oops!' he cried, and caught hold of her upper arms. 'What's the big hurry to get away?'

'I'm sorry, Doctor,' she said and suddenly she was over-whelmed with worry and lack of sleep, blurting out, 'Our Ben's lost, I can't find him anywhere, he wasn't at home when I got back last night and I looked for him everywhere and he wasn't—'

'Whoa there, take time to take a breath,' advised Tom. 'Your Ben?'

'My brother Ben, he's thirteen and—'

'Wait a minute,' said Tom, looking thoughtful. There was nothing urgent at the hospital – he just happened to have finished his rounds with a patient in town and had decided to give his workhouse patients a quick check before going home. But he could come back if necessary. 'Look, the trap is just over the road, I'll take you home. You'll see, Ben will probably be there. He'll have a perfectly good explanation for everything.'

Ben better have an explanation, Tom thought grimly, putting his sister through all this. He handed Merry into the trap and put the travelling rug over her knees for a cold wind had sprung up and she was shivering.

'Soon be there,' he said and they set off along Cockton Hill and into Newgate Street, then took the road out to Canney Hill. It was but a short ride from there to where the stile gave access to the path down the field to Old Pit.

'Warm enough?' he asked once and she nodded. She had struggled to regain her composure and now sat quietly, her folded hands under the cosy rug. When they arrived at the stile Tom tied the pony to the fence and handed her out of the trap.

'I can manage myself now, thank you very much, Doctor,' she said.

'I'll come with you, all the same. If Ben is still missing I will help you find him.'

Merry was too tired and miserable to argue. She allowed him to walk beside her to the bottom of the field and along the path to the deserted village.

At midday, in the light of the pale winter sun with frost glinting on the roof that remained, and blank windows looking out on the street, the place looked absolutely desolate to Tom. He hadn't realised just how desolate it would look. They reached the end house, the only one with a scrubbed and yellow-stoned step and clean windows, and went in.

Somehow it seemed colder inside than out with no fire in

70

the grate. Cold struck through his strong leather soles from the flagstones of the kitchen floor. The remains of a meal were on the scrubbed table, a pan on the fender by the fire.

'Ben? Are you upstairs, Ben?'

Merry stood at the foot of the rickety staircase and called up it. There was no answer but she went up anyway and looked.

'He's not here,' she said when she came down.

'I'll light the fire,' said Tom. 'Then we can decide what to do. Don't worry, we'll find him. In the meantime, I think a cup of tea would be in order, don't you?' There would be some tea, wouldn't there? Though there seemed precious little else. He looked around the kitchen – efforts had been made to make it comfortable, with home-made proddy mats on the flags. A mat frame stood in the corner with a half-made mat on it; there was a rocking chair by the range with a bright cushion on it and a settle along one wall. But everything in the place spoke of poverty. He looked at Merry's pale face, her red-rimmed eyes and concern and protectiveness strengthened within him.

71

Chapter Nine

'Full name of the missing person,' said the sergeant of police. He stood behind a high desk and looked at Merry over half spectacles. She was nobbut a lass herself, he thought, with those large brown eyes looking so anxiously at him.

'Benjamin Trent,' said Merry.

'Age?'

'Thirteen.'

'Do you have his birth certificate?'

'Oh! It must be in Granma's tin box,' Merry said to Tom.

'Well, if he doesn't turn up you can bring it in to-morrow,' said the sergeant. 'Just for the records, you understand.'

He looked from Dr Gallagher, whom he knew, to the young girl who evidently lived at Old Pit. He hadn't thought anyone lived at Old Pit, not nowadays. The place was nothing but ruined and broken-down pitmen's cottages.

'That's all,' he said. 'Let me know if the lad turns up.'

'That's all? Do you mean you don't even want a description? This is a young boy we're talking about, a lad of thirteen who's gone missing,' Tom said sharply.

'Not missing. Not officially, Doctor,' said the sergeant. 'He's only been gone for twenty-four hours. He can't be considered missing until it's a week at least.'

'But this is a young boy!'

'A young man, he is considered in law,' said the sergeant. 'Thirteen years old is old enough to work for your keep. He has probably run away to sea or somewhere. Lads do it all the time. It's in their natures, you see, Doctor.'

'But—'

Tom was interrupted by a young constable who came in holding a woman firmly by the arm. She was rolling drunk and he had to catch her once as she started to slide down to the floor. She was crying copiously, drunken tears which ran down her withered cheeks and stained wet the front of her dirty black dress.

'Yes, Constable?' The sergeant looked over to the pair with irritation.

'Excuse me, Sergeant Brown,' said the constable. 'I'll take her into the cells until you're ready for her.' As he took the woman through a door at the side the woman began wailing and when this had no effect she began cursing the constable, the sergeant and the police as a whole.

'As I was saying,' said Tom, 'I think you should put out a general alert for this young boy.'

'I can't do that,' said the sergeant. 'It's against regulations. No, come back in a week if he is still missing. Likely you'll have heard from him by then.' Why the doctor was so interested in the lad he didn't know. Or was it the lass he was interested in? She was certainly something of a looker, thin and pale though she was.

'But Ben would never go away without saying, without telling me,' said Merry. 'He wouldn't. I'm sure something's happened to him.'

Sergeant Brown was becoming impatient now. If it hadn't been for the presence of the doctor he would have indulged in some plain speaking about the young hellions from the mining villages he had to deal with every day. They were quite capable of doing anything, anything at all.

73

Anyway, if they lived at Old Pit they must have been living like gypsies, the pair of them. That was probably where the lad was when he thought of it, away with the gypsies.

'I have work to do, sir, if you don't mind?' he said pointedly to Tom. So Tom and Merry had no option but to go.

Outside on the road of High Bondgate they stood for a moment. Tom took out his pocket watch and noted the time – he was already late for his afternoon surgery.

'Try not to worry too much, Nurse Trent,' he said. 'I'm sure Ben will come home soon, you'll see.' Though he was not sure at all, really. 'I have to go now, to my surgery. I'll give you a lift as far as Winton if you like. You look tired.'

'Thank you, Doctor,' said Merry, taking her tone from him. 'You've been very good.'

As the trap turned into the market place Miles was just emerging from the Queen's Head Hotel with a woman, Miss Bertha Porritt. They had been taking tea in the lounge. Miles had met Miss Porritt, by design rather than accident, when she was looking at the latest winter fashions in Jones's Department Store. She had happened to mention on the last occasion he had visited her father that she liked to see what was new in the shops and usually on a Friday afternoon. The town was not so busy on a Friday. Thursday was market day when the town was thronged with people from the pit villages and the farming villages up the dale, all after bargains. Fridays, the shopkeepers had more time to give to their better clientele, she had informed the two men in her not quite strident tone.

When Miles met her in the street on this particular Friday and offered to give her a cup of reviving tea at the Queen's Head she had agreed instantly.

'Was that Dr Gallagher?' she asked, now leaning to one side to see round the corner where Tom's trap was disappearing behind the town hall. 'Surely he has someone in the trap with him?'

Miles smiled though his mood had turned black as thunder. 'One of his patients I shouldn't wonder. He has a practice in one of the colliery villages. He is a tender-hearted young man. No doubt he will learn as he gets older that it is impossible to help these people. I know, I've tried.'

'I'm sure you are just as tender hearted as your son, Mr Gallagher,' Miss Porritt gushed. 'I'm sure you just pretend to be hard, but if there is a truly deserving case or with those close to you ...' She let the sentence trail off.

'Do call me Miles, at least when we are alone,' he said. 'I think we know each other well enough now, don't you?'

'Indeed, Mr Gallagher – Miles. And you must call me Bertha.'

He was making progress, thought Miles triumphantly. It was all ridiculously easy. Really, she wasn't so ugly. Her eyes were quite fine in fact. He handed Bertha into her carriage, holding her fingers in his a little longer than was strictly necessary.

'Would it be convenient for me to call on you, Bertha, perhaps on Saturday afternoon? Say three o'clock?'

Bertha couldn't conceal her delight. 'Of course, Miles, I will look forward to it,' she replied and Miles indicated to her coachman to drive on.

This evening he would have a serious word with Tom, he thought. Anyone could have seen him riding through the town with what looked like a girl who was little more than destitute. He wasn't going to do his reputation any good, let alone his chances of building a practice among the decent people of the district.

Merry ran down the field after leaving Tom, hoping against hope that Ben had come back. When she reached the village she closed her eyes for a minute.

'Please God,' she prayed. 'Please God, let Ben be here. I don't care where he's been so long as he's safe home now.'

He was not. The whole place was hushed and silent. Even the goat wasn't bleating but laid on the ground with its legs tucked beneath it as it dozed in the early dusk.

Merry went inside and lit the fire and put the kettle on to boil. She took out the ashes and spread them on the old slag heap, then milked the goat which bleated sleepily in protest. Her milk was diminishing – she should have been taken to the billy before now, thought Merry. Ben had been going to do that. Oh Ben, what am I going to do? She laid her head against the animal's side and wept. After a while she dried her eyes and carried the milk into the house. She had not thought to buy in groceries so there was nothing much to eat apart from a heel of stale bread. She warmed milk and added a spoonful of sugar to the bread, pouring the milk over it to make broily.

When it was ready she forced herself to eat quickly, standing up. Then she went out again looking for anything that might give her some idea of where her brother was. The shadows were long across the grass as she climbed the stile into the field. This time she turned left along the old pack-donkey trail. She had the lantern with her so was not too worried about the approaching dark. As she went through the gap into the next field, she saw Mr Parkin herding cows back to the byre, ready for the evening milking. Curious as always the cows paused in their slow walking and turned to look at her. One or two came up to her and gazed straight into her face, their tails swishing from side to side. Merry waved her arms and they moved back warily.

'Did you find your brother then?' called Mr Parkin and 'U-urp u-urp!' at the cows as they headed off again up the field.

'No, Mr Parkin, I didn't,' Merry answered as he came up to her.

'Now where the heck has the lad got to?' the farmer asked, almost to himself. 'I'm sure it's not like him.'

'I don't know, Mr Parkin,' said Merry. 'I went to the police station in Auckland but they said it was too soon to say he'd gone missing. Anyway, they said, he might have run away to sea, he's old enough.'

'Tripe and onions!' Mr Parkin said. 'He's never run away to sea. The lad wanted to be a farmer.' He was walking away as he spoke, for the cows had reached the top end of the field and were waiting to be let through the gate. 'I'll keep an eye out,' he said over his shoulder. 'Don't worry too much, lass. I'm sure the lad'll be all right.'

Merry nodded and went on down the lonnen where generations of pack donkeys had carried coal along towards the coast before the days of the steam engine. It was almost dark now and she turned right with some idea of climbing the hill from where she might see something, anything that showed Ben had been this way. There was nothing. Oh, a few hoof marks where a horse had been ridden along, perhaps taking a shortcut across country to one of the villages dotted about the Durham plain.

By the time Merry reached the top it was too dark to see anything; she wasn't thinking straight, she told herself. She stopped beside the old stone-built ventilation shaft and leaned against it to get her breath. Away in front of her she could see the glow of a pithead, she wasn't sure which – Shildon or Winton perhaps. The sky was clear but for the dark plumes of smoke rising through the glow.

Merry had brought a lucifer to light the lantern and she struck it against the stone now and did so. It cast a circle of light around her, showing the bramble bushes where she had so often picked fruit to make jam. Or sometimes gran had made a suet crust, rolled out and filled with black-berries and sugar and rolled up in a pudding clout to boil. And it had tasted wonderful with a little goat's milk poured over the top. The purple juice would stain the white milk in little eddies and Ben had loved it. She must pick some late berries and make Ben a suet pudding – Ben. Merry realised her mind was letting go of reality, she was so tired. She must go home to bed, she had to work tomorrow. She set off, and stumbled almost immediately on something, stub-bing her toe. Bringing the lantern light to bear on it she saw it was the ladder, the iron ladder that had once run up the

77

side of the ventilation shaft. She looked quickly at the shaft. Had it just happened? Had Ben been climbing the shaft when he should have been digging over the vegetable garden for the winter? Had he fallen in?

Merry leaned against the shaft and shouted. 'Ben? Ben? Are you in there? Ben?' But there was no sound from the shaft, no human sound at least though there were rustlings and the distant sound of water slapping against stone. She stood the lantern on the ground and tugged and pulled at the rusty iron ladder until somehow she had it propped up against the stone shaft.

It did not reach to the top. From the top a piece of jagged iron jutted out, barely discernible against the dark of the trees and the sky above. Still, if only she could get nearer the top perhaps she could get a grip on the top stones, she thought. The bottom of the ladder dug into the soft earth at the base, so it should be safe enough. Merry put a foot on the bottom rung and stepped up; the ladder stood without wobbling as she climbed higher.

When she reached the second from last rung she was still about a yard from the top of the shaft. Merry clung with the fingertips of one hand to a stone that stuck out from the rest and with the other hand she clung to the ladder. Leaning her forehead against the stone she called again.

'Ben, Ben, answer me, Ben, please!'

An owl flew by suddenly, swooping low by her head and hooting as it snatched up something from the grass beneath a bramble bush. It startled her and for a moment she panicked as she felt her balance go, the ladder moving. Then she steadied herself and the ladder held. She looked up and for a moment crazily contemplated climbing the stones, but common sense prevailed. Much better to ask for help in Winton Colliery or Eden Hope.

Gingerly she climbed down and jumped out of the way as the ladder fell to one side once her weight was removed. She had kicked over the lantern as she jumped but luckily the light hadn't gone out. Merry picked it up and set off

78

back to Old Pit. She was tired to the point of exhaustion and had to get some sleep.

As she walked home Merry felt the blackness of despair. If Ben was inside the shaft he could be dead. Or he could be injured and unable to cry out. 'Or he could not be in the shaft at all,' she said aloud. What was the good of looking on the black side all the time? Pull yourself together, girl. She could almost hear Gran berating her for her attitude. She had to make proper plans, especially if Ben was somewhere in danger. She had to find him and she had to get other people to help her. The folk in Winton Colliery would help her; she knew they would. Tomorrow morning she would go there again and this time she would not be too timid to ask for help. This time she would knock on doors, get off-shift miners to help her. She would do it.

How she was going to manage without going in to work at the hospital she didn't know. But she would manage. By hook or by crook. The most important thing was to find Ben.

Merry got back to Old Pit, undressed and sluiced herself under the pump outside by the light of a half moon that shone fitfully down. She had never washed there since she was a little child and that was in the hot weather. But the cold water on her skin felt good and afterwards she towelled herself dry and went straight to bed. Her skin tingled and she was warm beneath the bedclothes. Anxious thoughts still filled her mind but nature took over and she slept the night through.

Chapter Ten

'I'm afraid we're short staffed today, Doctor Gallagher. The auxiliary has not turned up for duty. I'm beginning to think that Nurse Trent will have to go; we cannot have anyone who is unreliable.'

Tom looked up from scanning the patients' notes at Sister Harrison's stern expression. He had come early to do the rounds because he was bothered about Merry Trent and her brother. He wanted to know if the boy had come home, something he was naturally concerned about.

'She probably has a good reason for not turning up for work, Sister,' he said. 'Her young brother has gone missing—'

'Nothing should come before a nurse's duty,' said Sister. 'This will be a black mark on her record when the time comes for her to apply for training. She may not be accepted by the Board. After all, the Board will have to bear most of the costs of her training and if she is unreliable it may be a waste of the ratepayers' money.'

'Come on, Sister, have a heart,' said Tom. 'Her brother is her only relative now that her grandmother has gone. Besides, she must have years to go yet before she is old enough to do any formal training.'

Sister Harrison was affronted at the suggestion that she was being heartless. 'That may be so but my first concern is my patients, Doctor,' she said. 'Now the cleaning has not been finished and half the beds remain unmade. When Doctors' rounds begin everything has to be ready for the patients' comfort.'

By this Tom was to understand that he too had offended against hospital routine by turning up early for the ward round.

'Do you wish me to go and come back later, Sister?'

Sister Harrison's starched cap quivered and rustled against her starched collar. 'Oh no, certainly not, Doctor. It is entirely up to you when you wish to see patients.'

'Righto, then, let's get on with it,' said Tom, rising to his feet. He picked up the notes and handed them to the sister. 'The sooner I start the sooner I will get out of your way.'

It was half-past ten before Tom left the hospital. He set off along Cockton Hill, unsure what to do. He didn't have a surgery this evening as it was Saturday and so for the rest of the day he was free – Dr Macready, whose practice was at Eden Hope, did alternate weekends with him and this weekend it was his turn.

He would go to Old Pit, he decided. After all he could say he was concerned for Ben, as he surely was. First of all he would call in at home to see if there were any messages. Also, he might be in time to have coffee with his father, feeling a little guilty at spending so little time with him.

Miles was in his study when Tom put his head around the door. The coffee tray was on the table and he was sitting in one of the comfortable leather armchairs before the fire smoking his first cigar of the day.

'Morning, Father,' said Tom. 'I thought it would be your coffee time. I've told Polly to bring another cup.'

'Where have you been? Have you been out all night with that ... that pit lass I saw you riding round Bishop Auckland with yesterday for anyone to see?' Miles growled without any preliminary greeting. He had been

81

mulling the scene from the day before over in his mind and got angrier every time he thought of it. 'Don't you realise we are known in this town and have a position to keep up?'

Tom blinked. He couldn't remember seeing his father in the town. 'What?' he asked. 'What did you say?'

'You heard me well enough,' snapped Miles. 'There you were driving round the market place in Auckland in the trap with a miner's brat beside you. And you don't come in 'til this time of the morning. You're a disgrace, sir, a disgrace.'

There was a knock at the door and Polly came in with a cup and saucer. 'Will I pour, sir?' she asked, looking at Tom, but it was Miles who answered.

'That will be all, Polly,' he said. 'Close the door behind you.'

'Yes sir.'

She went out to tell Cook the master was in a right temper, fit to burst his boiler. They'd best keep out of his way, she reckoned.

When she had gone, Tom took time to pour coffee and sit down in the armchair opposite his father's. He crossed his legs and took a sip of the dark-brown liquid, murmuring appreciatively. Meanwhile, Miles was becoming redder in the face.

'Well?' he barked.

'First of all, Father, I was not out all night with anyone. I was asleep in my own bed upstairs. And I have just returned from Oaklands, the workhouse hospital in Auckland where I have a duty to attend the inmates who are old or infirm or both.'

'Hmm. Well, thank God for that,' snapped Miles. 'Now about this girl—'

'Yes, what about her, Father?' Tom was calm, his voice cold.

'What were you doing riding about through the market place with her in the trap? Our family has a name to

82

keep up, what are you doing associating with someone like her?'

'How do you know what I was doing yesterday afternoon?' Tom countered.

'What does that matter? As it happens Miss Porritt and I were just coming out of the Queen's Hotel when you came riding past, bold as brass, the pair of you.'

'Oh, Miss Porritt,' said Tom as though that explained a lot of things to him. As of course it did. His father would not want Miss Porritt to see his son associating with the lower classes.

'Yes, Miss Porritt. How do you suppose it looked to her?'

'Does it matter?'

'It does, I am thinking of asking Miss Porritt to marry me. It does not help when she sees my son keeping low company.'

'Merry Trent is a patient of mine!' said Tom. 'She works at the hospital and I was giving her a lift. She is in trouble and needs help, she is barely sixteen and lives alone with her brother in one of those broken-down old houses at Old Pit, and he has disappeared.'

The fact that his father did not reply immediately escaped Tom for the minute. He was thinking that Merry would have to move from Old Pit; she couldn't stay there on her own, not unless Ben came back. Perhaps he should try to get her lodgings near the hospital, for the moment anyway.

Miles had had a shock. He hadn't realised the girl in the trap was that boy's brother. Or thought she was at least. Wouldn't the baby who had been in the house that awful night have been the woman's granddaughter? What a flaming tangle everything was. Why hadn't he gone back to Old Pit himself since it happened? At least he would have known what was going on and done something about it sooner. As it was, he had avoided the place for thirteen years. Why hadn't the woman told him she was pregnant in

83

the beginning? He could have paid her to go away, though to be honest with himself he wouldn't have acknowledged he was the father. And of all the bad luck for the lad to grow up with such a striking likeness to Tom – and himself, of course, when he was younger, but that wouldn't have mattered as people forgot what one looked like thirty years ago.

'Father? Are you all right?'

Tom's voice broke into his racing thoughts. Miles got up abruptly and put his coffee cup on the tray.

'Yes, of course I'm all right. Her brother has disappeared, you say? Well, he's probably run off to sea, you know what these pit lads are like. Wild, you know. You've met them no doubt in your practice.'

'She says he would not do that. He wouldn't go without at the very least leaving her a note. I gather they are very close, those two. It probably comes from them growing up the only children in a deserted village.'

'Well, none of it is your business. I've always said that nothing would come of your practising in a mining village. Now, forget about this girl, and mix with your own kind. I've told you before, find a town practice and I'll help you with the cost. Why don't you find a suitable girl to marry? A doctor needs a wife if he wants to get on.'

'I'm happy working in Winton Colliery, Father. It is what I want to do.'

Miles lost his temper. 'Well I forbid you to talk to that pit lass! And don't ever give her a ride in your trap again, especially not where you might be seen by gentlefolk. I won't have people talking.'

'I'm afraid you're not in a position to forbid me to do anything,' said Tom calmly.

'Am I not, begod! You ungrateful young whelp, I've given you everything! You're living in my house and while you do so you will do as I say, do you hear me?'

There was a knock at the door and Polly opened it but

was stopped in her tracks by a bellow from Miles. 'Get out!' She went in a hurry.

'I couldn't get the coffee tray,' she told Cook. 'The master wouldn't let me in. They're having a row in there.'

'Well, girl,' snapped Cook. 'Get on with your work, you can help Edna upstairs. It's nothing to do with you whether they're having a row or not.'

Polly sniffed and left the kitchen. She would have a nice gossip with Edna over the beds, she thought. Cook could get so uppity sometimes.

In the study Tom drew himself up and stared levelly at his father. 'I can move out anytime, Father,' he said. 'I will not be told how to run my life; I am no longer a boy.'

'Go then,' said Miles. 'You've been nothing but a disappointment and embarrassment to me in any case.'

'If that's how you feel I'll go today,' said Tom.

'Do that.'

Miles heard himself say the words but he could hardly believe he was doing so. How had things escalated to this? He didn't want Tom to go, not really. But he was so stubborn, just as his mother had been. He had his mother's temperament even if he did look like his father.

'I will. If you'll allow me time to pack a bag. I'll send for the rest of my stuff when I'm settled.'

Ten minutes later as he stood at the window and watched Tom drive out of the gates and turn towards the town, Miles felt very sorry for himself. The lad had provoked him, it was true, but if he himself hadn't been so worked up and worried about the other one – for a moment he saw his face vividly, the eyes closed, a bruise forming on his temple, and he shivered. He didn't want Tom to move out – the house was too big for one man to rattle around in. There was the staff of course, but they were not company. Tom was his son and his heir and he ought to do what his father wanted.

Miles sat down in his chair again. He was supposed to be

going to call on Bertha but he'd never felt less like doing anything.

Merry stood on the patch of grass that surrounded the old ventilation shaft watching the party of men and boys milling around. They had rigged up a rope ladder and a lad of about nineteen was now sitting astride the top of the shaft, legs astride and bending down perilously low to peer inside.

'There's nowt to see down there, Da,' he announced, sitting up straight again. He gave Merry a sideways glance as he spoke to his father, who stood at the bottom with another rope slung over his shoulder. 'Nowt but water by the sound of it.'

'Give a shout, Robbie lad,' advised his father, who was Bob, the colliery joiner. 'Mebbe he might be on a ledge or something, asleep.'

Or mebbe dead, he thought but didn't say so, not in front of the bit lass. She was in a bonny taking over the lad, her brother she said it was. Though that was something of a mystery an' all – how could it be her brother? Everyone knew when the disaster at Old Jane Pit had happened.

It was a fine day and when she'd come into the rows a crowd of off-shift men were by the ball alley on the gable end of one of the houses. The lass was obviously in a state about something. He recognised her as the lass from Old Pit, Mrs Trent's granddaughter. So he had asked her what the matter was.

The miners were paid once a fortnight and this was the hungry week, so they couldn't afford the club or the institute. It had been easy to get a few of them together to go and search out the lad.

'I never knew she had a brother,' said one, looking puzzled. He had once worked at Jane Pit.

'Aye well, she has,' said Bob. 'He's nowt but a bairn, only thirteen, so howay, let's get going. I'll get rope from the joiner's shop.'

'Rope, what do you want rope for?'

Bob sighed. 'Will you stop asking questions and get the lads organised? The lass is worried to death, can you not see? We're going up by that ventilation shaft on the old pack-donkey trail. You know, on the lonnen to Eden Hope.'

So now the gang of them were here, on a sunny autumn afternoon, looking for the lad and picking a few late brambles while they were on and stuffing them in their mouths.

Bob climbed the ladder and sat atop the wall of the shaft by his lad. It wasn't exactly black down there; some light was getting in but it wasn't possible to see the bottom apart from the occasional glint of water, or at least something wet. He put his hand around his mouth and bellowed. 'Ben? Ben are you there, lad?'

The sound reverberated round the shaft but there was no answer.

'I can go down, Da,' said Robbie. 'If I tie a rope round me I can reach that platform there, anyroad.'

'Aw, I don't know,' his father replied doubtfully. 'I wouldn't dare go home if owt happened to you. Your mam would kill me.'

'Go on, I want to Da.'

In the end, the boy prevailed. The rope was secured on the outside and Robbie descended, walking down the wall with his feet as he held on to the rope. The men waited anxiously, ready to haul on the rope should it show signs of giving way, but it held firm.

An anxious ten minutes later Robbie was shouting to be brought up and they all joined in hauling on the rope.

'There's nothing to see, Da,' he said as he climbed onto the rim of the shaft, breathing heavily. 'I doubt he's not down there. Or if he is he's a goner.'

Merry, standing on the grass at the bottom, gasped and thrust her fist into her mouth.

'Mind what you say!' snapped Bob.

'Sorry Da.'

87

'It might not have been him that broke the ladder at all, pet,' said one of the pitmen. 'Look, if he's about here we'll find him, I promise you.' He turned to the others. 'Howay lads, spread out, we'll search the woods.'

Chapter Eleven

Miles Gallagher was writing a letter to the mine owner, his employer. Mr Bolton also owned the Arthur Bolton Ironworks in Middlesbrough and rarely came near the mines in south-west Durham, which supplied the ironworks with the coke needed to smelt iron. In many ways he was a remote figure even to Miles, his agent. Yet he insisted on detailed, meticulous reports on a weekly basis and, of course, the mines had to keep up the steady supply of coal for coking. Apart from this, Miles had a fairly free hand, he thought with satisfaction.

There have been some complaints from the local council concerning the general state of areas surrounding worked-out mines. Therefore I made time to ride around the vicinity of Old Jane Pit, the scene of the unfortunate explosion fourteen or so years ago. There is evidence of people living in the old cottages and also a tinker's encampment close by. I will give orders for them to be evicted and the site tidied up. This will easily be paid for by the materials still salvageable from the area.

Miles sat back and stared out of the window at the garden. All the flowers were gone now and the trees bare, the bushes sodden with rain and blowing in a northerly wind.

It was quite true that the council were making noises, prompted by the *Auckland Chronicle*. Only last week there had been an article in the *Chronicle* complaining about the areas of barren waste left behind when a worked-out mine was abandoned. It was as well to show a willingness to do something about it, especially when the expense would be minimal. And of course he had his own reasons for clearing the area of vagabonds, reasons that were nobody's business but his own.

Miles got to his feet and walked over to the fireplace, turning his back on the fire and lifting his jacket a little to let the heat of the flames get to his backside. His thoughts turned to his son, Tom.

Tom was living in the town in some poky boarding house in Tenters Street. It was ridiculous when this house was big enough to allow him three or four rooms should he wish for them – even if he himself did marry Miss Bertha, Miles thought. Tom could have his own rooms in the east wing; Bertha was unlikely to object, why should she?

He contemplated marriage to her with little enthusiasm. There was no quickening of the pulse at the thought, not at all like the time before he married Tom's mother. But what the hell, there were compensations, not least the prospect of managing the mines she would own when her father turned up his toes. Mr Porritt was just about in his dotage now; it would be a kindness to take the responsibility off his hands. The old man had made it plain that he wanted to see his daughter settled as soon as maybe, too.

He would go over there later on when he had seen to the matter of Old Pit. He crossed to the fireplace and rang the bell to summon Polly.

'Tell Johns I want Marcus saddled and ready in ten minutes,' he said to her when she appeared. 'And tell Cook I won't be in to dinner,' he added.

'Yes sir,' said Polly and withdrew. Johns was sitting at the kitchen table with a mug of tea and a piece of Cook's excellent fruitcake. He sighed heavily, took a large swallow of tea and stood up.

'That man seems to know when I'm having my ten o'clock,' he said. 'I suppose I'd best go then.' Stuffing the remains of his cake in his mouth he went out to the stable.

Cook compressed her lips. 'That man will suffer with his innards, having his eating interrupted like that,' she said. She watched him through the window, a stocky little man with rolled-up shirtsleeves and open waistcoat, and only a few wispy hairs on top of his head.

Polly glanced at Edna knowingly. Cook was soft on Johns; it was plain for anyone to see. It was becoming something of a joke in the kitchen.

'Now then, get on with your work,' Cook said sharply as she caught sight of their smirks. 'Have you even started on the dining room?'

Miles rode down the field and opened the gate that led onto the old line. Marcus nickered at an old pit pony that had been put out to grass and it trotted over. As he paused to open the gate the two horses rubbed noses; Miles looked at the galloway with disfavour. One of his eyes was milky and blind, the other looked to be going the same way; there were blue-black scars across his face and on his back, no doubt from when he had been working low seams where even his ten hands in height were too big.

Miles pulled his horse away, took him through the gate and closed it after him. He trotted along outside the hedge and the old galloway trotted along inside, whinnying. Lonely no doubt, Miles told himself. He would have to have a word with the manager – better to have the animal put down than leave him alone in that field in the cold of the coming winter. He would have a word with Mackay, the manager at Winton.

Merry scrubbed away at the bedpans in the sluice. Her fingers were red and raw from the carbolic acid solution she was using to sterilise the enamel pans, and even though she was used to that she winced as the solution got into a keen on her forefinger. She ran the cold tap on it quickly and the sharpness eased.

'Are you nearly finished, Nurse?'

Sister's voice behind her made Merry jump; she turned off the tap and turned to face Sister Harrison who was standing by the door.

'Yes, Sister. This is my last one.' She finished the bedpan quickly and put it in the rack.

Sister looked round the sluice for signs of slipshod work she could complain about but she had to admit there were none. The draining boards were scrubbed white and everything was spick and span. Her eye fell on Merry however, and she looked disapproving. The girl's hair was slipping down from under her cap and wisps were hanging on her neck. The heavy rubber apron she was wearing on top of her cotton one was twisted round and damp around the waist where she had leaned over the sinks.

'Go and tidy yourself up, Nurse,' said Sister. 'What Matron would think if she saw you like that I don't know. Be sharp about it too, we're almost ready to go to dinner. You are to go first turn today.' Sister Harrison didn't approve of Nurse Trent, though she had to admit that the girl had improved since she conveyed her doubts to Matron. It had been disappointing that the girl was not dismissed; instead she had received a severe warning from Matron. Perhaps someone had put in a good word for the Trent girl.

Merry gazed into the tiny mirror in the nurses' cloakroom. She had hung the rubber apron in the cupboard in the sluice, rolled down her sleeves and retrieved her stiff cuffs from the drawer. Now she took off her starched, enveloping cap and pinned her hair more securely before replacing it.

There were shadows under her eyes from lack of sleep and worry about the whereabouts of Ben. 'Where are you,

Ben?' she whispered into the mirror, but of course there was no reply, not even in her heart. Sighing she turned for the door; it wouldn't do to keep Sister waiting.

Merry was living in the Workhouse Hospital now. Not in the workhouse wards but in a tiny room of her own that Dr Gallagher had advised her to apply for. It was bare of furniture except for the bed and hooks to hang up her clothes, but at least it was handy for her work, which meant she could spend more time looking for Ben. All her spare time was spent in looking for Ben. Sometimes Robbie, the joiner's son, helped her. Robbie was sweet on her, she knew, but she hadn't time for anything like that. She was glad of him to help her in her search, though sometimes she felt a pang of conscience that she was using him.

'I don't care,' Robbie said to her more than once. 'I've nothing better to do.'

It was a fortnight now since Ben had disappeared. Merry was sure something terrible had happened to him. It must have done or he would have got in touch with her. Why would he run away to sea? Ben had shown no interest in going to sea; not once had he mentioned it. The police in Auckland weren't interested either. She had even gone to the police station in Shildon but they were uninterested too.

'Lads are always running away from home,' the desk sergeant had said.

'He wouldn't,' Merry had replied and the desk sergeant had sighed.

'Right then,' he had said. 'Let me have his birth certificate and I'll put out a call.'

That was the trouble; she didn't have a birth certificate for Ben; not a birth certificate or a baptismal certificate. She searched Gran's box where she kept all her papers. She found her own certificates, her mother's death certificate and also her father's. 'Killed in a pit explosion,' it said. 'Buried in the pit.'

The trouble was, the dates didn't match up. How could Ben be her brother when he was born so long after her mother and father were dead? Merry's thoughts went round and round it in her head whenever she had a moment to herself or lay down in bed to try to catch some sleep; and now, as she walked to the nurses' eating hall. They didn't eat with the paupers, getting marginally better rations.

The trouble was, the Board of Guardians kept back three-quarters of her wages to pay for her room and food, which made her only slightly better off than the paupers. Soon, when she had time, when she could spare an hour from her search for Ben, she would get a room in the town. Then she could save a little on food perhaps, towards a home for herself and Ben when he returned. For he would return, of course he would; the alternative was unthinkable.

She thought of that day when the off-shift men had helped her search for Ben. They had searched everywhere, but there were no more signs of him. Two men had even gone down the disused ventilation shaft again, climbing down from staging platform to staging platform. All rickety, all creaking alarmingly, but they had been tied securely together by a rope anchored at the top. Her heart had been thumping wildly as she waited for their shout, dreading the possibility of them finding Ben's body.

'Nothing to see down there,' they had reported. 'Nothing but an almighty stink.'

Tomorrow was the start of Merry's spell of night duty. If she went to bed as soon as she went off duty she could be up at six o'clock in the morning and go over the ground again. Also, she had saved enough money to put an advertisement in The *Northern Echo* asking for any news of Benjamin Trent, aged fourteen years, who was missing from home. And she had a wild hope that he might have been back to Old Pit and left a message for her.

'Any reward?'

The man behind the desk in the newspaper office looked over his spectacles at Merry. She was silent; for some reason she hadn't thought of the need for a reward.

'I could just put "reward",' the man said kindly, seeing

94

her dismay. 'If there is no answer it won't matter, if there is you will surely find something.'

'All right then,' said Merry. It was pay day on Friday. She had been going to buy badly needed new ward shoes but if she cut out cardboard soles and put them inside the ones she had, well, perhaps she could make them last for another fortnight. Or maybe she could sell Gran's rocking chair? She didn't really want to but she had left it at Bob Wright's house and worried that it was in their way, though Bob, being a joiner and superior to the miners, had a slightly larger house than they had.

She walked through the woods to Winton Colliery on her way to Old Pit. Going along the road towards the pit yard and waggon way, she almost bumped into Dr Gallagher as he came out of a back street, black bag in hand.

'Nurse Trent!' he exclaimed. 'Why aren't you at the hospital?'

'I start night duty this evening, Doctor,' said Merry. She could feel the colour rising in her cheeks at the unexpected meeting. She must look a mess, having come straight from the ward without bothering to wash or tidy herself. After all, she had thought to spend the day wandering the fields and old workings, just in case some clue to Ben's whereabouts had been overlooked.

Tom gazed at her and smiled, she looked so pretty with her cheeks pink and her eyes bright from the sharpness of the frosty weather. Yet there was still a shadow of unhappiness about her.

'Have you heard from your brother?' he asked and she bent her head quickly to hide her suddenly damp eyes.

'No,' she said and pressed her upper lip hard against her teeth to stop the tears coming. She rarely cried but, of course, wouldn't she just make a show of herself now, in front of Dr Gallagher? He would think her weak minded and silly.

Tom looked at her, noticing now how thin she had become. Her hands were red and chapped; seeing him look

95

at them she thrust them into the pockets of her coat, for she had no gloves despite the bitter cold.

'Come and have a cup of tea in Mary's teashop,' he said. 'It will warm you and we can have a talk. I've half an hour before surgery. I've been visiting Mrs Green, poor soul. I'm afraid there's little anyone can do for her.' Merry knew Mrs Green, though not very well. She was an old lady who was bedridden and lived with her daughter in the same street as the Wrights.

'Well?' Tom prompted.

'Thank you, I will,' said Merry. After all, what was half an hour? She could still go on with her search later and probably be better for the warm spell and the hot drink.

Chapter Twelve

Merry wandered along at the end of the lonnen, the old pack-donkey road now overgrown with straggly bushes and patches of dead nettles. She kept her eyes on the ground searching for what she didn't know – a sign, anything that told her Ben had been that way. It was silly, she knew it was silly but she felt impelled to search and search even though this was ground she had been over before. She even went around bushes to make sure she wasn't missing anything, then climbed over the gate and walked up the hedge at the other side.

She was into the edge of the woods now, the ground cold and dank. Dampness penetrated her old shoes and her toes were numb. A few flakes of snow were falling. Merry looked up at the patch of sky she could see between the trees; the clouds looked heavy with snow. She came to bushes overhanging the barely discernible path and kept in close to them as the snow increased.

Merry was bone weary with lack of sleep and being constantly on the go. She should go back, she knew, but really she wasn't so far from Old Pit – she would be able to shelter in her grandmother's house if need be. The path she was following was probably made by animals – rabbits or a badger – she knew that really. Yet she wandered along it, impelled to go on, further into the wood. She walked further round a bush, seeking for the shelter of a slight overhang of rock behind it.

There was an opening behind the bush. Quite a large opening with rotting wood lying about; wood that must once have been used to bar the entrance. Of course Merry knew what it was immediately: an ancient drift mine, driven into the side of the hill, perhaps centuries ago. There were one or two about, wherever a coal seam came near the surface.

She peered into the gloomy darkness inside as a dreadful fear began to form in her mind – if Ben was in here then he was dead. She found the box of lucifers she kept in her pocket and lit the storm lantern she carried with her. Looking around she saw broken, rotten pit props lying on the ground, a fall of earth and stone blocking the road a few yards in. It didn't look as though it had been disturbed at all.

If she had been less weary, if her thought processes had been working properly she would not have attempted to do what she did. There was a gap near the top of the tunnel; she could see the blackness of it above the fall of stone. She began to climb up, awkwardly transferring the lantern from one hand to the other as she needed whichever hand to dip into the stones.

Merry reached the top, lay panting for a minute or two, then slithered on her belly and held the lantern over the other side. All the time she feared she would see Ben's body lying there.

He wasn't there, at least not within the radius of her light. Merry relaxed suddenly, feeling as if all the breath had left her body. She closed her eyes tight and lay there while tears forced themselves between her eyelids and ran down her cheeks. After a few more minutes she began to slither back down the stone, not so careful now, simply wanting to get to the bottom and out of the tunnel. She was lucky and reached the ground unhurt but for a few scratches on her hands and legs where her skirt rode up. Shakily she got to her feet then stumbled and fell again, dropping the lantern and saving herself only at the expense of her hands, which thrust into the dirt and gravel and chips of stone.

Her left hand touched cloth and she froze, then scrabbled away at the stone until it was uncovered and she could draw it out. The lantern was still alight and she held the cloth near the flame. It was the patch from Ben's trousers; she was sure it was. Dear God, was Ben under the fall of stone? She took a step back and pain shot through her ankle – she had twisted it when she fell, she realised. But that was as nothing compared to the fact that she was becoming sure that she had found Ben. She lifted her skirt and tore a strip from her flannel petticoat; with trembling fingers she bound her ankle, cramming her shoe back on afterwards. Then she made her way back to Old Pit and from there on to Winton Colliery. The off-shift men would help her, she knew they would.

At least, that was her plan. Yet in spite of her determination she got no further than Old Pit for there her ankle finally gave out and it was all she could do to slither over the snow to the house where she was born, and crawl in. It was there that Tom Gallagher found her. The snow had stopped and the sun came out, though there was a cutting wind. Tom had finished his visits and had an hour or so to spare. For some reason he couldn't get Merry out of his mind. He told himself he was just going for a walk before it grew properly dark, to clear a slight headache. When he came across her footsteps in the snow he followed them, telling himself he would go as far as Old Pit then turn back.

The light from the lantern shone through the window of the house on the end of the row. Tom hesitated for only a minute before going to the door and knocking. When there was no reply he went in. The room was cold but dry and Merry was half lying, half sitting against the middle wall, fast asleep.

Tom went over to her and felt her forehead. At least the skin wasn't hot; for a moment he had thought she was ill but now he realised she was simply sleeping the sleep of the exhausted. Even as he thought it she opened her eyes and tried to scramble to her feet before falling back with a cry of pain.

99

'Doctor Gallagher! What are you doing here?'

'I was just passing, out for a walk,' he said, un-convincingly. 'But what are you doing here? It's far too cold for you and what's the matter with your leg?'

'It's my ankle, Doctor,' she said, grimacing. 'I turned it.'

'Let me see.'

Tom undid the makeshift bandage and felt her ankle, probing gently. It was swollen to twice the size of her right ankle and beginning to show bruising. He rebandaged it carefully before sitting back.

'You aren't going to be able to walk on that for a while,' he said.

'But I have to, I have to go to work, I'm on night duty,' Merry said despairingly. 'And I have to get help. I think I've found Ben. I must get help from Winton. He's buried under a fall of stone in an old drift mine entrance.'

'You're sure? I mean how do you know?'

Merry told him about the patch of cloth, then looked out of the window at the darkening sky and made another attempt to stand up. Tears streamed down her cheeks.

Tom caught her as she fell. She felt so thin and light, and his arms tightened round her protectively. He looked around. There was nothing in the room, nothing to provide any comfort or anywhere at all to lay her down, so he held her against him for a few minutes.

'I have to go,' she said weakly.

'You can't. It's snowing again, I'd never get you along the line or even up the path to Parkin's farm.'

He couldn't carry her along the line to Winton, which was where he had left his pony and trap, he thought. She was trembling with the cold and he was not surprised for he could feel it seeping into his bones. In the end he laid her gently down against the wall.

'Stay here, love, I must find something to cover you while I go for help,' he said. 'I'll light a fire, that will help too.' Neither of them noticed the endearment.

100

He took off his overcoat and put it over her then gathered handfuls of dry brown leaves that had collected in the corners and put them in the grate. He went up the rickety stairs and kicked off the door to the bedroom, then broke it into manageable pieces until he was at last able to set the lot alight – heat immediately began to penetrate the damp and bitter cold of the kitchen.

'Isn't there anything that might make you a bed or a chair?' he asked. 'Nothing at all?'

'There's hay next door,' said Merry. 'At least there should be some left from the goat.' She was beginning to feel decidedly light headed with the pain from her ankle and the heat from the fire after the intense cold. As he went out to look for the hay she closed her eyes and slipped off into a sort of half sleep, an escape from the misery of the day.

Tom came in with his arms full of hay and arranged it on the floor by the fire. At least it would provide some comfort, he thought. He picked her up and laid her on the hay. She was still trembling with cold and he held her to him to try to give her some of his warmth. Merry turned to him, snuggled against him and relaxed – only for a moment or two, he told himself. Then he would go and get help in Winton.

'I found a patch from Ben's trousers,' she whispered and clung to him, burying her head in his shoulder.

'I know, you said.'

'I have to get him out of there; he must hate it, not being able to move. Oh, Ben, why did you go in there?'

Tom held her close; put his cheek against hers; felt the cold and wetness of her skin. 'If he's there,' he said carefully, 'he won't feel it, love.' He could have bitten out his tongue because she began to sob wildly. He rocked her gently and waited for the storm to subside.

'What am I going to do? Ben is all I've got,' Merry said brokenly.

'You've got me,' said Tom.

Merry looked at him with drowned eyes and he kissed

her. A kiss that was intended to be comforting, brotherly. Except that it changed as she clung to him, put an arm around his neck and pulled him down upon her.

Their lovemaking was swift, their emotions already heightened so much, their feelings so intense. She cried out once but otherwise didn't make a sound and when it was over she lay quietly, her eyes closed. Tom lay quietly too, his ragged breathing gradually returning to normal. Then he got up, straightened her clothing and covered her with the overcoat. He replenished the fire with the remainder of the wood from the door and went out into the night. It had started snowing again and he had to bend into the wind as he walked along the waggon way in the direction of Winton.

Tom was filled with guilt. He was a doctor, who was supposed to look after people, not take advantage of them when they were vulnerable. He welcomed the stinging of the snow against his face as he trudged along, tripping occasionally on railway sleepers hidden under the snow. His jacket and trousers, without the protection of his overcoat, were soon soaked through, his skin icy and turning numb. He stumbled into the pit yard at last and turned into the manager's office. He had to get men to help him bring Merry in.

'Doctor!'

Jack Mackay was working late, going over in his mind what he was going to do about the latest orders from the mine agent. This was the wrong time of year to be clarting about out among the old workings; why not leave it until spring? He had asked Mr Gallagher but had been told to do as he was told and put some of the maintenance men on the job of tidying up the old workings.

'It means taking them away from more urgent work on bank and underground, Mr Gallagher,' Jack had protested.

'You'll do as you are damn well told!' the agent had snarled. So now Jack was trying to work something out. He'd got rid of Gallagher eventually and now here was his son, soaked to the skin an' all. Daft fool had been out without his overcoat. He stood there, just inside the door and dripped water onto the floor.

'Is something wrong?' Jack asked. 'Come to the fire, man, and thaw out.'

Tom moved to the fireplace where a coal fire was burning with flames climbing up into the chimney, held his hands out to the blaze and spoke over his shoulder to Jack.

'Miranda Trent is stranded at Old Pit. She's sprained her ankle or maybe it's broken, I don't know. The point is the place is a ruin, she'll freeze if we don't manage to get her down to Winton.'

'Miranda Trent?'

'That girl who used to live there. She's an auxiliary nurse at Oaklands. If you give me the names of some men who are off shift I'll get them to help me bring her down. Otherwise she could die in this weather.'

Trent. That was the lass who was making a fuss because her brother had took off, ran away to sea or something. Jack gazed at Tom wondering how he came to be involved with her. Still, she was a bonny lass; he'd seen her sometimes walking down the waggon way. He had meant to warn her off. The agent had been insistent that they should tighten up the rules on trespassing on company property.

'You should go home and get into some dry clothes, lad,' he observed. 'I'll send the maintenance cart up for her. A couple of likely lads can see to it. No need for you to go back. If you're not careful you'll be getting pneumonia.' Steam was rising from Tom's clothes and indeed, he felt decidedly unwell.

'Oh, but—' he began then saw the manager's knowing expression. 'Yes, of course, you're right.' He had to protect Merry's reputation. He walked to the door, then turned round. 'You'll see to it right away?'

Jack Mackay nodded. 'Aye, of course. I'll send a lad down to the rows. No, on second thoughts I'll go myself. It's on my way home.'

Tom went out and took his pony out of the stable, where it stood beside the manager's horse. He harnessed it to the cart and they trotted out of the yard. It was against all his instincts to go before he was sure Merry had been rescued but still he knew he had to. Gossip spread as rapidly in a pit village as anywhere else. Besides, in spite of the rug he had had under the seat and now draped over his shoulders, he was cold and shivery, with a burning spot right at the centre of his chest. Tom was well aware what that meant – he needed to get home and into a warm bath, and dose himself up or he would be in a worse state than Merry by morning.

His horse slowed to a walk, struggling in the six inches of snow as the road turned uphill. Tom closed his eyes and his head sunk into the rug. The horse pulled on manfully, making its way not to Tom's lodging but to his father's house and the warm stable it knew as home. It nickered softly as it turned into the gate and Tom opened his eyes with a start. He felt so ill he didn't even think of turning round and making for the town.

Chapter Thirteen

Robbie Wright was on fore shift and had been home since midday. He had been to bed for a few hours but now, in the early evening, the snow had stopped and he was sitting in front of the fire, idly teasing his little sister, Mona, by taking her rag dolly and holding it high above her head until Mona cried.

'Cry baby, cry baby,' Robbie laughed, and Mona's face crumpled.

'Will you stop teasing the bairn and give her her dolly back? I'll give you a crack about the ear in a minute,' his mother shouted at him.

Robbie threw the doll in the air so that it landed on Mona's head then fell to the floor. Mona wailed and picked it up and hugged it to her.

'Mam!' she cried.

'For heaven's sake, Mona, you're not hurt and neither is your dolly,' snapped her mother just as a knock came to the door. She turned to it in some relief and was amazed to find the pit manager standing on the step.

'Eeh, come in, Mr Mackay, come in do,' she said, though casting a quick glance round at the untidy kitchen. 'You'll catch your death standing out there in this weather.'

'I will for a minute, Mrs Wright,' said Jack. 'I'd like a word with your lad if you don't mind.'

Robbie had jumped to his stockinged feet when he saw

who it was. Something must have happened at the pit, flashed through his mind. Not that he was a safety man, so what could it be?

'It's that lass that lost her brother,' said Jack. 'She's hurt and laid up by Old Pit. You know, those broken-down houses. Well, Gallagher wants us to get a few lads together to bring her down.' He was careful not to say it had been Dr Gallagher and not the agent. That way it might be easier to get lads out in this weather. 'You can take the maintenance waggon up if you like,' he added. 'I don't think you need a pony, though. A couple of likely lads could push and pull it. It's not the weather for a pony to be out.'

Jack pulled his hat firmly on to his head and turned for the door, never doubting for a minute that Robbie would do as he was told. 'Goodnight to you then, Mrs Wright,' he said. 'I'll let myself out.'

'All right for lads to be out but not ponies, eh?' Mrs Wright commented.

'Aw, Mam, I don't mind. I'll get Davey to give us a hand,' said Robbie. He sat down and pulled on his pit boots. 'Any road, ponies cost money,' he added as he laced them up.

'Wrap up well, then,' said his mother. 'I don't want you going down with congestion of the lungs nor nowt.'

Ten minutes later Robbie and Davey were clattering up the line, pushing the cart with Davey's pit shovel on top and a blanket covered with an oilskin. The going wasn't too bad for most of the way as the wind was behind them and the waggon way was well maintained for the first mile or so. It was when the line branched off for Old Pit that their progress was slowed considerably. Here the way was not well maintained and the rails were rusty, in places uneven. They had to shovel snow out of the way and manhandle the cart over awkward parts. By the time they reached Old Pit they were both beginning to puff and blow with the effort.

They had to leave the cart where the line ended at the old colliery workings and walk to where the cottages stood in two lines facing each other. A faint beam of light illuminated the snow driving onto the water pump on the end of the rows.

'Sign of life, any road,' said Dave. He had been quite keen to come in the first place, but soon got fed up with the bitter cold and wet and had wished himself indoors many a time on the way to Old Pit. Now they took their own safety lamps, which had been hanging from their belts and lifted them high as they approached the house.

'Wat cheor? Are you there, lass?' Davey shouted before they pushed the door open and went in.

'Oh thank God you're here!' cried Merry. She had pulled herself along until she was almost on top of the dying fire. Tom Gallagher's overcoat was pulled around her and wisps of hay stuck to her hair. She gazed at the two young miners. 'Oh it's you, Robbie,' she said. 'And Davey too. Are you on your own?'

'Do you think we can't manage to get you down to Winton then?' Davey asked. 'Were you expecting someone else?'

'No, no, I'm ever so grateful to you both for coming to help me.'

'Well, we can manage you fine. We've got the maintenance cart on the end of the waggon way, and a nice blanket to keep you snug.' Robbie knelt down beside her and looked her over. 'Your leg, is it? Your ankle, eh? You'll see, we'll manage fine.'

They did, of course, wrapping her up in the coat and making a chair with their hands to carry her between them to the cart, where they covered her with the blanket and the oilskin on top.

When they finally reached the pit yard at Winton Colliery the snow had stopped and the sky cleared. The moonlight created an eerily beautiful landscape with the slag heap covered in snow like an Alpine mountain towering by the side and the winding wheel whirring above them. The cage came to bank and decanted the men from the heat

107

of the mine to the icy cold of the north wind blowing through the yard; they stood for a moment shivering as long drags were taken on the first pipes lit after ten hours, and men coughed deeply before heading home.

It was all like a dream to Merry as she lay on the maintenance waggon. But she had to sit up now, shrug off her weariness and decide where she was going to go and how she was going to get there. There was no possible way for her to get back to Oaklands tonight. Robbie was before her, however.

'You canna go back the night. You'd best come to me mam's,' he said. 'Me and Davey will take you there. You can sleep in our Mona's bed.'

'Mona might not like it,' said Merry.

'She's nowt but a bairn, so she'll do as she's told,' Robbie asserted. 'Howay, Davey, give us a hand here.'

Davey opened his mouth to say something – he was tired and wet and wanted his supper and had had quite enough of tonight's adventure.

'It's a working day the morn,' he muttered.

'What? Did you say summat?' asked Robbie, giving his friend a hard stare.

'Nay. I said nowt,' said Davey and held out his hands to make a cradle with Robbie's.

'You understand, Dr Macready, the lad was caught out in the snowstorm last night. I'm a little worried about him; this morning he seems to have a fever. He should have had more sense than to go out on call to a panel patient in such atrocious weather. There was probably nothing much the matter with her anyway. You know what they're like.'

Dr Macready grunted, a sound that could have meant anything. He thought of the family he had just left – four children down with whooping cough, two of them frail and unlikely to survive. But there was no point in fighting the prejudices of men like the mine agent who seemed to be permanently at war with the workforce.

108

'I tell you plainly, I wanted Tom to take a private practice in the town,' Miles went on. 'What future is there in practising in a place like Winton Colliery?'

'There is the satisfaction of helping people who need it,' said Dr Macready, who had never been in a position to buy into a private practice and didn't want to in any case.

'If I could see my young colleague?' The doctor grasped his black leather bag and turned to the stairs. 'I have a surgery in half an hour.'

'They'll wait,' said Miles but he led the way up the staircase to Tom's room. Polly had been sitting by the bed but now she rose to her feet hurriedly and bobbed a curtsey.

Tom appeared to have been dozing but when the two men came into the room he came awake. His face was flushed and his eyes bright; a pulse beat at his temple, fluttering.

'Perhaps you will help me, my dear,' the doctor said to Polly and she stepped forward to unbutton Tom's nightshirt so that Dr Macready could examine him. He took his time, making a thorough examination, then he smiled at Polly. 'Cover him up, my dear,' he said. 'Thank you.'

'You don't have to tell me, Doctor,' Tom said in a voice barely above a whisper. 'I can feel it.'

'Rest easy, Doctor,' Macready replied. 'You have nothing to do but get well. You know the importance of rest as well as I do.' He motioned to Miles who had been standing silently by, almost as shocked by the deteriorisation he saw in Tom as he had been by the appearance of his son late the evening before. He followed the doctor out of the room.

'How do you find him, Doctor? You should have been here sooner! But the weather, we couldn't get hold of you—'

'I don't think a few hours delay would make a great deal of difference,' Macready interrupted. 'You did the right thing, putting him straight to bed and keeping him warm. I got here as soon as I could.' In fact he had been up all night, first with a difficult birth and then the children with whooping cough. These he hoped to get into Oaklands today if the roads were clear enough for the horse ambulance – then, perhaps, he would be able to snatch a few hours sleep this afternoon. Except that Tom's surgery would have to be attended now as well as his own.

'He has acute double pneumonia and will have to have professional nursing,' the doctor said now. 'I can arrange for that if you wish; a day and a night nurse is essential. I won't hide the fact that the crisis could go either way when it comes.' Miles paled and Dr Macready looked at him keenly. 'Sit down man, you've had a shock. I assure you I'll do my best for him, apart from his being a friend of mine he is a very good doctor and we can't afford to lose anyone of his calibre. But with poulticing and the right treatment . . .' He let the sentence trail off.

Miles had recovered himself and now rose to his feet.

'Thank you Doctor, I'm sure you will. I'll let you go now, I'm sure you need to get on with it.' He led the way to the door, his attitude plainly saying waste no more time. After Macready had gone, he stood in the hall for a moment, biting his lip. Briefly he thought of the other one – was he being paid back for his treatment of *him*? Miles shook his head, dismissing the thought. It was stupid; he didn't believe in such things. He climbed the stairs to Tom's room. The lad would recover – why shouldn't he? He would have the best treatment he could possibly get.

Merry was laid on the horsehair settee in the corner of the Wrights' kitchen. Apart from the fact that her ankle throbbed and the horsehair pricked her legs through her thin skirt, she was desperately uncomfortable.

Mrs Wright didn't want her there; she made that fact obvious having said hardly anything to her since Robbie and Davey brought her in.

'Merry lives at Oaklands,' Robbie had explained to his mother. 'She can't get home tonight, not when she can't walk. I knew you wouldn't mind if I brought her here, Mam.'

110

Mrs Wright didn't answer, nor did she smile a welcome. She simply stared at the girl so that embarrassment filled Merry. She considered asking Robbie to take her to the Hawthornes, for surely they wouldn't turn her out. But Robbie was taking off his pit boots and stretching his legs out on the fender towards the fire. She couldn't ask him to go out again.

Doris Wright lifted the heavy iron kettle from the fire and mashed the tea in her large brown pot with the cracked lid. When it was brewed she poured tea into a pint pot and added three sugars before handing it to Robbie. Robbie glanced up at her.

'Give Merry a cup of tea, Mam,' he said mildly. He winked at Merry and said by way of excusing his mother, 'She always thinks of me and Da first, like.'

His mother poured a cup of tea and added a spoonful of condensed milk and took it over to the girl. 'What sort of a name is Merry, then?' she asked as she held it out.

'It's short for Miranda. My gran said it was her mother's name,' said Merry. 'Thank you for the tea.' She took a sip of the dark-brown liquid, which was hot and sickly sweet.

'It sounds daft to me,' said Doris. She looked at her son and back at the girl. Merry could almost see what was going through her mind. Mrs Wright thought Merry was setting her cap at her only son and she didn't like it.

'We can't help our names, Mam,' said Robbie. He smiled at Merry. 'How does your ankle feel now, lass?'

'Not so bad,' said Merry, though in truth the pain from it was making her feel sick. She was beginning to think a bone was broken and if it was, what would she do? Already Sister thought she wasn't reliable, coming on to the ward tired and late because she had been out looking for Ben.

The thought of Ben brought it all back – finding the piece of cloth yesterday in the entrance of that ancient drift mine.

'What's up?'

Robbie had been watching her and noticed immediately when her expression changed to one of distress. 'Is it

111

worse? Should I go and get the doctor?'

'Don't be so bloody daft, man,' said his mother. 'Dr Gallagher would be spitting blood if you called him out on a night like this just 'cause a lass has sprained her ankle.'

Something stopped Merry from saying the doctor had already seen her ankle. 'No,' she said, 'I was just remembering –' how could it ever have slipped from her mind? '– I was up in the woods looking to see if I could see any sign of where Ben had gone and I found this.' She pulled the square of cloth from her pocket.

'What's that?'

'It's a patch from Ben's trousers.'

'Where did you find it?' Robbie leaned forward to get a good look at the piece of cloth. 'We were all over there when we were looking for the lad.'

'In the entrance of an old drift mine.'

'Eeh, I didn't know there was one there.'

'Yes. Up by that rock overhang, behind the bushes. The entrance is all overgrown but if you look hard enough you can see it. It was covered with wooden planks at one time but they've rotted away. And so has one or two pit props from just inside. There's been a fall of stone there, where the pit props have fallen.'

Merry began to cry, suddenly overwhelmed by everything – the realisation that Ben was probably under the rubble in that forsaken mine entrance; that she had forgotten him because she herself had a bit of pain from a sprained ankle. She had even acted like a loose woman with Dr Gallagher, letting him do what he liked. The inside of her thighs and her knickers still felt wet with it. And Ben lying there under the rubble unheeded. She was bitterly ashamed of herself.

Robbie walked over to her and knelt beside her. 'Never mind, lass, I'll get the doctor the morn when I get back from the pit. I have to go in a minute, I'm on fore shift, but I'll go for him, I promise. And me mam will look after you, won't you, Mam?'

He patted her head clumsily and offered her a grimy handkerchief. 'You'll be all right, Merry, I'll look after you. See if I don't.'

Robbie was absorbed in her and so didn't see his mother's expression as she stood behind him, but Merry did. Doris Wright was spitting fire, and looked as though she was ready to consign Merry to the flames of hell or at least throw her out of the house into the snow. But she said nothing, at least, not in words, though her gaze at the girl was full of hate and spoke volumes.

Chapter Fourteen

The Guardians have decided that in view of your poor work record they have no alternative but to rescind their offer of financial support for you to train as a nurse at Newcastle General Hospital. We are reluctantly making this decision, especially as you showed such promise when you first applied.

Reliability and dedication to the work is essential in nursing staff and we feel these are qualities of which you do not show sufficient evidence. Dedication especially is essential and nothing must interfere with your duty.

We have to tell you therefore that your employment at this hospital is now terminated.

The letter was addressed to Merry at the house on the end of Middle Row, the Wrights' house, for she was still there. It was signed by the Clerk to the Guardians and it was from the Wrights' house that she had written to the Board two days before, explaining her absence from the wards.

She stared at it in disbelief. It just couldn't be true; it must be some nasty prank being played on her. How could she help it if she had broken her ankle? For that was what was wrong with it, Dr Macready had told her, when he put it in a splint of gutta-percha bound with a flannel bandage.

'It should heal quickly if you don't put any weight on it,

lassie,' he had told her. 'Come to see me in a month's time at the surgery. It's not a bad break, I'm sure.' In fact he was not entirely sure it was broken at all but in such cases he considered it best to treat a suspected break like an obvious one.

Merry hardly believed it was broken, preferring to believe Dr Gallagher who had said the night it happened that he didn't think it was broken at all, but was merely sprained. Tom Gallagher – the thought of him made her tingle. She couldn't think of him, not now.

'Are you sure it's broken, Doctor?' she had asked Dr Macready anxiously. He had frowned blackly and Merry had blushed – it was an impertinence to question a doctor's judgement. Yet her time working at the workhouse hospital had taught her that doctors did not always know as much as ordinary people thought ... though she trusted Dr Gallagher.

Hurriedly Merry got to her feet with the aid of a sweeping brush with a clean duster over the bristles; it made a reasonable crutch. She limped over to the table and began to clear the dirty crockery left there since breakfast into an enamel bowl. Every time she saw the frowning disapproval of Robbie's mother she felt she ought to be trying to find somewhere else to live – anywhere – a spare corner out of everyone's way where she could wait until she could walk on her damaged ankle.

Now she hopped to the fireplace, lifted the kettle and poured hot water over the pots. She added soda and a grating of coarse yellow soap, and began to wash up, standing on one foot and bending the other leg so that she was supporting it on a chair.

Doris Wright came in from the yard where she had been dashing pit clothes against the coalhouse wall to get rid of the caking of coal dust which covered them after every shift underground. She deposited them in the corner by the fire where they would be ready for Robbie to wear. He was on night shift this week and would be going out at three o'clock. She spoke in a low voice because he was in bed.

'Haven't you done those pots yet? Oh, get out of the way, I haven't time to wait all day for you.' She shoved Merry aside, almost causing her to topple to the floor. As it was, Merry saved herself by grabbing hold of the table. Doris didn't appear to notice. Feeling utterly defeated, Merry sat down.

'I've got the sack from the hospital,' she said.

Doris looked at her, her thin lips tightening. She turned away and walked to the door as though going out, then turned back.

'And what are you going to live on, miss? 'Cause it's bloody certain you cannot live on us, nor our Robbie neither. It's time you found somewhere else an' if the only place is the workhouse you'll have to go there, won't you?' She glared at Merry, her hands on her hips.

'I'll keep meself, thank you!' said Merry.

'Oh aye. And how are you going to do that exactly? Live on fresh air, can you?' Doris taunted. 'You had a good job an' a better chance than most other lasses around here and what did you do wi' it? Chucked it away, that's what. No, you're angling to trap my lad so you'll have a meal ticket for life, that's what. Don't think I haven't seen you making eyes at him 'cause I have!'

'I haven't, no, I haven't,' cried Merry, feeling sick, but Doris Wright was past listening. All the pent-up resentment she had been harbouring since Robbie brought the girl into her house was pouring out now.

'My Robbie's a good lad; he's going to take his under manager's ticket. He could marry a lass wi' a bit behind her. He doesn't have to marry a nowt like you that's been living up in Old Pit among falling down houses 'cause she couldn't get anything better. An' that's another thing, all this tale about a lost brother, why man, nobody believes a word you say about him. Ben Trent? There never was a lad called Ben Trent. If there was he never went to school here. He wasn't baptised at the chapel neither.'

116

'There was, of course there was.' Merry was amazed that anyone should say such a thing. It was as though Ben was of no account, had never been of any account. It was true that Gran had kept them away from Winton Colliery, and Eden Hope an' all for that matter, and Ben had gone to school in Shildon. But he had gone to school, she could prove it.

Suddenly she remembered that the policeman at Bishop had been sceptical when he discovered she didn't have a birth certificate for Ben, after which he hadn't bothered looking for him much.

'Ben was my brother! No, I mean, he is my brother, I'm telling you.' He was alive, she was sure Ben was still alive. Robbie and his marras hadn't found a thing when they moved the pitfall in the old mine. Though of course they hadn't been able to move it all. But Doris was speaking again, cruelly and sarcastically.

'Oh aye? Then mebbe you can tell me how it is your mam died when you were born? I know she did 'cause Etty Morrison told us before she went off yon side of Durham. So what was it, a miracle birth? Or did your gran pinch him from the gypsies?'

Doris laughed, a hard, amused, cruel laugh. That was a good joke she'd made.

Merry looked at her, fighting back the tears, for she wasn't going to let this spiteful biddy know just how much she had been hurt. 'I'll go,' she said. 'I'll go as soon as I can.'

'Aye well, you haven't got much to pack,' Doris jeered.

'Don't worry about that. I have plenty of clothes in my room at the hospital.' She had a spare shift and pair of knickers and petticoat, much patched. And of course, her Sunday best dress.

'Aye well, you won't have far to move them, will you? Just to the workhouse next door.'

Merry opened her mouth to retort but both women were stopped in their tracks by the roar from upstairs.

117

'What the hell is all the racket? Can a man not have his sleep in peace without being woken up in the middle of it?'

Robbie came thumping down the stairs in his bare feet, his trousers pulled on anyhow over his nightshirt and his braces hanging down by his sides.

'Did she wake you up, son? Eeh, I'm sorry, she just wouldn't shut her gob,' cried Doris.

'Aw, Mam, you were shouting an' all. How a man is supposed to go to work when he cannot sleep—' Robbie stopped as he saw Merry pulling on her coat and wrapping her head and neck in a shawl. 'Where are you going? You're not fit, man, you cannot walk yet!'

'She's going back to the workhouse where she belongs,' his mother said calmly and Robbie shot her a venomous look.

'I have to go, Robbie,' said Merry quietly. 'I have to get my things, anyway. I've lost me job.'

'But where are you going? You've nowhere to go, have you?'

'I can always go back to Old Pit,' said Merry.

'Aye, go on. I heard there was a gang of tinkers there any road, and like goes to like,' Doris jeered. Robbie ignored her.

'You can stay here, never mind what she says,' he said and his mother gasped.

'Robbie!'

'No, I have to go, Robbie,' said Merry. 'Thank you both for having me,' she said formally. 'I hope I can borrow the broom. I'll bring it back when I can.' She slipped out of the door.

'Wait! I'll get me boots on—'

But Merry was away, hastening down the yard as fast as she could considering her splinted ankle, and set off down the row to the corner where she hoped to get the ten o'clock horse bus that went into Bishop Auckland. The cobbles were slippy with ice where the sun had not yet reached them, so her progress was slow and she was panting by the

118

time she got to the end of the row, but luckily the bus was standing there with only a few people sitting on it.

The driver was untying a nosebag from his horse's head. ''Ere lass, I'll give you a hand up,' he said and took hold of her arm.

'Never you mind, I'll do it.'

Merry glanced round. Robbie had come after her, his jacket slung on anyhow and his pit boots unlaced. He was collarless and his shirt neck was open.

'Robbie, you shouldn't. I told you I could manage,' she said. 'You need your sleep, you're on shift the night.'

'I won't sleep now, not a wink,' Robbie said grimly. 'I'll follow you down. I'll take the path through the woods and be there as soon as you, likely. I'll just get me coat and scarf.'

The women already on the bus watched the two with interest.

'It looks like Robbie Wright is sweet on that lass,' one observed to her friend.

'I bet Doris Wright is spitting feathers about that an' all,' her friend replied.

As the horse clopped its way down the road and around corners, stopping now and then to pick people up – it was Thursday and market day in Auckland and the town would be full of housewives from the surrounding pit villages – Merry allowed herself the luxury of thinking about everything that had happened.

She had been so sure that Ben was under the rubble in the entrance to the ancient drift mine. Yet she hadn't wanted to believe it. Desperately she wanted him to be alive, to be at sea, to be somewhere, anywhere on this earth. But she knew him too well – Ben would not have deserted her, she was certain he would not. She rubbed her forehead with her forefinger, felt the pulse that beat there. A fog of unhappiness clouded her mind.

Merry allowed herself to think of Tom, remembering the feel of him beside her in the house in Old Pit. The warmth of him, the touch of his hands, how he made her feel safe

119

and taken care of. He had aroused feelings in her she had never suspected she was capable of. In a way she felt guilty at the strength of those feelings for surely all her thoughts should have been concentrated on the fact that she thought she had found Ben, on her grief for Ben.

The bus was approaching the market place in Bishop Auckland and the passengers were stirring, gathering together shawls and baskets. She could hear the fishwives from Shields, calling their wares.

'Caller herring, fresh cod, drawn from the North Sea this very morning!'

The horse stopped at the edge of the market, puffing and blowing with distended nostrils. Merry limped down the steps, the pain in her ankle excruciating for, of course, she hadn't brought the makeshift crutch made from Doris Wright's sweeping brush. Still, she had a small store of money, one pound eleven and twopence to be exact, and she could buy a cheap walking stick from the stall next to the fishwives. It cost one and threepence but it had a rubber tip so wouldn't slip on the cobbles. It was a long walk up to Oaklands and all uphill. She hobbled along, stopping at times as the crowds surged around her up the road that was straight as a die, for it had been a Roman road.

In spite of her predicament, Merry was feeling a little hopeful. Though Tom had not been to see her at all since *that* night, and must have known where she was, Dr Macready had said something about having to do two men's work, so there could have been a good reason for it. But surely he would be at the hospital; this was his time to be there. She could bump into him at any time. She paused and gazed into Lipton's window, not at the display of tinned goods and packets of tea but at her reflection against them. She wished she had had time to tidy herself better, but she could go to her room and wash and comb her hair – perhaps even put on her good dress now that she was no longer expected to wear a uniform apron. She did look a bit like a waif at the minute.

There was his overcoat too, though it was still at the Wrights' house. She had the coat to return to him; she could mention it. Her thoughts were interrupted as a shadow came behind her, blotting out her image in the glass.

'Robbie! You shouldn't have come, I can manage. You need your bed if you're to work tonight.'

'I'll get a couple of hours later. I wanted to make sure you would be all right. Howay, you can lean on me to walk up to Cockton Hill.'

Merry looked at him and sighed. He acted as though they were going together and they weren't – she was nobody's lass. And she didn't want to meet Dr Gallagher while she was leaning on Robbie's arm.

'If any of the other lads see you they'll have a laugh,' she said and it was true. Men, proper men didn't link arms with lasses, not pitmen didn't. His marras would call him a Nancy-boy if they caught him doing that.

Robbie wasn't a bit bothered. 'They wouldn't dare, man,' he said cheerfully. 'If they did they might end up with a smashed nose or a broken head. Nay, they won't mess wi' me.'

Merry had to admit it was a great relief to have his hard, well-muscled arm to lean on. It didn't take long to reach the workhouse and the hospital wards behind.

'Wait out here, please, Robbie,' said Merry. 'I won't be long. I just have to see Matron and collect my things. Then you can help me find a lodging house.'

'You can come away home wi' me,' said Robbie. 'I'll soon put me mam straight, she won't bother you.'

'I'd best be on my own,' said Merry and he was silent. He might say what he would do but Merry knew Doris was the boss in their house.

The interview with Matron was short. It was a waste of time appealing to her, the meeting of the Board of Guardians had made the decision and Matron could do nothing about it even if she wanted to, which evidently she did not.

121

'You have proved yourself unreliable, Miss Trent,' she said. 'I would have thought you would be grateful for the chance to train properly that the Guardians were prepared to give you. You let them down badly, didn't you?'

'I couldn't help hurting my ankle, Matron,' Merry ventured.

'No excuses, Miss Trent. I cannot abide excuses.'

'No Matron, I'm sorry. But I hoped I would be able to use my room at least until my leg is better.'

Matron looked affronted. 'Use the room? Certainly not, Miss Trent. It will be needed for someone more deserving. You may go now and please ensure you clear your things and have the room clean and tidy within the hour. If you don't mind, Miss Trent.'

'But—'

'Miss Trent, if you are desperate for somewhere to stay perhaps you can satisfy the Guardians you are destitute and want to enter the workhouse?'

'No. No, I don't,' Merry said quickly. 'I can manage. I just thought ... well, never mind. I will find somewhere, don't worry about me.' She lifted her chin in the air and limped to the door. Dare she ask about Dr Gallagher? She had nothing to lose, she told herself, and turned back to Matron.

'I wonder if you could tell me if Dr Gallagher is in the hospital, Matron. He was kind to me and I want to say goodbye.'

If it was possible, Matron looked more affronted than she had before. 'No he is not, and if he were I shouldn't think he'd want such as you bothering him.'

'He's not here?' Merry was despairing and Matron's expression became even more forbidding.

'That's what I said. Dr Gallagher does not work here any more.'

Matron was not prepared to discuss a doctor with this girl any more. 'I think you should go, Miss Trent,' she said, rising to her feet and Merry went.

He didn't work at the hospital any more and he wasn't working in his practice at Winton Colliery. Tom had disappeared, just as Ben had disappeared. Merry was defeated. It was obvious that Tom had left to get away from her, she thought. Otherwise he would have got in touch with her – he could surely have found her in a small place like Winton Colliery?

Miserably she went to her tiny cubbyhole of a room where she packed her straw box and tied it round with her grandfather's leather belt. Then she went out of the workhouse grounds to where Robbie was waiting, leaning against the high wall, watching the folk go by.

Chapter Fifteen

'I'd best stay in a lodging house tonight,' said Merry. She and Robbie were standing in the market place. They had been waiting for the horse bus to take them back to Winton Colliery, but thinking about it as she stood there waiting, she had decided not to go after all. She fingered the purse in her pocket, feeling the few coins through the thin fabric and wondering how much it cost to stay in a lodging house. Perhaps she had enough to last the week at any rate.

'You'll come away home with me,' declared Robbie. 'Me mam's bark is worse than her bite, man, she won't let you stay out in the cold.'

'Will she not?' Merry murmured. She thought Doris Wright would cheerfully let her stay out in the cold, would even chase her out with a broom, the one she herself had been using as a crutch. She put her bandaged foot on the ground experimentally, trying her full weight on it. 'It feels a bit better, Robbie. I don't think it is broken. If I find a place in the town this afternoon I can look for a job the morn.'

Robbie snorted. 'Don't talk so daft, lass. You'd be much better coming home. There's others would take you in any road.'

Merry thought about it. Of course there were the Hawthornes, but she didn't really know them that well,

124

even though Jim Hawthorne had sold them the goat. No, she would not put herself back in the position where she was beholden to anyone as she had been at the Wrights' house.

'I'll stay in the town,' she said. 'Tomorrow I'll get a job, you'll see.'

'Oh aye, and what about your leg?' asked Robbie. 'Going to hop to work then?'

'It's getting better,' said Merry. 'I've got my things now an' all. If I stay here I can start looking for work first thing in the morning.' She lifted her bundle. 'I won't come back with you now, Robbie, I'll find a place don't bother about me.'

'Don't be a bloody fool!'

Merry looked at him going red in the face, his temper rising in a way that reminded her of his mother. But he wasn't going to stop her, not now she had made up her mind.

'I'm off,' she said. 'Thanks any road.' With a tremendous effort she managed to stop herself from limping as she made towards Bondgate.

'Merry!'

Robbie started after her and caught hold of her arm. 'You'll do as I say, or—'

'No, Robbie, I won't,' she said determinedly. People were in the market place, waiting for horse buses or wandering round the stalls and they were beginning to take notice. One burly stallholder started towards them as though he was going to intervene.

'Let the lass alone,' he shouted and Merry took advantage of the fact that Robbie turned away to face the stallholder to slip away in the crowd, and was soon walking along the narrow street that was Bondgate. There were a couple of small lodging houses there; she had often seen the notices in the windows. Once she heard Robbie shout her name but she didn't look back.

He had helped her a lot and she should be grateful to

125

him, she knew, and felt guilty. But she wasn't about to let him tell her what to do. And she wasn't going back to his mother's house, not even if she starved. Besides, she had a plan. She wasn't going to starve, she was going to make something of herself even if she had to start scrubbing floors or working on the coal screens at some pithead.

It was almost dark when Merry made her way up the drive of Miles Gallagher's house. She hadn't been thinking of it as the agent's house at all, just as somewhere she might get news of Tom. Once she had got somewhere to live the worry about Tom came to the front of her thoughts, for something must have happened, she was sure of it. Tom would not just abandon his work at the workhouse hospital, nor his surgery in Winton. Nor was he the sort of man who would take a girl down then forget about her, no, he was not.

She would just ask at the house if he were there, if he was all right. Her leg throbbed as she hobbled up the drive and she knew she should rest it – she would, just as soon as she found out about Tom.

Merry had rented a tiny room in Back Bondgate. She had had to pay 3/6d in advance and she knew there was no way she could pay for a second week unless she got a job. She was walking now with the help of the stick but tomorrow she would have to walk without it, she knew that. No one would take on someone who needed a walking stick.

A horse came trotting round the corner of the house and Merry shrank into the hedge for it was Mr Gallagher, Tom's father, the man she had been dreading meeting. But of course he had seen her and pulled up his horse beside her and glared down.

'What are you doing here? Get off my property or I'll call the constable,' he said, his tone as harsh as his expression.

126

'I want to see Dr Gallagher,' said Merry, standing her ground. She hadn't done anything wrong, so he had no right to speak to her like that, she thought and lifted her chin, determined not to be browbeaten by him.

'Do you indeed? And why did you want to see him?'

'I have a message for him. I have his coat; he left it.'

'Well, you won't see him here,' said Miles. 'And if you have his coat why haven't you brought it?' He stared at Merry searchingly. 'Aren't you the girl I saw with him in his trap once? Pestering him, are you? Well, you won't any more, my girl. Now be off with you before I do call the constable. Or take this to you!'

He raised his whip threateningly and she shrank away instinctively.

'Go on, you heard what I said.'

Miles was grinning, now he'd seen the flash of fear in her eyes. Merry turned and went down the drive, forcing herself to walk rather than run. Behind her she heard the horse start to follow her but she did not look round. She had forgotten all about her ankle though her hand gripped the stick, ready to do battle if she had to. At the gate she turned for the market place, still not looking back, on edge, her pulse racing, her tense muscles aching. She did not relax until the sound of the horse's hooves faded away as Miles Gallagher took the opposite direction. Suddenly her ankle throbbed painfully, though it was not as painful as her feeling of humiliation.

Back in her attic room in Back Bondgate, Merry sat on the bed, for there was no chair, and munched the penny dip she had bought from the butcher down on the street. The bread bun contained no meat but it had been dipped in the juices and fat that had come out of the meat the butcher had roasted only that morning and it was tasty and satisfying. Then she drank the sweet tea she had brought up from the kitchen she shared with all the other tenants and lay back on the bed.

She needed to rest her leg – had to if she was ever

127

going to get work to pay for her room and food. She closed her eyes but sleep didn't come, not at first. She thought about Tom and his father. She had been wrong about Tom; he must be keeping out of her way. He didn't want to see her. Maybe he was just like his father and despised her. She saw his face in her imagination and she couldn't really believe that. No, his eyes were kind; he worked hard for workhouse folk, didn't he? And the people of Winton spoke well of him. Anyway, he looked more like Ben than his father, she thought drowsily. Even if all three had the same colour eyes, his father's were cold and hard.

Something niggled at her as she drifted into sleep – there was something about the Gallaghers, what was it? But the warmth of the bed and a full stomach lulled her and she slept.

At nine o'clock the next morning Merry was walking down Newgate Street once again. She was thankful that the swelling in her ankle had almost gone, as had the pain, so at least that meant it wasn't broken. She had even been able to leave her stick behind in the lodging house. She wore her black serge skirt, which she had sponged and cleaned only a day or two before when she was living at Winton Colliery, and her only decent blouse under her shawl.

The sun shone and there was an air of coming spring about. Everyone she passed seemed to look cheerful at the change in the weather, and Merry's natural optimism bubbled inside her. She would go up one side of Newgate Street and down the other, she decided, looking at all the notices in the windows for any that advertised for help wanted. Surely someone would employ her? Of course they would, all she had to do was persevere. Hadn't Sister Harrison once said that anyone could get work if they tried hard enough? Merry had wondered about that at the time but now she was going to put it to the test.

She had walked all the way to Cockton Hill and back on the other side of Newgate Street, almost into the market place once again, when she saw a notice in Turner's newsagent shop.

'Boy wanted to sort and deliver newspapers and do odd jobs,' it read. 'Apply within.'

She could do that, she thought and better than any boy.

'I can do it,' she insisted to Mr Turner. 'As good as any boy and better.'

'It's not the job for a lass,' said Mr Turner.

'What's the difference? I'm strong, let me try, please. I need a job, really, mister, I do.'

Mr Turner hesitated and looked at her searchingly. She was a little under average height but she was young and strong – he could tell by her hands she had been used to hard work. And he was sick of training up boys who more often than not got up to tricks when they should have been doing their rounds and were less than useless in the shop.

'I'll work for nothing for two days and show you what I can do,' said Merry. 'Please, mister.'

'It only pays seven shillings a week any road,' said Mr Turner. He had reduced the amount by sixpence on the spur of the moment.

'That's all right,' said Merry though she had been hoping for more. She stared at the grizzled man with pepper and salt sideburns and stomach bulging slightly under the waistband of his trousers. Please say yes, she prayed.

'Three days trial for nothing?' he asked.

'I . . . all right,' Merry said, though she would have to do without her dinner for one of those days.

'Can you start now? Mind though, today will just be a half day. It's twelve o'clock already.'

So Merry found herself unloading boxes from the carrier's cart out the back and carrying them into the storeroom. Then she was running about the shop fetching

129

and carrying for Mr Turner until Mrs Turner came in with his dinner plated up and in a basket. The sudden smell of the food made Merry's stomach flip over and Mrs Turner must have noticed the hungry look in her eyes. She was a stout, middle-aged woman with iron-grey hair pulled back in a bun at the back of her head and a black-beaded dress.

'Is this your new boy then?' she asked Mr Turner ironically.

'Now Mrs, don't you create,' her husband answered. 'She's doing a trial for us for nothing, just to show that she's as good as a lad.' He grinned at his wife but she did not smile back.

'Is she then? Well, in my humble opinion a labourer's worthy of his hire even if he's a she. It's three o'clock already; has she had any dinner hour?'

'She didn't start 'til twelve, man,' Mr Turner protested. 'By, lass, you'll have me bankrupt before you know it. I've said it before and I'll say it again. You're too soft by half.'

His wife ignored him and addressed Merry. 'Have you had any dinner, lass?'

'It's all right, I'm not really hungry,' said Merry, though the smell of Mr Turner's dinner in the basket was making her stomach rumble.

'Rubbish,' Mrs Turner said briskly. 'A lass your age is bound to be famished by this time of day.' She turned to Jos and handed him the basket. 'Go and eat your dinner in the back. I'll go over the road and get the lass a bit to eat.'

She came back with a roast beef sandwich with more meat in it than Merry had eaten in a fortnight. 'Get that down you, lass. No, don't thank me, you'll work the better for it. I can see you're doing a good job here.'

She glanced around at the shop. The counter was gleaming where Merry had polished it, the glass front sparkled from her application of a chamois leather, and the papers

130

were laid out in neat rows. Then she nodded to Merry.

'Right then, I'll go in the back and make a cup of tea. Just watch the shop for us.'

Merry went back to her room at six o'clock more content than she had been in an age. At least about that part of her life. The thought of Tom was ever present though, but she tried to hold it off for she couldn't bear to let it fill her thoughts. She bought a bag of chips at the fish shop in Bondgate, filled a bottle with water from the tap in the yard and sat on her bed to eat her supper. Her ankle throbbed a little but it was back to normal size and she massaged it a little before going downstairs for a basin of hot water from the kitchen. There was no one there, in fact there were no sounds in the house at all. It was that time of the evening, she thought. As she went upstairs she heard voices behind one door but that was all.

Merry washed herself all over and slipped into bed. There were noises – laughing and shouting in the street below – but that did not disturb her. She was asleep in minutes but was plagued with dreams of Tom and his father and woke up in a sweat in the early dawn. The pain of humiliation of the previous morning seared her mind, together with the bittersweet memories of Tom as he had been in the deserted village. She had to forget him, she told herself fiercely. It was obvious he didn't want her or he would have sought her out. It wasn't that he was bad, he had just given in to a moment's temptation. And anyway, he was far above her, wasn't he? His father had made that plain enough.

A pale grey light was coming through the threadbare curtains. She had to get up, had to be at the shop in time to help Mr Turner sort the newspapers for the morning rounds and then she had to go out on deliveries. She had to forget about Tom, she told herself again.

Outside on the street there was a cold wind channelled down the narrow, medieval street and she drew her shawl around her shoulders. At least she'd thought to wear both her vests and warm petticoat. She would be a couple of hours out in the cold, she reckoned, delivering papers to South Church Road and Kingsway.

Chapter Sixteen

'We will be married at St Anne's of course,' said Bertha. She nodded to emphasise her words and the bird adorning her hat wobbled dangerously. 'Next month I think, so we must go to see the vicar.'

'Yes dear, of course, I'll make an appointment with him.'

Miles spoke absently, watching his son's reactions to the news that he was marrying again. Tom was sitting in a winged armchair between the fireplace and his bed. This was the first time he had been allowed out of bed by Dr Norton, the specialist Miles had brought in.

'I'm very happy for you both,' said Tom, his voice so low Miles could hardly hear him. It was an effort for him to lift his head and smile at his father and his intended bride. Of course he knew in theory that he would be left very weak by the illness but hadn't imagined it would be so bad.

'I expect you to be well enough to come to the wedding, Tom,' Bertha said with an arch smile. 'So you must hurry up and get better.'

'I'll do my best, Miss Porritt,' he replied.

'Yes. Well, I must be off, there are a thousand and one things I have to do before then,' said Bertha. 'Come along, Miley, you may take me home.'

Tom leaned back against the cushions as the door closed behind them. Miley, he thought, as for the first time he

133

smiled genuinely and not for the sake of politeness. What on earth was his father thinking of?

His mind wandered and he stared into the fire as he watched smouldering coal break and fall with a small shower of sparks. Was Merry all right? Had the miners taken her down to the village and was her ankle better now? It ought to be; the bone wasn't broken he had been fairly sure about that.

Tom moved uncomfortably in his chair. He had not treated her right, in fact his behaviour had been disgraceful. But it wasn't just a man taking advantage of a girl, it had been more than that. He had genuine feelings for her, he loved her and as soon as he was able he would seek her out and tell her so. But for now he couldn't do it. He felt so incredibly weak he could not believe it. Of course he had known anyone recovering from pneumonia would feel like that but that had been theory.

There was a knock at the bedroom door and Edna poked her head round. 'Will I make the fire up now, Doctor Gallagher?' she asked.

'Thank you, Edna.'

She came in and knelt by the hearth, raked ash from the embers and added coal, piling it high for it was a raw day in March and the wind was rattling the windowpanes. Tom watched her idly. She was a middle-aged woman who had been with them since Tom was a child. Her figure had thickened at the waist and there were grey hairs showing beneath her cap, but she was a capable woman and her movements were agile. Edna had never married but her family still lived in Winton, her brothers and father still working at Winton Colliery. The thought gave him an idea. She would know where Merry was, so perhaps she could take a message to her.

'Edna, do you know the girl who lives at Old Pit?'

'Miranda Trent, do you mean, Doctor?'

'That's the one.'

Edna sat back on her heels with the small brush and shovel

134

from the companion set still in her hands. 'Yes, I know her. She doesn't live there any more, she lives in Winton Colliery. With the Wrights. Bob Wright, the colliery joiner.'

'She's lodging with them? Is she all right?' Tom noticed Edna's curious expression. 'I ... last time I saw her she had injured her ankle and I wondered how she was getting on, living out there by herself.'

Edna hung the brush and shovel on the stand and got to her feet. 'Well, she's fine as far as I know,' she said. 'Fallen on her feet, I think. That Robbie Wright is besotted with her, me mam said.' She walked to the door before turning.

'Will there be anything else, Doctor?'

'No. No thank you Edna.' He felt the need to explain a little further. 'You see, she works at Oaklands hospital; I know her from there.'

'She doesn't work there any more, Doctor. That's what I heard. Got dismissed for bad timekeeping. And now I come to think of it, someone said she'd moved.'

After Edna had gone Tom resumed staring into the fire, trying to sort out his jumbled feelings. Robbie Wright – he knew him, a young man not long out of his time. Good looking he was too in a brash sort of way. The sort who swaggered about with his mates, his marras as he would call them, getting drunk on a weekend and often missing his shift on a Monday morning. Robbie had come to see him one Monday morning with a deep cut on his wrist which Tom had cleaned up and inserted surgical clips. Surely Merry wasn't interested in Robbie Wright? Tom felt a sudden surge of jealousy followed by frustration. There was nothing he could do until he was better himself.

Suddenly his tiredness deepened into exhaustion and he fell asleep like a child, his head lolling against the arm of the chair.

Just as she thought she was beginning to make a fresh start in the news agency business Merry came to suspect she was

135

pregnant. For nearly two weeks now she had had to rush outside to the sink in the yard and had been sick and dizzy every morning. Standing over the sink, shivering and retching until she thought her very stomach would come up and desperate to get to work in time to see to the newspapers, she faced up to the fact.

Merry could hardly believe it, for there had been only the once and didn't the women say it never happened the first time? Questions ran through her head at breakneck speed. Could it be true? Where was Tom? Had he really just cast her off like an old shoe? What was she going to do? What about her job? Would she end up an inmate in the workhouse?

She stood up straight and waited for the world to stop spinning round her then wiped her mouth. On her way to work through the half-light of the morning she decided she would try once more to see Tom. She had been to the house where he had lodged and the landlady had refused to tell her anything except that he had left.

'I hope you're not sickening for something,' said Mrs Turner when she came into the shop with her husband's dinner. There had been a brief lull in customers and Merry was leaning against the counter doing nothing – something very uncharacteristic of the lass in Mrs Turner's opinion. 'You're as white as a sheet.'

Merry straightened up guiltily. 'I'm fine. I was just going to tidy the shelves at the back.'

'Well, mebbe you should have a bite to eat first, you're as thin as a lathe,' declared Mrs Turner.

'No, I'll wait until Mr Turner's had his,' Merry protested.

'Indeed you won't,' said Mrs Turner and going to the shop door she closed it and shot the bolt before turning the sign hanging there to closed. Just as she did so someone came to the door and knocked hard.

'Go away, we're closed,' mouthed Mrs Turner.

'Let me in,' shouted the man and Merry turned in surprise for it was Robbie.

136

'It's . . . my friend,' she said and went to the door. Mrs Turner glanced at her in surprise – this was the first time anyone, let alone a young man had sought Merry out in the shop. Merry opened the door and Robbie stepped inside. 'Robbie,' was all she said.

'I want to talk to you,' said Robbie. He was unsmiling as he glanced at Mrs Turner. 'Come away out with me. We can take a walk.'

'I cannot. I have to mind the shop,' said Merry. This was the first time she had seen Robbie since she came to work in the newsagents and she wasn't particularly pleased to see him even now. She had so much else on her mind.

'I'll mind the shop for half an hour,' Mrs Turner intervened. 'You get your dinner. Any road, you're due to half an hour. Mr Turner won't be long now.'

'Are you sure?'

Merry didn't really want to go. Yet after all, she did owe Robbie something for all his help when she needed somebody. And she had to admit, his horrible mother too. If it hadn't been for the both of them she would have had to go into the workhouse or be without a roof over her head. She put on the coat she had bought from the second-hand stall on the market. It was a dark-blue serge which fitted her well and was good protection against the wind and cold when she was delivering papers. But it was shapeless and a size too large for her.

Mrs Turner, who was watching curiously, was struck by how pale and thin she looked in it. There were dark shadows beneath Merry's eyes too. Mrs Turner was beginning to suspect there was something else too. If so she was going to need her young man.

'Be back at one o'clock, mind,' she said as they closed the door with the bell jangling behind them.

They walked the short way down the street to the market place and on the corner Merry stopped and looked up at Robbie.

'Where do you want to go?'

'In here.'

Robbie indicated a small café, which usually did a roaring trade with the market traders. Today it was fairly quiet, it being a Monday. He led the way in, leaving Merry to follow.

'What do you want to eat? You look fair famished to me, you've no meat on your bones. What have you been doing to yourself?'

Merry warmed to him a little. He did sound concerned about her, so he must care for her. He wasn't the type to bother if he did not.

'I'll have a bacon sandwich. But I'll pay for my own, mind. Here's the money.' She held out fourpence but he pushed it away.

'You keep it. You look as though you could do with it.'

Soon they were sitting back at the scrubbed wooden table with the bacon sandwiches before them, together with steaming mugs of tea. He ate his with gusto then watched as she finished hers, leaning forward with his elbows on the table and his large, capable hands holding his mug of tea.

'Now then, lass,' he said. 'Are you ready to come back wi' me?'

Merry paused, the half-eaten sandwich in her hand. 'I cannot do that, Robbie, I told you. I cannot live with your mother. Anyway, I'm all right, I have a nice job with the Turners and a room up Bondgate.'

'You won't need the job or the room, Merry, not when you're married to me. An' make no mistake, I'm going to marry you, I've made up me mind.' Robbie still spoke quietly but with determination.

'Oh Robbie,' Merry said helplessly and looked down at the bacon sandwich she no longer had any appetite for. What a tangle she was in, she thought. She took a sip of tea and suddenly felt the need to be out in the fresh air. The atmosphere in the café was hot and steamy and the smell of the food beginning to turn her nauseous. She stood up and

138

pushed back her chair. 'I have to go,' she mumbled and made for the door.

Outside she leaned against the doorpost breathing deeply of the cold air. The wind which always deemed to be tunnelled down the straight length of Newgate Street revived her. Robbie came out and towered over her so that she stepped away.

'What the hell's the matter with you?' he asked. 'Anybody would think you hated the idea of us getting wed.'

'No,' Merry replied. 'No, it's not that. It was just too hot in there.'

'An' too bloody cold out here,' he snapped. 'Look at you, you're shivering. Howay round the corner out of the wind.' He put an arm around her shoulders and steered her along. Once out of the wind he stopped, but still kept his arm around her, holding her close. The thought ran through his mind that if any of his marras saw him at the minute he would be taunted to death on shift that night. But at the minute he didn't care, she felt so good held against himself.

Merry stood there for a moment. She felt light-headed and was glad of him to lean on. I'll tell him it's no good, she thought. It was never any good.

Just then Robbie pulled her back against the wall as a horse and trap came trotting by, slowing to turn the corner into Newgate Street. She looked up and was transfixed to see Tom Gallagher staring at her with such an expression on his face as she had never seen him wear before. Beside him, his father gave a thin smile and leaned towards Tom to say something. He too was looking straight at Merry and Robbie.

'Tom!'

Merry stepped away from Robbie and called. Behind her, Robbie put out an arm and pulled her back. Tom gazed at them for a moment then looked away along the length of the street. The horse quickened its pace and the trap sped off.

'What do you want with the doctor?' Robbie asked suspiciously.

'Nothing,' Merry said dully. She wanted nothing with him and it was glaringly obvious that the doctor wanted nothing to do with her. Of course he didn't. He had probably forgotten all about her and that snowy night in the deserted village at Old Pit. But how could she forget?

'Robbie,' she said, 'I'll have to go now, I'm needed at the shop.'

'I told you, you should just leave the flaming shop and come home wi' me. Me mam won't say anything to you. She knows she daren't. I told her what I was going to do before I came out.'

'I'm going back to the shop,' said Merry and set off up Newgate Street. After a second, Robbie caught up with her.

'I'll see you tomorrow,' he said. 'I mean what I say, Merry, you'll find out I do.'

Tom rode through Cockton Hill beside his father. The wind was bitterly cold but he didn't feel it. He was well wrapped up in overcoat and scarf, and with a fleecy rug over his knees; he sank back against the padded seat unseeing and unspeaking. He was deep in his own bitter thoughts; his father had been right, he told himself.

Miles looked sideways at him and smiled to himself. It couldn't have happened better as far as he was concerned, seeing the miner with his arm around the girl. If anything it would put Tom off seeing any more of her, that would.

They were going to see Bertha Porritt's father. Tom had not met him before and as the wedding date was looming it was certainly time he did.

Chapter Seventeen

'You're going to have to get wed to your young man,' said Mrs Turner. She had been watching through the window of the back room to the shop and seen Merry's headlong rush down the yard to the lavatory. Now, as Merry came in the back door looking white and shaken the older woman shook her head sadly.

'I'm all right,' said Merry.

'Aye, I see that,' Mrs Turner replied dryly.

'I am. I must have eaten something that disagreed with me, that's all.'

'Like you did yesterday and the day before?'

Merry's shoulders slumped for she couldn't think of an answer.

'Do you think I'm daft, like? I've been around a few years, you know. No, I'd say you're carrying. Fallen wrong, going to have a bairn, put it how you will, it comes to the same thing.' Mrs Turner sighed. 'Eeh, lass, you'd best sit down afore you fall down. I've got the kettle boiled, so I'll make us both a nice cup of tea.'

Tea, the cure-all for everything, thought Merry wearily, but she sank down on a chair after glancing at the closed door to the shop just in case Mr Turner might have heard.

'I suppose it means I'll lose me job,' she said.

'Well you can hardly run about with a bag full of papers when you have a big belly, can you?' Mrs Turner thrust a cup of tea into the girl's right hand and a sandwich into the other. Merry looked at it bleakly.

'Get it down, you'll feel better, you'll see,' she said. 'I might not have any bairns but I carried a few and I know what it's like.' Merry remembered the time Mrs Turner had told her how she'd lost two children stillborn and felt a new sympathy for her. To go through all this and more and not have a baby to show for it! She took a small bite from the sandwich and a sip of tea and after a minute realised that she did feel better.

'I don't know what I'm going to do,' she said. 'I have to work and I'm not going into the workhouse.'

'Nay lass, there's no need for that, is there? The lad's keen to wed you, anyone can see that.'

Merry looked up at her, unable to tell her the truth; it wasn't Robbie's baby was it? And when he found out about it he wouldn't have anything more to do with her, would he?

'Besides, I won't say a word to Jos,' Mrs Turner nodded her head at the door behind which Jos Turner could be heard speaking to a customer. He was becoming deaf as he got older and his speaking voice had got louder to compensate. 'You can work here a few weeks longer if you have to, but the best thing you can do is have a word with your lad, as I told you.'

'Oh, thank you, Mrs Turner,' Merry breathed. She took another bite of sandwich and realised she was ravenous so finished it off quickly. Even a few weeks would give her time to work out what she was going to do. And this week Robbie was not coming by the shop for he was on night shift, going out at midday and working until almost midnight. On Sunday though, she would have to tell him about the baby. She put her hand on her stomach, imagining it was already beginning to swell. She would look after it somehow, she told herself.

'We'll walk through the wood back to Winton Colliery,'

said Robbie. 'I told me mam I was bringing you back for your tea.'

It was Sunday and he had picked Merry up at the corner of Bondgate; now they were walking along Kingsway.

'No, Robbie, I don't want to,' Merry protested. 'I have to talk to you anyway, so we're best on our own.'

'You can talk on the way back,' said Robbie, taking hold of her arm and pulling her along with him. Merry dragged her feet.

The one thing she did not want to do was meet his mother. Not until she had told Robbie about the baby and then he wouldn't want to take her to his home. But Robbie was refusing to take no for an answer and walked on determinedly. Well, she thought, she would wait until they were away from the town before saying anything. It would be better in the woods when they were truly on their own. As it was there were people about, taking advantage of the bright sunshine and the fact that at last there was some warmth from the sun.

In the wood the sunshine was dappled under the trees and there was a smell of wild garlic and fresh new growth. There were clumps of bluebells in bud almost ready to open and patches of new grass, a pure bright green. Robbie slowed his pace and took hold of her hand. His felt hard and there were calluses, but it was also large and warm and capable.

'We could get wed at Whitsuntide,' said Robbie and Merry came to an abrupt halt. He turned to her, smiling. 'I know, I know you haven't said yes yet but you will, lass, you will. It's going to happen, I told you.'

'Robbie,' she said.

'What?'

They had reached the stile that led on to the path to Winton and he leaned against the fence, prepared to humour her.

'I have to tell you something.'

'Go on then.'

143

'You won't like it.'

'Well, spit it out, whatever it is. If we're late for tea me mam will go mad. You're not wed already, are you? Tell us an' I'll kill the bugger.'

Merry bit her lip and she too leaned on the fence for support. 'I'm not married, no. But mebbe I should have been. I'm having a bairn, Robbie.'

There was a silence that seemed to stretch out for minutes. Merry kept her head bowed. Her heart beat so loudly she thought he must hear it too.

'Say that again.'

This time Merry did look up. Robbie was standing up straight and seeming to tower over her.

'I said, I'm—'

'I heard,' he said savagely. 'Who was it? Did some lad take you down?' He caught hold of her by the upper arms and shook her. 'Say it! Say who the bastard is. By God I'll murder him.' His fingers dug into her flesh, bruising the bones.

'No! I can't, Robbie, I can't. I don't know who it was, I don't. Leave go of me, Robbie, please.' An image of Tom flashed before her but she lied, improvising wildly. 'It just happened, that's all. I'm sorry, Robbie.'

'Sorry are you? Why, you little whore, I'll make you sorry all right.There was that many you don't know who it was, eh? Well, I'll give you something to be sorry about!'

Robbie was pushing her down the bank towards the river. At the bottom he flung her on a patch of grass and started to unbutton his trousers. Merry realised what he meant to do and tried to scramble away but he was too quick for her, caught her and dragged her back before she even got to her feet; in a second he was on top of her and had her skirt over her head. He held her down with an iron hand on her already sore breast and when she cried out he moved his hand to her mouth.

'Everybody else seems to have had a slice; I reckon it's my turn. Lie still, you whore or it'll be the worse for you,'

144

he grated out through his teeth. Tearing her drawers aside he began thrusting into her, grunting and panting like a wild animal.

The pain was excruciating. She couldn't move, she couldn't cry out and in spite of her struggles all she could do was pray for it to end. When it did, he still lay on top of her, panting. She could feel the wetness on her belly, warm and slimy.

'Get off me,' she croaked, hardly able to talk. The inside of her lip was bruised from being pressed against her teeth and she could taste blood.

Robbie didn't move so she pushed up at him, trying to heave him away but to no effect. Eventually he did roll off her and started to get to his feet.

'What's the matter? You're used to it, aren't you?' he asked. He was buttoning his flies and hitching his braces. 'By, you had me fooled all right there, I was going to marry you. You lying little—' He broke off and turned away. 'You're lucky I don't give you a bloody good hiding for making a fool of me.' He fingered his belt and for a minute Merry shrank back, her pulse racing even faster.

However, Robbie turned on his heel and set off up the bank to the stile and the path to Winton Colliery. She waited until he was gone and then went to the water's edge and stepped in. The icy water made her gasp, but she welcomed it. She took her torn drawers and bent down to soak them in the peat-coloured water and used them to wash herself; to wash all traces of him from her body. Her skirt got wet in the process but she didn't care.

What a fool she had been to think even for a moment that he might stand by her, that he might even think enough of her to take her on, though the baby wasn't his. Why should a man do that? Why should a man like Robbie do anything he didn't want to do?

Oh God, the baby, please don't let the baby be hurt. As if in reply or reassurance she felt a tiny tremor inside her. She paused in the act of climbing out on to the bank. It

145

couldn't be, of course it couldn't. But yet it was over four months since that night in Old Pit. It had been snowing, she remembered, every minute of that night etched in her memory. It was the worst snowfall of the winter – was it before Christmas or after? She couldn't think straight so pulled herself out of the water. Her feet were numb with the cold as she sat down on the grass and rubbed at them with her skirt. After a minute they began to glow with heat and she pulled on her stockings and shoes. She got back to her feet and the tremor came again. She laid a hand on her stomach but there was nothing to feel from the outside.

She climbed the bank from tree to tree and rested at the top, leaning against the solid trunk of an oak. She was bruised and battered, humiliated and angry at the same time but her baby was alive.

The smell of wild garlic was pungent but she breathed it in, for it smelled of spring. As she set off along the path back to Auckland she saw a flash of blue to one side. A bluebell bud had broken open and the flower danced gently in the breeze. She walked back, her thighs and back aching and her lip swelling against her teeth, but she was determined not to think of anything, not until she was in her own little room in Bondgate with the door closed against the world.

Surprisingly she was hungry but she had the heel of a loaf in her cupboard and a scraping of pork dripping. She made herself a cup of tea in the communal kitchen and took it up with her, then got out of her damp clothes and pulled on her flannel nightgown. She climbed into bed, ate her bread and dripping and drank the tea, sweetened with a little condensed milk. The memory of Ben, which was never far from her thoughts, came again. She prayed for him – surely he wasn't dead, she didn't feel that he was dead. The men had said he wasn't there among the rubble at the entrance of the old drift and that had given her hope. She wept inside a little for him. Then she lay down and slept.

*

Merry had forced herself not to think while she was awake but she could not control her dreams and nightmares. And her nightmares were of the workhouse and also of Robbie Wright, so she slept restlessly, tossing and turning and waking every now and then. But towards morning she fell into a deeper sleep and eventually dreamed of Tom.

'Come with me, Merry,' he said to her, holding out his arms to her and she ran towards him, her whole being flooded with happiness. Then she woke up, still feeling happy and sure everything would be all right. Not only all right but better than that. She would find Tom. But of course, as she got out of bed and dressed in the meagre light from the moonlit window, her thighs and back still ached, her mouth was sore and she remembered yesterday. She remembered too the last time she had seen Tom and the way he had glanced so impersonally at her in the street. He didn't want her and if she did manage to see him and tell him about the baby it would just be an embarrassment to him. She had to face the fact that he did not love her.

Merry went to the shop and sorted the newspapers, before slinging the bag full of them over her shoulder as she prepared to go out with the paper boys.

'Put your shawl over your head,' said Jos, surprising her. He didn't usually take an interest in her welfare. 'That's a raw wind out there and you look a bit femmer to me. I expect you're not sickening for something.'

'I'm all right,' Merry replied. 'You needn't worry about me.'

'Aw, I don't,' said Jos, 'but if you were off work I'd have to train up that gormless Charlie there and that might be well nigh impossible.'

Charlie looked round on hearing his name and grinned, then went out into the dark morning whistling. Merry followed him, smiling herself. She might have known Jos Turner was more interested in how it would affect the business if she were poorly rather than how she was herself.

*

147

'Have you told your lad yet?' Mrs Turner asked a few days later.

Merry nodded. 'I did.'

'Well, are you going to get wed?'

'No.' Merry couldn't say any more. She wished Mrs Turner would just shut up. She couldn't bear to discuss it with her, not Robbie or why he didn't want to marry her any more.

'The dirty swine,' said Mrs Turner forcefully. 'He's had his fun and now he won't pay.'

'It's not like that, Mrs Turner.'

'No? Then what is it like? Something will have to be done about it, you know it will. And the sooner the better in my opinion. You should go after him, lass, he was keen enough, hanging after you like a dog after a bone—'

'I don't want to talk about it, Mrs Turner.'

Merry turned her back and began dusting the shelves behind her, tidying the pencils and stacking the notepaper evenly, trying to think only of what she was doing.

'Well, if you feel like that I'll away home,' said Mrs Turner, sounding very offended.

'Oh, Mrs Turner,' said Merry, looking round at the older woman, but Mrs Turner was tight lipped and with heightened colour she picked up her basket and went out, the shop bell jangling behind her.

'Has she gone?' Her husband emerged from the back shop looking annoyed. 'I wanted to ask her to get me something different for me tea the night, I'm sick of cow's heel, every Friday night it's jellied cow's heel.'

Merry said nothing; she turned back to the shelves, knocking over a box of indelible pencils as she did so that she had to scrabble about on the floor to retrieve them. She heard the bell jangle again but didn't see who had come in until she heard Robbie's voice asking for her. She began to tremble, the last time he had been with her vivid in her mind but she wasn't going to let it show if she could help it. Taking a tight hold on her emotions she got to her feet.

'Good afternoon, Robbie,' she said. Jos Turner glanced at her then went back into the back shop muttering about invoices and paperwork he had to do while trade was quiet. Thursday was the busy time, being market day. Fridays were usually quiet before the bustle of Saturday when the miners' wives usually came into the town.

'I want to talk to you,' said Robbie. 'When do you get off?'

'I don't want to see you, though.'

'I said, what time do you get off? Howay, Merry, don't cut off your nose to spite your face.'

Merry leaned over the counter towards him. 'How do I know you won't do it again?' she hissed.

Robbie shook his head. 'I won't. It's not in me to force a lass. But you made me so mad I hardly knew what I was doing.'

'So that makes it all right, does it?'

'Merry!' Robbie's voice rose. 'I want to talk to you!'

Jos Turner was out of the back room like a shot from a gun. 'Hey, what's all the shouting?' he demanded. 'Get out of my shop, lad, before I call the polis!'

'It's all right, Mr Turner,' said Merry.

'No it bloody well isn't,' Jos snapped, going close to Robbie and glaring fiercely into his face. 'Out, I said.' He poked a finger in Robbie's chest.

Robbie looked down at Jos who was a good six inches shorter than him. For a minute Merry thought he was going to hit the older man but after a tense minute Robbie relaxed.

'Right,' he said. 'I'm going. But I'll be waiting outside.' He strode out of the shop and took up a position on the pavement just outside the door.

'What was that all about?' Jos asked Merry.

'Nothing. It was nothing,' said Merry.

'Aye well, I'll not have a commotion in the shop, mind,' he replied. 'Just think on that.' He stamped through to the back shop again.

149

Merry could see Robbie as he stood outside the shop, not budging, just standing there even when it started to rain. Every few minutes he cast a glance over his shoulder at her, just in case she slipped away out the back, she surmised.

Jos usually told Merry to get away early on Fridays and this Friday was no exception. He put his head round the door and told her she could go at four o'clock. 'An' take that daft loon with you,' he snapped, nodding at Robbie. Merry sighed, she was going to have to face him, so she might as well do it now, she thought.

She went out the back and put on her coat and hat and when she came back into the shop Robbie was standing staring through the glass, making it plain that if she hadn't reappeared he would have come in looking for her, polis or no polis. Calling goodnight to Jos, Merry went out to meet him.

'Let's away down the park,' said Robbie, taking hold of her arm with a firm grip.

'No,' Merry answered. 'I don't want to be on my own with you and I won't be.'

'Aw, man, I told you I wouldn't hurt you again, didn't I?'

'I don't trust you,' said Merry. 'We'll walk up the street and you can talk as we go.'

Reluctantly, Robbie had to agree and they set off along Newgate Street, Merry refusing even to turn off into one of the quieter side streets.

'Well, what did you want to say?'

Robbie stopped by the entrance of the Bishop Auckland Co-operative Society, the Store, as everyone called it. 'Merry, I'm sorry for what I did, I am, honest. It was such a shock, that's all. I know you were likely taken down, it happens with lasses sometimes. But I can't get you out of my head. I'll marry you, I don't care. I'll bring the bairn up as me own, even. Merry, I think the world of you, I do.'

'I don't think I want to marry you, though,' said Merry.

'Don't be daft lass, what else are you going to do? Go to the workhouse? Have the bairn taken off you – that's what happens, isn't it?'

Merry was silent, thinking of Tom – oh, she had been taken in by him all right. She had thought he was a real gentleman but he had proved to be just a nowt, as her gran would have said. By, it was a good thing her gran was dead so she couldn't be shamed by all this. Ben an' all. No, no, Ben wasn't dead a voice cried out inside her. But she wasn't so sure now. Oh, she felt so mixed up.

A woman came out of the Store and pushed past them, her loaded shopping basket catching against Merry's leg.

'Hey, watch where you're going, Mrs,' said Robbie and pulled Merry aside. To Merry it felt novel to have someone look out for her, even in such a little thing. Her heart warmed a little.

'Well?' asked Robbie. 'Look, if you like I'll get taken on at Eden Hope; they have some empty houses along there, two bedrooms an' all. I'll ask the morn, go along and see the manager. What do you say?'

'All right, I'll wed you,' said Merry. At least it would keep her out of the workhouse, though that wasn't a great reason for getting married, she thought, as Robbie looked around to make sure no one was watching, then gave her a quick hug.

Chapter Eighteen

'Now then, Miranda, what's wrong with the children today?'

Dr Macready turned his swivel chair and looked keenly at Merry and the children over his glasses. She sat on the hard chair in front of his desk with Alice sucking her thumb on her knee and one arm around Benny who stood beside her, leaning against her side. Before she could say anything Dr Macready had seen how pale Benny looked, with great shadows under his eyes. He was holding his left arm awkwardly too and his head drooped.

'It's Benny, Doctor, he's hurt his arm and I'm worried about it.'

'Let's have a look, son.' The doctor got to his feet and came round the desk. Benny pushed harder at his mother but said nothing.

'Go on, Benny, let the doctor see,' said Merry. She held Alice with one hand and gave Benny a gentle push. 'He's a bit shy, Doctor,' she excused him.

'No, no, he knows me well enough, don't you, laddie?'

He drew the boy towards the pool of light coming in the window. 'Now, let's have a look.'

The boy's arm was bruised from shoulder to wrist, and the wrist swollen. 'What happened, Benny? How did you do this?'

'He fell down the stairs,' Merry said quickly.

Dr Macready glanced over to her; she looked anxiously back. There was something there, he thought, something she's not telling me. 'Can you turn your hand, laddie?' he asked. Benny turned his hand, albeit slowly. He waggled his fingers in obedience to the doctor, wincing as he did so.

'I don't think there's anything broken,' Dr Macready said to Merry. 'But it is badly bruised. How did you say it happened?'

Merry repeated that the boy had fallen down the stairs. The doctor sighed. This was not the first time Benny had hurt himself. He would have to watch him.

'Is everything all right at home, Miranda?' he asked.

'What? Yes, yes of course,' Merry answered, but he picked up the hesitancy in her voice.

'And Alice, she's well? She certainly looks it.'

The little girl was struggling to get down from her mother's arms; she was plump and rosy and determined, almost too strong for her mother to hold her.

'Good, good. Well, I think I'll put a sling on this young man's arm. Keep it on for a few days and it should be fine. And you, laddie, be careful how you come downstairs in future.'

Merry walked home with the children, passing the school on the way. The schoolchildren were in the yard, the boys at one end behind a fence and the girls at the other. They were shouting and laughing and chasing each other, deep in a game of tag and Benny paused to watch.

'Can I go back to school, Mam?' he asked. Benny was a quiet child, saying little but he was still quite popular with the other boys in his class. Now two of them noticed him, came towards the railings and as they began to chatter to him he seemed a different boy. But a teacher came out and rang the bell three times so they hurried over to join the lines ready to march into school.

Merry looked down at Benny – the lively expression he had worn when talking to the boys had faded and his face had a closed-in look.

'Can I, Mam?' he asked.

'I'll have to go in and see Miss High,' Merry said doubtfully.

'Me go! Me go!' shouted Alice. She was at the age that whatever anyone else wanted she wanted.

'Come on then, we'll have to hurry.'

If they weren't back at the house before Robbie was back from fore shift there would be trouble, even though his dinner was in the oven and would be ready for him. But she went through the school gates with a child on each hand and into the school. The headmistress's study was just to the left past the entrance. Merry knocked and went in.

'We can't be held responsible if anything happens to him,' Miss High said, looking dubiously at Benny's sling.

'He wants to come, Miss High,' said Merry. 'Benny likes school.'

'He's doing well, Mrs Wright. He's a good worker,' Miss High replied. She tapped a pencil on her teeth then smiled. 'All right, Mrs Wright, after all, it is his left arm so he can still write. But as I said, we can bear no responsibility for anything that might happen.' She turned to the boy. 'Go on, Benny, go to your class. Tell Miss Gunner I said it was all right. Go along now, and don't run.'

Benny's face lit up and he hurried out, if not at a run at something very close to it. Only at the door did he remember and turn back, 'Ta ra, Mam,' he said and was off.

Merry hurried home as fast as she could with Alice hanging back beside her; the interview with the headmistress had taken longer than she had thought. Benny had been glad to go; she could see that only too clearly. He was a changed little boy away from his home. Especially when Robbie was there.

'Where the hell have you been?' Robbie greeted her as she went in the back door. 'Is it too much for a man to ask for his wife to be home when he's finished his shift? Where's me dinner, any road?'

'I'm sorry. I'll put it out now,' Merry answered. She

154

hurried to the range and got the dish of panackelty out of the oven and put it on the table. It smelled delicious; in fact it had smelled delicious when in the oven so he knew it was there. All he had to do was spoon it on to his plate. But he could only have been home ten minutes; he hadn't had to wait long.

'Daddy, daddy,' said Alice and leaned against him. Robbie's expression altered to one of fond indulgence as he bent down and swung her up in his arms.

'Now then, me little lass,' he said, 'what have you been up to? Tell your old dad.'

Alice babbled a long incomprehensible string of words; only she knew what she meant. She patted her father's cheek and shiny bits of coal clung to her hand.

'Put her down, Robbie, you'll have her all black,' said Merry. 'Eat your dinner.' She took Alice from him and the little girl started to wail until she was sat beside him on a cushion and a small plate of panackelty put before her. Merry put a bib under her chin, though there were black smudges on her dress from her contact with Robbie. Merry sighed. She would have to steep the dress before she washed it. For the thousandth time she wished Robbie would bath before eating but she knew that few miners did. They had eaten nothing but a snack in the pit, their bait as they called it, and it was a long time since he had had a meal.

Robbie was tucking into his dinner, all his attention on it as he reached for a slice of bread with hands that gleamed white against the black of his wrists. At least he washed his hands under the pump before he ate, she thought. Some didn't bother.

'Coal dust isn't dirty,' she had heard many a time from them. 'Just black.'

Merry had just spooned out dinner for herself, and a plate to put in the oven for Benny when he came in from school, when Robbie pushed back his plate, took a long swig of tea from his pint pot and felt behind his ear for the

155

dog end of a cigarette he had there. He went to his chair by the fire and lit it, inhaled deeply and leaned back, stretching his long legs out on the steel fender.

'I'll have me bath as soon as I've finished this,' he said. 'I want to go down to see the pigeons. There's a race on Saturday. They're to put on the train.' Most of his spare time was spent down at his allotment with his pigeons. Merry hurriedly ate a few more mouthfuls then went outside to bring in the tin bath. With a bit of luck he would be out of the house before Benny came in for his dinner.

'Don't think I've forgot about it,' Robbie growled as he went out of the door, his hair still wet and his pit clothes left in a heap on a newspaper by the side of the range. 'I just haven't time now. I want to know where you've been.'

He hurried off down the yard and out of the gate. Merry picked up Alice and followed him to the end of the street to watch for Benny as he raced round the corner with his friend, Jimmy Morrison. Jimmy turned off into the next street and Merry watched as Benny's pace slowed and he began to slouch, trailing his feet. But he looked up and saw his mother and sister there and gave them a small smile. Merry held out a hand to him and he took it, his other arm held close to his body in the sling.

'Your dad's gone down the allotments,' she said as sadness washed over her. 'And there's panacklty for your dinner. I bet you're hungry.'

Benny smiled and nodded; he never wasted words. But he straightened and began to pick up his feet as he walked. Alice was yawning by the time they got back so Merry put her down for her nap. Then she poured herself a cup of tea from the pot on the hob, not caring that it was stewed by now and sat down at the scrubbed wooden table to watch Benny eat. He started well enough then seemed to flag, rested his elbows on the table and picked at the food with his fork.

'Eat it up, Benny,' Merry encouraged him. He was so thin and just at the minute he looked so small and vulnerable. Her

156

heart ached. Benny put another forkful into his mouth and chewed slowly, though in fact the food was fairly soft and the pieces of bacon in it were the only bits to chew.

'I've got you an apple for after your dinner,' said Merry. 'If you eat it all up, that is.' Benny ate another forkful.

Merry remembered the evening before; it was late, about seven o'clock when Robbie had come in from the allotments. His face darkened when he saw Benny, playing in the corner with a 'wheelie' made out of a cotton reel, elastic and a short stick of wood. The stick was used to wind up the elastic and then when the contraption was put on the floor it slowly rolled along the flags as the elastic unwound. Jimmy's dad had shown him how to make one, helped him do it even, and Benny was proud of it.

'What's he doing up at this time of night?' Robbie demanded.

'I was getting him ready for bed in a minute,' Merry replied. 'Benny, it's bedtime.' Benny didn't look up; he hadn't even noticed his father had come in, being so absorbed in his game.

Robbie bent and grabbed Benny by his arm, lifting him up off his feet. The boy began to scream at the shock of it and that further enraged Robbie. He picked up the 'wheelie' and threw it on the fire.

'Robbie!' Merry shouted and went to take the boy from him. Robbie pulled him away roughly but put him on his feet at least and the boy's sobs subsided to a hopeless crying. The only sound he made was an occasional sniff.

'There was no call for that,' Merry said flatly. 'Leave loose of him, you great bully or I'll . . . I'll bang you over the head with the frying pan. I'll scream the place down and tell everyone how cruel you are to the bairn.' The walls between the houses were single brick and any commotion could be heard two doors away at least. Robbie wouldn't like that, she knew – he liked everyone to think he was a great fellow.

Robbie sneered at her but he let loose of Benny and

157

Merry breathed her relief. She rushed to the boy and gathered him up in her arms. Benny buried his face in her shoulder.

'I wasn't going to hurt him, woman,' Robbie growled. 'He's as soft as muck. I was just trying to make a man of him.'

'He's only five years old,' Merry reminded him. She could smell the beer on Robbie's breath now; he must have been to the Club on his way home. Of course, the Pigeon Fanciers meetings were held at the Workingmen's Club, and it was a good excuse for a drink.

'You smell like a brewery,' she went on, bitter about the way he had treated Benny. 'I expect you're fit for the pit tonight.' She could feel Benny trembling in her arms. 'Howay, son,' she said to him. 'I'll make you another wheelie. I saw how it was done. Now it's time for your bed.'

Robbie scowled. 'Aw, you have the lad like a little nancy boy. Why don't you dress him in a skirt an' be done with it?'

Merry didn't reply – she couldn't. She felt if she did she would give him such a mouthful he would be sure to hit her, and it wouldn't be the first time. Oh God, she thought, mebbe I should have gone to the workhouse as it couldn't have been worse than this. She rushed upstairs with Benny, undressed him in the icy bedroom and put him to bed. At least he had stopped his silent sobbing and his fair eyelashes, beaded with tears, were beginning to fan his tear-stained cheeks.

When he was asleep Merry checked on his sister, asleep on the other side of the room in a cot that had been Robbie's when he was a boy. Then she went downstairs. Robbie was dressing in his pit clothes which she had dashed against the wall in the yard to get rid of the excess coal dust and then dried by the fire. He was about ready but for his boots when Benny began to scream.

'That little sod, he'll wake my bairn,' Robbie shouted

and pushed Merry out of the way as he ran upstairs. Merry followed full of dread.

'Don't touch him!' she cried. 'Don't you dare touch him.'

'Touch him? I'll murder him,' said Robbie.

Benny was standing up in a bed drenched with urine, his night shirt wet at the front. 'Mam, mammy!' he was shouting.

'You dirty little tyke, I'll mammy you,' said Robbie. In her cot, Alice stirred and sat up. 'Look what you've done now.' He advanced on the boy and Benny, his face full of fear, dodged him and ran for his mother. But Robbie grabbed him from her and pushed him ahead of him to the top of the stairs. Merry tried to get between them but he pushed her out of the way so violently she fell to the floor.

'They'll hear next door.' She tried to stop him the way she had the last time.

'Bugger the neighbours,' he said savagely. Merry staggered to her feet, but even as she stepped towards the landing she heard Benny fall, bumping on each step, taking an eternity to get down to the bottom.

'What have you done?' she cried. 'You pushed him, didn't you?'

Robbie was standing at the top of the stairs, quieter now, looking down at the huddled figure of Benny at the bottom.

'I did not push him, he fell,' Robbie said as she took the stairs two at a time and bent over the small figure.

'He's all right. He isn't dead. Oh, God be thanked,' Merry breathed.

She relived that terrible moment when she thought he was dead as she gazed at him the following night. She was going to have to do something, she knew. For the sake of her son she must do something. But what could she do? She had no one to turn to, no one at all. Very well, then she would do something herself. She vowed it now as she laid her hand on her son's head, smoothed his pale hair, so different from her's or Robbie's. If she didn't, Robbie

159

might kill Benny. She went back down into the kitchen. Robbie was putting on his pit boots.

'I'd swing for you if it wasn't for the bairns,' she said quietly. 'Make no mistake, one of these days I'll take a knife to you if you don't leave Benny alone.'

Robbie laughed. 'Oh aye? Then who'll look after your precious lad? Me mam will take Alice but she won't take that little bastard. I've told her the truth, you know, I told her last week.'

Chapter Nineteen

Miles gazed out of his study window in Winnipeg Colliery with profound dissatisfaction. It was just like his fool of a father-in-law to give the place such an idiotic name, he thought. Old Porritt and his wife had been on honeymoon in Canada when news had come through that the engineers sinking an experimental shaft on the north side of Bishop Auckland had struck coal, Busty seam in fact. So he had called it Winnipeg, where they were actually staying at the time.

Damn fool of a man. Old Porritt, as Miles was in the habit of calling his father-in-law though he was but ten years older than he was himself, was a fool. Far from turning over the reins of his business to Miles as any man of his advanced years and waning powers would normally do, he treated his daughter's husband as an errand boy, or just about. He certainly never let Miles anywhere near decision making. In fact, anything Miles suggested was usually barely considered by him.

At least he was still agent for the group of mines and the land surrounding to the south of the river. But he wanted more, he wanted his own mines, and he wanted to market his own coal from them too. He was sure he would make a success of it. The coal from Eden Hope and the rest belonged to his ironmaster boss and went straight to Teesside for it was good coking coal for making steel. Marketing didn't come into it. But there were great possibilities to take the odd waggon load or two and add them to that of Winnipeg Colliery. Were it not for Porritt. Why, he was almost decrepit. He was past bothering about new markets.

The door opened and Miles turned, irritation rising in him. Bertha came in, her long nose pink at the end for she had a perpetual cold. She was wearing a pink dress too and it was completely unsuitable for daytime wear with its ribbons of a deeper pink. He watched her critically as she came up to the desk. Her bodice was cut low but only showed up her lack of bosom. She was altogether too thin, all angles and hard bones, and uncomfortable to lie beside in bed. All this went through his mind but he still managed to smile at her.

'Now then my love, I'm rather busy. You know I'm delighted to see you but if my work is interrupted—'

'Oh, shut up,' said his wife. 'I'll go anywhere I like in my own house. But I came to tell you that I want to go over to see Father this morning. So be good enough to harness the horse to the trap. You can take me and then you can go and do what you like.'

'But I have to go to Winton today to see the manager—'

'Rubbish, you can do that later. I need to see Father. And another thing. It's time we had a proper carriage, something as befits our station in life. I'm ashamed to be seen riding through the town in the old trap.'

'Really, my dear, I don't know if we can afford—' Once again he was interrupted.

'Of course we can. And if we cannot, Father will buy one for me. I'll ask him today.'

Miles groaned inwardly. He knew what would happen then, he thought. The old man would go on and on about how Miles wasn't treating his daughter as she deserved; couldn't afford to. Miles capitulated. He rose to his feet and sighed. 'Very well, my love, I'll take you now.'

As they drove down the bank to the ancient stone bridge over the Wear then up the other side, the horse slowing to a walk, his thoughts were dark.

162

'Be back for me by three,' Bertha ordered as he handed her down at her father's door. 'There'd be no need for this, you know, if you'd come and live here. This house is superior to yours.'

She never let anything go, thought Miles. Every day she said something about moving in with her father. But on this he was adamant. Mr Bolton, the ironmaster, liked his employees to stay where he told them; the agent's house was there, overlooking the valley and hillside studded with mines, and there he expected his agent to live. He would be very suspicious if Miles moved to live with another owner nearby, even if that owner was his wife's father. Mr Bolton had a keen eye for his company's interests.

Miles held out his arm for Bertha to take and led her to the door. 'I must stay where I am, my dear,' he said. 'It is a condition of the position.'

Bertha sniffed. 'You could take up my father's offer,' she said.

'No Bertha, I could not,' he replied. She might wear him down, he thought wearily as he returned to the trap. But the position old Porritt had offered was one without power – he would be a glorified office boy. He would fight to the last to avoid it. One of these days the old man would be completely past it then he would have total control.

He drove the horse out onto the road, took the turning back into the town and out the other side, turning off onto the road for Winton Colliery. It was a nice day, the first warm day of the year. He would leave the trap in the colliery yard and walk up the line to Eden Hope. He had plenty of time before he had to go back for Bertha so he might as well stretch his legs, get some fresh air in his lungs.

As he drove through Winton Colliery village he gazed sadly at the surgery where Tom had used to practise. He could have gone so far, that lad. Instead he was working in another colliery village over by Durham. Miles had to admit he missed him. Tom was maddening at times with his

163

funny ideas about working for the pitmen and their families, but he was a hell of a lot better company than Bertha.

When Miles came out of the manager's office with an obsequious Jack Mackay showing him off the premises as it were, the sun was warm on his face. The winding wheel was whirring against the blue sky and the cage came up, spilling a load of men out. They blinked in the brightness of the unaccustomed sun, and the light twinkled and bounced off the coal dust on their clothes as light does off sequins. They looked over at the two gaffers but all they were really interested in was that first draw on a fag for eight or ten hours and getting home for their dinners.

'Get the horsemen to see to my horse, Mackay,' said Miles and strode off up the waggon way towards Eden Hope.

The wind was slightly chilly in his face but fresh and bracing. He strode out with a will, trying to work out in his mind the best course of action for him to achieve what he wanted. When he came to the offshoot that led to the abandoned Jane Pit and its deserted village he paused, distracted by memories. On impulse he turned off along the overgrown track, past the ancient pithead. The memorial was almost obliterated by dead weeds, brown and sere. A nettle bed had new growth almost six inches high already, growing right up to the stonework. Anyone walking past would not recognise the structure for what it was.

The double row of cottages faced each other, still not demolished. But there was very little to salvage from them, Bob Wright the joiner had told him years ago. He paused at the end house with the water pump opposite, rusty now but still standing solid and sturdy. There was glass in the bedroom window still. Undergrowth and even taller trees encroached on the houses.

Miles thought of the woman who had lived there with the little girl. A real woman she had been, he thought, not like Bertha. As he turned away and took the track that led out of the village towards Eden Hope, he felt even more dissatisfied with his life than he had that morning.

He was abstracted as he conducted his business with the manager, Mr Jessop, absent-minded almost, less critical. When he had finished he went outside to find the day was darkening, rain beginning to fall, stirring the dust in the yard and turning it into black mud.

'Blast the bloody weather!' he said savagely to the manager. 'I've left my trap at Winton.'

'I'm going home for dinner today,' said the manager. 'I'll take you over to Winton if you like.'

'Thank you. I think I'll take you up on that,' Miles replied.

They were going through the village of Eden Hope to the road that led to Winton when Miles saw the boy. He was with a woman and a younger child but the younger child looked different. The boy was the same colouring as Tom and that other one; even as he himself had been when he was younger.

'Is something wrong?' Jessop asked. The gaffer looked as though he had seen a ghost.

Miles looked quickly away from the woman and her children, but not before she had caught his eye and he realised with a shock who she was. Was he to be plagued with that family forever? He turned to Jessop and forced himself to smile pleasantly.

'No, why should there be?' he asked.

'Oh, nothing,' Mr Jessop replied. He turned the pony out onto the road that meandered out between farms on its way to Winton Colliery. 'Giddy up,' he said and coaxed it into a canter. He was looking forward to his dinner, which would be waiting for him.

Morosely, Miles picked up his own vehicle and drove home. His spirits lightened as he went inside. Polly brought his meal on a tray to the dining-room table. It was steak pie today and there was an abundance of vegetables and rich gravy. What could happen anyway? he wondered. That brat couldn't possibly be his, though it could be Tom's. Miles

165

doubted it, Tom was too goody-goody to leave a girl and his child. Or maybe he wasn't? Perhaps he didn't know about the child.

'Isn't that the girl who lived at Old Pit?' he'd asked Jessop.

'Mrs Wright? I believe she did,' Jessop had replied, glancing curiously at Miles but Miles's expression gave nothing away and he volunteered no information as to why he was interested. Maybe it was just a casual enquiry.

Inwardly Miles was telling himself it didn't matter; Tom was unlikely to find out. He himself was married to Bertha now, so there wasn't the same threat.

Thinking of Tom he decided he would go over Durham way and see him at the weekend. Have one more try at getting him to see sense and take up a more lucrative private practice, something that paid more than the pennies he got from the Panel.

Tom was driving back home himself after his rounds. He was tired, having been up since two o'clock when he had been called out to a small boy with a fever. The tiny body was hot and the skin dry, the face flushed with the fever.

'It's his throat, Doctor,' said the mother. 'I was waiting for morning to see if he was any better before calling you but he's not getting better, he's getting worse. He can't take even a sip of water now. I'm sorry to call you out like this—'

'Don't worry about that,' Tom had said. 'Let's have a look at him.' His heart sank as he realised that the boy had a membrane beginning to block his throat, typical of diphtheria. It was early in the year for it to appear, so now there was every chance of an epidemic. 'We'll have to get him into the fever hospital, Mrs Johnson,' he said to the mother. 'I fear it is diphtheria.'

It had taken hours to check the boy's brothers and sisters, send for the fever cart ambulance to take him to the hospital, instruct the mother on the proper method of disinfecting the house with carbolic acid and see the boy taken away. By that time it was daylight and almost time to open surgery. He had been home of course and bathed and changed himself, so the surgery was late and consequently he had been late going on his rounds.

He had to order a new supply of diphtheria anti-toxin. Well at least he had a telephone to do that with. What a difference the telephone made. He ate the dinner his housekeeper put before him, not because he was hungry but because he knew he had to keep up his strength.

Afterwards he had an hour or so before evening surgery to relax, barring another call out. However, he had barely taken off his shoes and put on his house slippers when he heard the jangling of the telephone in the hall and Mrs Minton, his housekeeper, answering it. A moment later she knocked on the door and came in.

'Your father is on the telephone, Doctor,' she said, full of disapproval. Neither Doctor's father nor anyone else should disturb him when he was having his quiet time, she thought. The telephone was the instrument of the devil in her opinion, invariably bringing bad news or bringing Doctor more work.

'Thank you, Mrs Minton,' said Tom, perfectly aware of her feelings on the matter. What did the old man want now? he wondered as he went out into the hall. Miles came straight to the point.

'I'm coming over to see you this weekend,' he said. 'Saturday afternoon, probably.'

'Well, I had been going out—'

'Put it off,' said Miles. 'See you Saturday then.'

Tom was left looking at the receiver. He had thought of taking Jane Hall, the manager's daughter out for a drive on Saturday. Perhaps they could go into Durham, walk by the river. It was time he had some female company and she, he knew, would accept any invitation from him eagerly. She was a nice-looking girl too, gentle and pleasant, and there was no doubt that he needed a wife. Oh well, another time. At least he hadn't asked her yet.

167

For some reason the image of Merry Trent flashed through his mind, bringing with it the usual feelings of regret. Was she happy with that miner she had married? he wondered. She had two children now, or so he understood when dropping a casual enquiry last time he was in Winton. Oh well, he hoped she was happy and contented, he told himself. He glanced at the grandfather clock in the corner. It would soon be time for surgery. He sat down in his favourite armchair before the fire in his study and relaxed. He had learned to take advantage of these odd half hours whenever they came. But today, he was unable to clear his mind of the worry of an epidemic of diphtheria. It could decimate the children of the pit rows – any epidemic did for there was no proper sanitation. Only the officials' houses had running water and water closets. The rest had ash closets in the middle of the back streets and a water pump on the end of the row.

He would write yet another letter to the mine owner and a copy to the Board of Health, he thought. Sometimes it was like battering a brick wall, though.

Chapter Twenty

It was the week after Easter when Benny came home from school half an hour late.

'I wonder where he is,' Merry fretted aloud as she ladled out stew and dumplings for Robbie who had just come in from back shift at the pit.

Robbie picked up his knife and fork and began to eat. 'This isn't as good as me mam's,' he said through a mouthful. Merry took no notice, he said the same thing about everything she cooked.

'I think I'll just have a look up the back row,' she said.

'That lad o' yours wants his backside kicking,' said Robbie. 'You're a bloody fool, he'll only be playing down the sandpit or something.'

'No he won't, not in this weather,' said Merry. She took a shawl that was hanging behind the back door and put it over her head. 'Watch the bairn, I won't go further than the end of the row.'

Robbie began to mutter about a man coming in from the pit and not having a minute's peace to eat his dinner, but she ran out to the gate and turned up the row. She didn't have to go far for Benny was coming down, walking as though he hardly had the strength to put one foot in front of the other. He had lost a garter and one of his socks was hanging over his shoe. It was a good job Robbie hadn't seen him first; he would have got a belting for that, she thought. Poor bairn, she felt so guilty about him. But she had plans, oh yes she had – it was going to stop.

Anxiety crowded out all her thoughts as the boy got near to her. He looked so flushed and the circles under his eyes were very dark.

'Benny!' she cried and went down on her hunkers to take hold of him. Alarmingly he collapsed in her arms.

'Mammy,' he croaked. 'I feel bad.'

Her heart beat fast as she took his weight while his legs gave way beneath him. Fever, he had a fever, the heat of it went through both their clothes and she could feel the fire in him. Staggering to her feet she turned and hurried back to the house, bursting in the back door so that Robbie looked up in irritation.

'What the hell's the matter, woman?' he demanded.

'He's got a fever,' she replied breathlessly and laid him down on the horsehair sofa near the range.

'Keep him away from Alice!' Robbie shouted and grabbed the little girl. 'Hadaway, take him into the room. I don't want the little bastard by my bairn.'

'There's no fire on in there,' said Merry, 'It's too cold.' The sitting room got no sun through the small window and was used only on special occasions.

'Light one then, go on, do as I tell you for once.'

'Will you get the doctor, Robbie?' Benny was lying quietly but breathing hard through his mouth. She hurriedly took the coal shovel and dug into the fire in the range, taking a few glowing coals and carrying them through to the grate in the other room. Oh God, she prayed, tell me what to do. With a few sticks from the pit prop end Robbie had brought home she soon had the fire going. Running up the stairs she got a blanket and pillow and made the boy a bed on the sofa in the room. Robbie still sat by the table with Alice squirming on his knee. He would not help her, she knew, not until she had Benny away from Alice.

'Go for the doctor, please, Robbie,' she cried as he made no move to go.

170

'I'm not,' Robbie replied. 'Get the doctor yourself. I've had a long shift.'

Merry argued no more, instead she ran down the yard and up the one next door.

'Whatever's the matter, missus?' Annie the woman next door rose to her feet. She wasn't to tell twice. Grabbing her shawl from behind the door she ran up the street in search of Dr Macready.

'He's out,' she reported from a few feet down the yard. 'I won't get too close 'cos I don't want to carry anything to my bairns, you understand. How is the lad?'

'Badly, he's really bad, Annie. I don't know what to do. But where is the doctor, did they say?'

'It was the maid, you know, that daft lass, Maisie. She said he'd gone into Auckland, or something. He has no surgery the night. But she'll tell him as soon as he comes in.'

'Will you be quiet down there? A man cannot get his sleep when he's off shift for women gabbing!'

Robbie had pushed up the sash of the bedroom window and poked an angry face out. Annie looked up at him in disbelief.

'Why, Robbie Wright, you should be ashamed of yoursel' when the lad's so bad!' she yelled at him and Robbie's face darkened. 'You should be getting up and helping your lass at a time like this any road.'

'Go to hell!' Robbie pulled in his head, banging it against the window as he did so; the sash, in poor fettle as it was, snapped and the top section came down on his hand. They could hear his yell of pain and fury all down the row. Annie grinned.

'Serve the bugger right,' she said. 'Anyway, pet, I'll have to go and see to the bairns. Give a bang on the wall with the poker if you need me.'

It was half-past eleven when Dr Macready came to the door. Merry was just about past herself with worry. She had sponged Benny down three times during the afternoon

171

and evening in an effort to get down his temperature. He had opened his eyes and smiled faintly at her, only wincing when she moved his arm, still showing signs of bruising from when his stepfather had handled him so cruelly. She had tried to give him a little broily – bread steeped in milk and sprinkled with sugar – but he couldn't swallow. His mouth was open all the time and his tongue looked dry and swollen.

Thankfully, Robbie had said little when he got up, simply swung out of the house a couple of hours before his shift was due and gone down to the Club for a pint. Alice was unusually quiet too, bless her, Merry thought, going to bed without a word of protest.

In the end, Merry knocked on the fire back with the poker for Annie and asked her to send one of her lads to the doctor's house. And at last, Dr Macready had come. She stood by the bed watching his face anxiously. It was impassive for the most part. He felt the boy's throat and looked down it with the aid of his silver spatula and bit his lip. He put a tiny tablet on Benny's tongue.

'Don't bother trying to swallow it,' he said, 'It'll go by itself.' Pulling the blanket back over the boy he got to his feet. Merry knew what he was going to say before he opened his mouth but still she hoped against hope.

'The laddie has diphtheria,' he said. 'He'll have to go to the isolation hospital.'

Merry sagged. 'Why didn't you come?' she asked. 'Why? If my bairn dies I'll . . . I'll—'

'Nay, lass, I'm sorry,' said Dr Macready. 'I had a round of golf and when I got back Maisie forgot to tell me.'

'A round of golf?'

Merry knew she sounded stupid but she couldn't help herself. A round of golf? It was another world, something beyond her experience altogether. He had been nancying around hitting a ball with a stick while her lad was here, dying mebbe?

'It's too late to get the ambulance now,' Dr Macready

172

was saying, oblivious of her anger. 'I'll have it here first thing it the morning. Now, the Board of Health has to be notified and the house will have to be fumigated. You have a little girl, too, haven't you? She will have to be inoculated. Then—'

'Dr Macready, if my bairn dies I'll have your head on a platter,' said Merry as he blinked and looked straight at her.

'We'll do our level best not to let that happen,' he said. 'I'm sorry I didn't get here sooner. But even doctors have to have time off, you know.'

'You should—' The words rushed hotly to her lips but Dr Macready interrupted her.

'We're not helping him standing here arguing, are we?'

Merry looked down at Benny, his eyes wide open and so unnaturally bright, looking up at her. 'What can I do?'

'At the moment, just watch him. Don't attempt to get him to drink. I'll go and see to everything and come back when I can.'

It was the worst night of Merry's life even though the boy slept fitfully at intervals. She felt the sound of his rasping breath would haunt her forever. Dr Macready came in twice.

'Good, good,' he murmured. 'He's no worse.' The doctor was there when Robbie came in from work, early in the morning, for he'd started on fore shift.

'What's going on?' he shouted from the back door. 'Where's me breakfast?' She didn't reply and they could hear his pit boots drop to the floor as he took them off in the kitchen. He came through to the room in his stockinged feet and pushed open the door.

'I said, where is my breakfast?' he enunciated slowly, menace creeping into his tone.

Dr Macready looked up at him coldly. 'Don't make so much noise,' he said. 'This child is seriously ill.'

Robbie glanced at the two of them standing by the bed, then at the boy lying in it. 'Aye well, I suppose I'll have to

173

see to meself,' he said and went out, clashing the door behind him. They could hear Alice begin to cry upstairs.

'Let your husband attend to her,' the doctor said as Merry took a step forward automatically. 'I will immunise her after we get Benjamin away. Though I doubt it's too late.'

Merry was not allowed to go in the ambulance with Benny. At least he was too ill to realise that. And afterwards Robbie was unusually quiet, even when Alice developed the disease within a few days and followed her brother to the isolation hospital.

Merry and Robbie took the horse bus into the town on the Saturday afternoon, both of them smelling faintly of carbolic acid as everything in the house had been fumigated. It was the first time they had gone anywhere together since they were married. They stood outside the window of the ward where the little patients had had their beds turned round so that they could see their parents outside. The window was opened a little way at the bottom so they could hear.

'Mam,' Benny croaked when he saw them. He didn't look at Robbie nor did he plead to come home as all the other children in the ward were doing. 'Our Alice is bad, I heard the doctor say.'

'Howay, you've seen the lad now. We'll go and see Alice,' said Robbie.

'I'll come back, pet,' Merry promised.

They couldn't see Alice because she was in a steam tent. In the office at the end of the ward the sister, looking formidable in her starched, square linen cap, told them that the dreaded diphtheria membrane was growing across the little girl's throat.

'Doctor is going to do a tracheotomy, that is he will cut into the child's windpipe and put in a tube so she can breathe,' Sister said.

'No bloody doctor is going to cut my bairn's throat,' Robbie said forcefully.

174

'Would you rather we left her to choke to death?' asked Sister and the brutality of it struck Merry to the heart.

Robbie opened his mouth to shout but just at that moment the doctor in charge came in, nodded impersonally to the parents and spoke to Sister.

'Is everything ready?'

'Yes sir,' she replied and Merry and Robbie found themselves ushered out of the office. Robbie, collapsing in the face of such authority, keeping to the side and with his head down, walked along the corridor to the door at the end and into the fresh air with Merry behind him. Outside, he took a Woodbine from a crumpled packet and lit it with a match cupped in his hand against the wind.

'This is all your bloody fault,' he growled at Merry. 'It was your little bastard that brought it into my house.'

Merry didn't answer him. She walked back along the outside of the ward to the window where Benny's bed was still turned round so he could see outside. His eyes brightened as she came within his view.

'I brought you a bar of chocolate,' she said to him. 'But I had to give it in to the nurse. She said you would get some at tea time. You will eat it, son? It's good for you.'

Benny nodded. 'I'll save some for Alice,' he promised.

'I don't think she'll want it, not today,' she replied. He at least looked a little better, she thought thankfully. The fever seemed to have left him or at least gone down.

The bell rang for the end of visitors' hour so she blew him a kiss and smiled, though how she managed it she didn't know. He looked so frail lying flat and with only one thin pillow. That was because they worried about any strain on the heart; she knew that. He wasn't allowed anything to read either, in case it damaged his eyes. And Alice was worse; oh God, what did she look like?

The visitors were trailing down the path to the road outside the hospital. Robbie was there, yet another cigarette cupped in his hand, his cap pulled down over his forehead.

175

'Let's away,' he said when he saw her. 'I cannot stand this damn place.'

'I'm going back to see how she is,' Merry said suddenly and turned on her heel. She got as far as the reception desk.

'I'm afraid you can't go any further,' said the sister there, a different sister than the one she'd seen before.

'I have to know how my bairn is,' said Merry and the woman sighed as she stood her ground.

'Very well, I'll send a nurse,' she said. It was all a waste of time really, Merry thought as she walked back to where Robbie was standing by the gate.

'As well as can be expected,' the nurse had reported.

Benny came home six weeks later, taller and thinner and looking as though a puff of wind would blow him over. Alice did not come home. Dr Macready explained to Merry how the toxins from diphtheria could seriously damage the heart and little Alice had succumbed. Benny was left with weak eyes and a heart murmur.

'He must be kept in bed for a few weeks,' said Dr Macready. 'He will improve, you'll see. I'll come in to see him when I can. Meanwhile try to build him up, feed him as well as you can.' Dr Macready was very kind.

'It's because he feels guilty about not being here for the bairn when he was needed,' said Annie from next door.

'He's due to some time to himself,' said Merry. 'He wasn't to know.'

'He should get somebody with a bit of common sense instead of that daft Maisie,' Annie said tartly.

Merry walked up to Mr Parkin's farm to get fresh milk for Benny. Mrs Parkin gave her six eggs, still warm from the nest and the butcher in the Co-operative Store slipped her some beef dripping with a liberal layer of jelly.

She was terrified Benny would have a relapse and had to try to feed him up. Benny was all she had left now Alice lay in the churchyard on Eden Bank. There were a number of

176

small graves there, the earth freshly turned and jam jars with wild flowers beneath the cheap markers. Merry called in on her way back from Parkins' Farm, staying longer than she ought to have done so that when she arrived home Robbie was already there.

'Where the hell have you been?' he asked truculently.

'I called at the graveyard,' she said, putting her basket down on the kitchen table. 'Where's Annie?' Annie had said she would keep an eye on the lad; pop in and out.

'I sent her packing. He's old enough to look after himself.' Robbie never called the boy by his name.

'I've got a cow heel in the oven for you, it won't take a minute,' said Merry.

'An' what have you got in here? You've been spending my hardearned money on the bastard, have you?' Robbie peered in the basket and saw the can of milk and the eggs.

'Eggs? Fresh eggs and milk, be buggered! Well, I'm blowed if he's going to get them. I haven't had a nice boiled fresh egg since I don't know when. Put them on now, I'll have them.' He lifted the can of milk, took off the cap and put it to his lips.

Merry sprang at him and grabbed for the can. 'Put that down, it's for Benny's dinner,' she shouted. Taken by surprise he let go of the can and it fell to the floor, spilling half its precious contents. She went down on hands and knees to save what she could but he kicked her out of the way, her head landed against the table leg and she was knocked out.

Chapter Twenty-one

'Do you want me to have a word with him?' Dr Macready finished off the dressing he had put on the side of Merry's head and reached for a roll of bandage. He secured the dressing with the bandage then stood back and regarded his handiwork. 'Not bad, really,' he murmured. 'Should have had a stitch though. Well, what about that man of yours?'

'No, don't do that, Doctor, please.' said Merry. The wound on her scalp stung and her whole head throbbed. 'He'll be angry enough as it is. He'll think I've been moaning to you about him.'

Dr Macready knew she was right. Any trouble between husband and wife, short of actual murder, was considered a private matter. If a man hit his wife, well then, she must have done something she shouldn't. That was the accepted thinking and not just in the pit villages.

'What about the boy?' he asked. 'This is doing him no good. He hits the boy too, doesn't he?'

'All fathers leather their lads, else they go wild.' But even as Merry said it a vivid picture came back to her of the last time Benny had annoyed Robbie. Robbie had taken off his belt and gone for the lad until Merry couldn't stand it any longer and she got in between them. She had felt the belt across her own back for that. If Alice hadn't started to scream in fear and panic it would have gone further. She

178

felt the familiar feeling of desolate loss as she thought of Alice, and swallowed hard.

'He doesn't hit the lad, not since Benny was in hospital,' she said.

'It's going to start again though, isn't it?' Dr Macready persisted. 'The boy is not strong enough to stand it, you realise that?'

'What can I do?' The cry was agonised as Merry sat down suddenly, the pain in her head intensifying.

She had come to to see Benny out of bed and bending over her, touching her face with trembling fingers. There was no sign of Robbie; he must have gone down the allotments.

'Mam! Mam!' He was crying.

She managed to get Benny back to bed and was sitting on the edge of it herself as the room swam around her when Dr Macready walked in, pausing only to give a brief knock at the back door.

'Morning, I was in the street anyway so I came in to see how—' he began and stopped as he saw them through the open door of the room. 'What's happened here?' though he already had some idea.

'Me dad hit me mam,' said Benny before she could hush him. 'He wanted to drink the milk.' Benny's face was white with red blotches and his eyes glittering with unshed tears.

'No, Benny,' said Merry. 'It wasn't just like that.'

Dr Macready thought it probably was just like that and he began to get angry. He checked Benny's pulse and felt his forehead, gave him a tablet and told him to stay still. 'I'll just see to your mother,' he said. 'Be a good boy and lie very still. It would be best if you had a nap.'

He led Merry out of the room and sat her down on the horsehair settee before looking at her head, probing the area round the wound with firm but gentle fingers.

'Where is he now?' he asked.

'I suppose he went down the allotments,' Merry replied. 'Or he could be at the Club with his marras.'

'Have you ever thought of leaving him?'

179

Merry could hardly believe the doctor had asked. No one left their husbands, not in the mining communities, not around here. How would they live, her and Benny? Not even the workhouse would take them in if she left Robbie. But still, she had dreamed of it. Dreamed of finding work, of living in the deserted village at Old Pit as she had done when she was growing up. But no one would help her, she knew, not if she left her husband.

'What could I do? Especially now with Benny the way he is. He needs looking after, good food and that. You said so yourself, Doctor.'

'Yes, he does. But you have to face it, Mrs Wright, he's in danger here. You both are.'

Dr Macready was well aware that he was advising her to go against all the public opinion of the age. For a woman to leave her husband was unheard of, but he liked Merry, knew her for an intelligent woman who had had more than her fair share of knocks in her young life, physical and mental. And he had a plan. But first of all he had to talk it over with his wife.

'I'll have to get on with my rounds,' he said. 'Please think about what I said. I'll say good day to you now.' He picked up his hat and bag and went out.

She watched him through the window as he walked down the yard and turned into the back street, a short, thickset figure with greying hair and kind blue eyes. He meant well, she knew, but what did he know of her life really? He was from the Scottish highlands or some such place, miles away from the Durham coalfields.

Merry peeped into the room. The furniture had been pushed back against the wall to make space for Benny's narrow bed. He was asleep, his breathing soft and hardly discernible so she went in and bent over him, feeling his forehead; it felt cool to the touch though his eyes were still a little red. He muttered something and turned over onto his side. She heard footsteps in the backyard and went out to the kitchen quickly, closing the door behind her. If Robbie

180

didn't see the lad he might forget about him for a while.

It wasn't Robbie but his mother who opened the door and came in without so much as a knock or word of greeting. Merry's heart sank even further and the throbbing in her head began anew.

'Who the hell do you think you are, madam?' Doris Wright demanded. Her cheeks were mottled red with anger and she strode in towards the range, then turned to face Merry.

'Good morning, Doris,' said Merry. 'I'm afraid I don't know what you're talking about.'

'Our Robbie's just been in and he's in a right state with himself. I had to give him something to eat an' all, as his own wife couldn't be bothered. Too busy running about after fresh milk and eggs for your by-blow, my Robbie said. He works all the hours God sends down the pit and you spend his money on that . . . that—'

'Watch your mouth,' Merry advised and Doris Wright fair danced with rage.

'Watch my mouth, is it? By, Robbie said he only had a drink of the milk an' you went berserk! Everybody else has to make do with tinned, concentrated milk but not your precious darling. No, if you'd looked after our Alice half as well as you do him, she might be alive today. I told our Robbie that. He reckons the bairn always came second to Benny, he reckons—'

'How dare you come in here and say that!' Merry said angrily. She sat down on the settee suddenly for her head felt fit to burst and she saw flashing lights before her eyes. But this was nothing compared to the fury rising in her.

'I'll say what I like – this is my lad's house, not yours. If it wasn't for him you'd be out on the street, and I doubt the workhouse would have you after your carrying on. Somebody has to tell you, Robbie's too soft hearted. He—'

'Soft hearted?' Merry began to laugh. She put a hand up to the dressing on her head. 'Do you see what he did to me?'

181

'No more than you deserved, I'll warrant. It'll be nowt more than a scratch but you have to play it up, haven't you? You're a bloody actress an' what's more you have the morals of one.'

'Mam? Mam?' The raised voices had awakened Benny in the room.

'It's all right, pet, I'm coming,' Merry answered. She got to her feet, took hold of the older woman and forced her out of the door, her anger lending her strength. She didn't even answer Doris's jibes but thrust her out and closed the door after her and shot the bolt. She could hear Doris shouting outside but she ignored her and went through to the boy. 'It was nothing, just someone shouting in the back street,' she said.

'I thought it was Granny Wright playing war with you,' Benny sighed and leaned against her as she put an arm around him.

'It wasn't anything,' Merry insisted. Benny's eyes were closing again, his fair lashes fanning his cheeks. She could feel his bones through his nightshirt; he felt incredibly frail to her.

Dr Macready was right, she thought. She had to get away. If Annie would keep an eye on Benny tomorrow while Robbie was out of the way on shift, she would go and ask Jos Turner if he could give her her job back. It was the only way out she could think of. Then if she could get a place of her own with a little bit of land she could keep a nanny goat as she used to do at Old Pit. Goat's milk would build Benny up. Robbie wouldn't allow her to have one on the allotment as some did.

Merry went out to the kitchen and looked at her reflection in the looking glass over the mantelpiece. She didn't look too bad, she thought, though the bandage didn't help. Still, she could pull her hat down over that to hide it. Her headache was lessening as she tried to work out a plan. If Annie kept an eye on Benny she could be in and out of Bishop Auckland in a couple of hours. Robbie often stayed down the allotments for that long then went down the Club for a pint before coming home.

Now she had made up her mind, Merry was afire to get on with it. Within twenty minutes she was on the horse bus going to the town and half an hour later she was hurrying down Newgate Street to the newsagent's on the corner.

'Mind, you're a stranger,' Jos Turner commented by way of greeting. He gazed at her. She had her old brown hat pulled down over the bandage on her head; an equally old brown coat, which he seemed to remember from before her marriage, hung loosely on her shoulders. She was thinner and paler than she had been before and there were shadows under her eyes. 'I cannot say that being wed seems to suits you; by the look of you it does not.'

Merry sighed. 'No, Mr Turner, it does not. I'm going to have to start again on my own and I need a job and somewhere to stay.'

Jos was scandalised. 'Leave your husband, you mean? Nay lass, you cannot do that! What about the bairns?'

'My Alice got the diphtheria and died,' Merry said baldly. Saying it didn't make her emotional at all. She felt as though she was saying it about someone else's child. Just now she had to think about the living; fight for the survival of Benny.

'Benny got it too but he's out of hospital now. He needs building up.'

'I'm sorry to hear about the bit lass, but, well, it's best you stay with your man, isn't it?' Jos Turner shook his head. 'Especially if the lad is still sickly, like.'

'He's not the lad's father,' Merry cried desperately. 'I have to get away; he hits my Benny and me and all. Look.' She took off her hat and showed him the bandage on her head.

Jos took a step back away from her. 'Well, I mean, it looks like the man has good cause, doesn't it? I'm sorry, Merry, but I can't help you, you've made your own bed and now you'll have to lie on it.'

183

'But Mr Turner, I'm a good worker, you know that, I never let you down, did I?' Merry appealed to him. She felt as if he was taking away her only chance to escape. 'If you only knew—'

'I think I know enough, lass. Now go on, get back to your man.' He turned back to the papers he was sorting, shaking his head. By, he'd never thought Merry was a lass like that.

Merry found herself walking back along Newgate Street, despair gripping her so that she could hardly see in front of her. Where could she get work that would pay enough to keep her and Benny? There was nowhere. Always there were lots of girls looking for work; she had been lucky to get the job with Mr Turner the first time.

In the mining villages around the town there were no jobs for women, or very few apart from housework in the officials' households. So Auckland was always saturated with girls out of work and chasing after every vacancy – most girls had to go into service miles away. But even if she tried that, no one was going to take on a woman with a young and sickly boy.

Merry thought she had some time to spare so she decided to walk through the woods and save the tuppenny bus fare. Besides, she wasn't ready for what faced her at home in Eden Hope. Her head had started to ache again, clouding her thoughts as she tried to find a way out.

Maybe she could go back to Old Pit, get a goat from Mr Hawthorne, do farm work for Farmer Parkin. She remembered the days when she had lived there with Ben and her gran with a yearning nostalgia. The houses hadn't been completely destroyed, she knew, though they were more and more dilapidated as the years went by. But she didn't know if it was possible.

Merry emerged from the wood near Winton and began to hurry along the waggon way to Eden Hope. The walk had taken longer than she had thought it would and she began to worry that Robbie would be home. If so he was sure to

184

have upset Benny. Oh Lord, what had she been doing, taking so long? She ran along the end of the rows and down the back street to the house, her head thumping at every step.

Robbie was home, standing in the window looking blackly down the yard; behind him she could see his mother smiling maliciously at her. The door was locked against her. She couldn't believe it.

'Robbie! Let me in!' she shouted.

'Go to hell,' he replied.

'Robbie, Benny will be frantic, let me in.'

Robbie pushed open the bottom sash of the window. 'You're not getting in here again so you might as well take yourself off. An' your by-blow isn't here, I put him out an' all. I've kept the bastard long enough.'

'Where is he?' she screamed. 'If you've hurt him I'll swing for you, I will, I'm telling you.'

Doris poked her head out by the side of her son's. 'If you're that worried about him why did you leave him?' she taunted. 'Well, I'll tell you, we put him out with the rubbish when the muck cart came round.' She laughed, a hard sneering sound. 'I've packed your box an' all – if you don't take it away it'll go the same way.'

'Where is he?' Merry shouted. 'Robbie, if you've hurt him I'll—'

'I never touched him,' said Robbie. 'Not but what the little bastard didn't deserve it.'

'Merry? Merry, we've got him round here.' Merry turned to the high wall between the yards. It was Annie's voice. She turned and ran down the yard and up her neighbour's. Annie had gone back in the kitchen to where Benny was lying on the settee, his blue eyes the only colour in his pale face. She gathered him up in her arms and held him to her.

'He didn't hurt you?' she whispered.

'No, Mam,' he replied. 'I didn't see him. Where've you been, Mam?'

185

'Never mind that, I'm here now.' Merry breathed a long sigh before turning to Annie.

'I saw the pair of them turning the corner into the rows,' said Annie. 'I lifted the bairn and brought him round here.' Anyone can see the lad's not well yet. He's best out of the road.'

'Eeh thanks Annie,' said Merry.

'I'll put the kettle on. It'll be a while before Jack comes in. Mind, I don't know what you're going to do. You can't stay here, pet. I haven't the room and any road Jack wouldn't have it.'

'No, no, Annie, I wouldn't think of it,' Merry said hastily but her mind was racing round in circles, as she tried to think of what to do, where she could stay.

Chapter Twenty-two

Dr Macready ate his dried-out meal stolidly as he sat at the dining table and stared out of the window at his small front lawn. He wasn't tasting his food nor seeing the lawn; in his mind's eye he was seeing the young woman whose head he had bandaged that morning and her young son, just recovering from diphtheria.

Miranda Wright was an intelligent woman trapped in an impossible situation. Perhaps the situation had been of her own making, for anyone could see that the boy was not her husband's, but still, as a doctor he was not here to judge. All he knew was that Merry needed to get away from her brute of a husband before he killed her or the child, or even both of them. The child reminded him of someone he knew but no, that was impossible. In any case, that wasn't the issue.

Pushing his plate, which was edged with dried-up gravy and curled-up scraps of meat, away he dabbed at his mouth with a napkin and took a drink of water before sitting back in his chair. He was tired, very tired. Before he came to County Durham he knew nothing about it or the people there. Now he was deeply involved with them and didn't want to work anywhere else. It was just as well Kirsty, his wife, didn't care where she lived. She was a painter and spent her days sketching in the surrounding countryside when the weather was clement, and when it was not she practically lived in her studio in the attic.

It had been a hard summer and it wasn't over yet but at least the diphtheria epidemic seemed to be waning. In its place measles and mumps were on the go. He needed help – Dr Moody who had replaced Gallagher in Winton shared emergency cover with him now but that wasn't enough. Maisie just wasn't good or reliable enough to take messages properly, though the poor girl tried. Kirsty wandered into the dining room and dropped an absent-minded kiss on his sparse grey hair. 'Did you enjoy your meal?' she asked, not noticing the dried-up remains on his plate.

'Very nice, dear,' he replied. She wandered over to the window and gazed out.

'I think I'll walk up Canney Hill this afternoon,' she murmured, almost to herself. 'There is such a view of the valley and the town there and I want to catch the effect of the afternoon shadows along the bottoms. The light is so . . . golden almost in the late afternoon, don't you think so, dear?'

Dr Macready grunted in reply. He looked up at his wife; though her thoughts were so often wrapped up in her art, she had a good mind and surprised him often with her common sense and straightforward approach to his problems. Now was a good time to talk to her.

'Come and sit down, dear,' he said. 'I want to talk to you; it won't take long.'

'Yes of course, what is it?' Kirsty was immediately alert. 'I know you've been busy with the diphtheria epidemic and there are all the other infectious diseases that come with the warmer weather.' She sat down opposite him. 'You look tired, dear. Perhaps you need some extra help.' As usual, she surprised him by her perception. She gazed at him steadily, waiting for him to speak.

'I have been busy, but no more than I would expect in a mining village with no proper sanitation. Dear Lord, the powers that be here think they have modernised when they changed from open middens to ash closets. I dread to think what would happen should the cholera sweep down this

188

valley as it has done over Sunderland way. 'I've tried talking to the Board of Health but to no purpose.' Dr Macready paused and looked at his wife thoughtfully.

'You have a plan?' she asked.

'Not for the big problem, no, I'm afraid I haven't,' he said. 'But I do have a plan to get some help for myself and at the same time help a young woman I know. She has a young boy just recovering from diphtheria and a husband she is desperate to escape from. He is violent, both to her and the boy.'

The doctor sat back and waited for Kirsty's reaction.

'Go on,' was all she said.

'There are the two rooms above the surgery. We don't use them and they wouldn't take much doing up. Being attached to the main house her lout of a husband won't bother her, I don't think. I have long been dissatisfied with Maisie answering the telephone, you know that. And Mrs Wright has some limited experience of nursing. She could be a great help to me.'

Dr Macready paused to take a breath. In the end his ideas had come out in a rush. After all, he was asking a lot. Aiding a woman with an ailing child to leave her lawful husband was unheard of even if they were entering more enlightened times with the coming of the new century.

'It might cause you problems with the locals if you take her on,' Kirsty said thoughtfully.

'Yes. But I'm sure they would blow over.'

'I think you should do it, Ian,' She said. 'Ask her at least, anyway.'

Dr Macready smiled and got to his feet. He had known what she would say really – he just needed to hear her say it. He had to go into the rows to see a baby who had been suffering from measles; the measles had gone but the disease had left him with severe bronchitis. He had left instructions for nursing the child and with luck he would be beginning to improve by now. Then it would be almost time for surgery. At least the surgery was by the house and

189

wasn't far to come home. The house was apart from the miners' rows on a small rise but it was still close for his patients. And the pithead, should there be an accident, which God forbid.

'I knew you would understand,' he said and dropped a kiss on his wife's head. 'Well, I'll be off. Don't stay out sketching if the weather turns too cold, dear.'

The doctor decided to take the trap into Eden Hope, though it wasn't far. If there was time he wanted to go into Winton later and have a word with Dr Moody about the possibility of approaching the council concerning the open-topped carts that were used to empty the ash closets. If he passed one in the street he was obliged to hold his breath until it passed. Surely they were the perfect instrument for spreading infectious diseases?

As he came around the corner to the top of the rows he was amazed to see Merry walking towards him. She was carrying the boy, Benny who was lying against her, his head on her shoulder. The bandage on her head had been knocked askew somehow and the edge of the livid bruise on her temple could be seen. Dr Macready stopped the cart.

'Goodness, Mrs Wright, what are you doing? The boy should not be out here, not this late in the afternoon. It's already turning cooler.'

'I'm going into the town. I'll have to find somewhere to live or I'll have to go to the workhouse,' she said dully. Her head ached and her arms felt as though they were being pulled out of their sockets. Benny's thin little body had felt like no weight at all at first but now, after only a few minutes, it was becoming heavier by the minute.

The doctor got down from his seat on the trap. 'Give me the boy,' he ordered. 'And you, get in and sit down before you fall down.' He waited until she had done as she was told, then went on. 'Now, what's all this about? I didn't expect you to be leaving your husband quite so quickly. Has he been violent again?'

190

'Robbie has locked us out,' she said. 'I have to find somewhere to stay.'

The doctor looked around. Two women were walking along the top of the rows and they slowed as they approached. They gazed open mouthed at Merry and the boy on the trap and Dr Macready standing beside them. The doctor sighed. Goodness knew what tales would be passed around the community now unless he said something. Not that he cared for himself but there was the girl and her son. He beckoned the women over and they came almost at a run, lifting eager inquisitive faces to him.

'Mrs Wright is suffering from concussion,' he said. 'I wonder if you could let Mrs Robinson know I have been delayed as I have to take her to Bishop Auckland. I will be back to see the Robinson child as soon as I can.'

That should do it, he thought. Surgery might be late this evening but it couldn't be helped. 'Gee up,' he called to the pony and cracked the reins, setting off at a steady trot for the town.

He turned into the gates of Oaklands, the workhouse hospital. Merry's heart felt like a great leaden weight in her chest. Weak tears sprang to her eyes; her head throbbed.

'I don't want to go in, please, Doctor,' she pleaded. 'They'll take Benny from me and put him in the children's Ward. They might put him in the Children's Home, mightn't they?' The Children's Home on Escombe Road had recently been built and children were no longer kept in the Workhouse.

'No they won't,' soothed Dr Macready. He gazed at her keenly. Perhaps she really was suffering from concussion, in which case the sooner she was put to bed the better. 'Give me the boy.' But Merry was clutching Benny desperately and her son was clinging just as hard to her.

'Look, they won't separate you, not tonight,' said the doctor. 'I'll see to that. I am on the Board of Guardians.' Not that it did much good, he thought to himself. His was a lone voice among the rest. 'Come on, the boy will catch a

191

cold if he's out here much longer.' He held out his arms again and reluctantly Merry handed him over.

'You promise me?'

'I do,' said Dr Macready. At least he had enough clout to see they stayed together for the night. 'I'll take you in now. You will be looked after for the night. Then I'll see you in the morning. Don't worry now, just try to have a good night's sleep.'

They were put to bed in a narrow, cell-like room that Merry knew was meant for someone who was dangerously ill or suffering from an infectious fever. Not that there was any danger, the smell of Lysol was so strong it seemed to burn her nostrils. There was a bed and a baby's cot and Benny was laid in the cot. His thin legs reached to the iron rails at the bottom but he didn't appear to mind; his eyes were closing almost before the blanket was laid over him.

The day had been altogether too much for the bairn, Merry thought as she looked down on him. She lay back on her hard pillow and sighed. She had to make plans for the future, she told herself; she would never sleep until she did. She vowed they wouldn't stay another night in the workhouse even if it were the hospital part of the institution; the shame was too much. Until now she had not met any of the nurses she had worked with in what seemed another life, but she was aware that it was only a matter of time before she did.

Tomorrow, she thought drowsily, and fell into a deep sleep from which she was only awakened when the nurses began clattering in the adjacent ward with bedpans and washing bowls.

'Mam? Mam?' Benny was awake too as he sat up in the cot and turned to her in fright. 'Mam? Where are we, Mam?'

'It's all right, pet,' she soothed. 'I'm here. Lie down again and the nurse will bring you a drink in a minute.'

But Benny was not to be reassured so easily. He clambered

over the side of the cot and onto her bed, diving under the blanket to cling to her fiercely. She could feel his heart beating rapidly against her ribs and anxiety filled her. He wasn't strong enough for this upheaval, she thought. Dear God, what was she going to do?

The nurse came in and gave them tea and porridge made with water and a drizzle of milk on top. 'He should be in the cot,' she said disapprovingly. 'I don't know what Sister will say.' But she made no effort to make him leave his mother's bed and said nothing else. Merry asked what time Dr Macready was expected but the nurse simply shrugged and went out, though not before giving mother and son a strange look.

When the doctor did arrive later in the morning Merry was sitting on the single hard chair in the room with Benny on her knee.

'I'm sorry I've been so long, Mrs Wright,' he said before turning to Sister who came puffing out of her office. 'Don't let me disturb you, Sister, I have just come for Mrs Wright and Benny.'

'If you're taking them you will have to sign them out according to the rules, Dr Macready,' said Sister.

'Yes, I will see to it. Now I know you're busy, Sister, so don't let me keep you.' He waited until Sister had swept back into her office before turning to Merry. 'Now, how do you feel today my dear? Sleep well?'

'I did, thank you, Doctor,' she replied.

'Then we'll go.'

Go where? Merry thought as they left the ward and walked to where his pony stood patiently waiting. But there was still the throb in her head from the wound and she was happy to let him take over. She trusted the doctor completely.

Jogging along in the trap with Benny sitting between them and a warm rug over their knees, for the weather was cool and overcast for August, she began to feel a little more herself. The air, in spite of the slight smell of coal dust as

193

they passed small collieries on the way, was greatly better than the air in the hospital with its pervasive stink of disinfectant. She breathed deeply of it and her head began to clear properly for the first time since being knocked unconscious when she fell against the table.

'Where are you taking me?' she asked as they passed by the miners' rows of Winton Colliery. 'We can't go back home, not after yesterday.'

'No, I know,' said Dr Macready. 'There are a couple of rooms above the surgery which my wife and I thought would be just the thing for you. I was waiting until we got to the surgery to tell you, or rather ask if you agreed.'

'Agreed?' Merry echoed. She couldn't believe what he was saying. 'But ... you don't have to do this for me. I haven't managed to get any work so I won't be able to pay rent.'

'I am doing it for me, primarily at least,' said the doctor. 'I want you to help with the practice. You can take messages and help with the patients in the surgery hour, can't you? It would help me enormously if I had someone to help with medicines, apply bandages, that sort of thing. I know you have some knowledge already as you worked on the wards at Oaklands – as for the rest a quick girl like you will soon pick it up. I have a man to collect the panel money from the miners' families. You wouldn't have to do that. The most important is taking messages; you know what can happen when these things are left to Maisie.'

Oh, she did, Merry remembered the day and part of the night she had waited for him to come when Benny caught diphtheria. She might have lost him besides Alice. A stab of pain went through her at the thought of Alice. Sometimes it caught her unexpectedly and was almost physical in its intensity. She took a deep breath and forced her attention back to Dr Macready.

'I do,' she said simply.

'Then you agree? We can talk about wages later.'

Merry felt the tears spring to her eyes; she looked away

194

towards the whirling pitwheel of Winton Colliery, which they happened to be passing as she willed them to stop.

'You have saved my life, Doctor,' she said and turned back to him. 'I was at my wits' end. Of course I agree. I'll do my level best for you.'

Dr Macready smiled and turned his attention to the pony as they approached the gates of his house and surgery on the hillside on the outskirts of Eden Hope.

Chapter Twenty-three

'It will be the usual nine-day wonder,' said Dr Macready. 'Don't let it upset you.'

'No. No, I won't, Doctor,' Merry replied. This was the third day in her new job and it seemed to her that every patient who came in the surgery looked at her as though she was a scarlet woman. The first day when she handed over bottles of cough mixture or horse liniment to treat the crop of miners with bad backs or 'miners' cough' that were always at the doctor's on Mondays after a heavy weekend, the recipients looked at her sideways as though she had grown a pair of horns.

With the women it was sniffs and curled lips, though one or two gave her a sympathetic or even admiring glance – the ones with bruises of their own who would have liked to do as she had done mainly, or so she thought. Mostly they went away with the comforting thought that they at least had not been locked out of their own houses by their men.

Apart from the attitude of some of the people, Merry was happy, even beginning to relax. She loved the flat over the surgery. It was sparsely furnished with only a couple of single beds and a chest of drawers in the bedroom, and two old leather armchairs Mrs Macready had sent in from the house, a wooden table and four kitchen chairs in the living room; but it was a delight to Merry. There was a small kitchen with a proper sink and wooden draining board with a cold water tap on the wall over it. There was even a sort of boiler beside the tap that gave out hot water. It was just as well Merry had worked at the hospital or the boiler would have frightened her to death with its hissing and spluttering. As it was she had seen them before on the wards. The best thing of all was the fact that there was a real water closet.

Oh yes, Merry told herself, this was a lovely place to live. Having to answer the door and the telephone and take messages for the doctor was a small price to pay. And when the doctor was called out in the evenings or even during the night she hadn't to go outside at all, just downstairs to the surgery and there was a connecting passage to the house.

Now she stood behind the partition that screened off the dispensary from the surgery, measuring out the medicinal mixtures from the carboys into smaller bottles and adding water ready for patients. On the other side of the partition a patient was standing up ready to leave.

'Mrs Wright will give you the liniment,' the doctor said and the man thanked him. Merry picked up a bottle of liniment and went out into the surgery proper. She looked at Jack Suggett, for that was who it was, full in the face as she handed it over. He didn't acknowledge that he even knew her, simply nodded, took the bottle and walked out. Merry followed him to the door.

'Next for the doctor,' she called and her heart sank as her mother-in-law got up from the form which lined the wall and came towards her. She stood back as Doris swept past her and stood in front of the desk.

'Please sit down,' said Dr Macready pleasantly. 'What can I do for you?'

'You can get rid of that whore for a start,' replied Doris.

The doctor looked up sharply. 'What did you say?' He rose to his feet and stared disdainfully at her.

'I said you could get rid of your assistant,' said Doris. Though her eyes flickered in the face of his authority she stood her ground.

197

Dr Macready gazed at her in silence for a moment and her cheeks turned a beetroot red.

'She's not fit to live with decent folk,' she said. 'God only knows who the father of that bastard of hers is.'

Dr Macready did not raise his voice. 'Is there anything wrong with you?' he asked.

'I just thought you should know how folk felt, she—'

'Shut your filthy mouth, woman!' the doctor interrupted her. 'If you don't get out of my surgery I will call the police.'

'I have a right—'

'You have no rights at all here,' he interrupted her again. He rang a small bell that stood on the desk; almost immediately the door to the waiting room opened and a man came in. It was Jim Hawthorne, a miner of about sixty who was now retired through a mining accident that injured his leg. Jim had taken over collecting the fourpence a week the miners paid for their families to be on the panel. The miners themselves were covered by the Union.

Merry stood still, humiliation washing over her in waves.

'Escort this woman off the premises,' said Dr Macready.

'What? What?' Doris gasped. 'She let my grandbairn die!'

The doctor ignored her.

'Yes Doctor.' Jim Hawthorn grasped Doris's arm in a grip hardened by years of wielding a pick and shovel at the coalface. But she wasn't going to go so easily. Taking him by surprise she wrenched her arm away and swung round on Merry and spat in her face.

'You bloody whore,' she cried. 'I bet you don't even know yourself who fathered that lad.'

Merry fell back, as white as a sheet.

'Get her out,' Dr Macready said to Jim and he did so, propelling Doris through a waiting room full of patients, all wide-eyed to see it.

'Take a minute,' the doctor said to Merry who was

shaking. 'Breathe deeply now, you'll be all right. Sit down, the next patient can wait five minutes.'

Merry sat down and stared at her hands, which were clasped tightly in her lap. The doctor left her alone and got on with writing up patients' notes. After a minute or two her pulse steadied and she felt better. She took a long breath and got to her feet.

'I'm all right now, Doctor,' she said. 'Thank you for dealing with her for me.'

'Nonsense, I won't have anyone coming into my surgery shouting the odds. I would deal with any troublemaker the same way.'

'Shall I call the next patient, Doctor?'

He nodded and she went to the door and opened it. 'Next to see the doctor,' she said. All faces in the waiting room were turned to her but she held her head high. A woman with a little girl got to her feet. 'Howay now, Nellie,' she said and walked in. She smiled at Merry as she passed her, a smile that told Merry she was on her side and Merry felt a small uplift of spirits.

Kirsty looked out over the lawn to the rear of the house and smiled when she saw Benjamin playing with a ball. It seemed so strange having a child about the place, she mused. She and Ian had never had any children and to be honest, she hadn't missed them, being entirely wrapped up with Ian and her art. Yet somehow, since she had told the boy he was welcome to play in the garden, the sight of him there seemed so natural and right. She stepped through the French windows and called to the boy.

'Would you like some lemonade, Benjamin? Mary has made some fresh this morning.' She always called him Benjamin because when they had first met this was what he said his name was. In fact she had been there when he had told his mother his name was Benjamin and not Benny. 'Benny is a baby's name,' he had said.

The boy came running to her. She could hardly believe

199

the change in him since that first day. There was actually some colour in his cheeks and she could swear he had grown a couple of inches, though it was barely six weeks later. Mainly though, it was the change in his manner that was so noticeable. He was no longer the timid child he had been but more sure of himself, not so quiet, even mischievous at times.

'Sit down and have a rest,' she said. 'I'll get the lemonade.' Benjamin sat down obediently and waited until she returned carrying a tray with a jug of lemonade, two beakers and a plate of biscuits. His eyes sparkled – he had not tasted lemonade until he came to live at the doctor's house and he loved it. He took the beaker eagerly and drank thirstily.

'Slowly, Benjamin,' said Kirsty and he stopped and looked apprehensive until he saw she was smiling. She offered him the plate of biscuits. Carefully he put the beaker down and took one.

'Ta, Missus,' he said and began nibbling round the edges. By, it was lovely, he thought. Was this Heaven?

'Say "Thank you, Mrs Macready", Benjamin,' she prompted. She was slowly trying to improve the way he talked. At least his mother didn't mind her doing that – she wouldn't have if Merry did.

Kirsty looked out over the lawn towards the small wood at the bottom of the garden. The leaves on the trees were already beginning to turn shades of russet and yellow even though there was still warmth in the sun and against the blue sky the ash and willow trees looked amazingly beautiful. There was a copper beech in the corner and the brightness of its leaves was dimming to what it was in the summer but it was still beautiful against the leaves of the two sycamores behind it. She would sketch them, she decided, and went into the house for her pad and pencils and watercolours. Perhaps she would even have time to finish it before the light went.

*

It was a couple of hours later and she was finishing the colours off from memory when Ian walked through the house and into the garden. He saw her sitting at her easel with Benjamin beside her, the boy paying close attention to everything she did. In his hand he held a drawing of his own.

'Here you are,' said the doctor. 'Benjamin, I think your mother wants you to go home for tea.'

'Yes, Doctor,' said Benjamin without lifting his head.

'Go on then,' Ian said gently.

'In a minute, I just want to—'

'You had better go now,' Kirsty advised him. 'I've finished anyway.' She began to pack up her materials. 'You can help me tomorrow if it's fine.'

'Promise?'

'I promise. Go home now, love, and show your mother what you've done.'

Benjamin got down from the bench and trotted off round the side of the house to the entrance to the surgery and flat above.

Ian took his place on the bench. 'You like having him here, don't you, Kirsty,' he said.

Kirsty smiled. 'I do,' she replied and showed him her watercolour sketch. Sitting cross-legged on the grass below the beech tree she had drawn the small boy. He was leaning over a board with a pencil in his hand, obviously absorbed by what he was doing. The likeness was striking; she had even caught the pale colour of his hair as the sunlight touched it.

'Has he made you wish you had had children of your own?' the doctor asked.

'No, not really. We're happy as we are, aren't we?'

Ian nodded, relieved. 'Come on in now, dear,' he said. 'I'll get us both a drink before dinner.'

'Can I have a box of paints, Mam?'

Merry took the plates of Welsh rarebit out of the oven

and put them on the table. 'Mind the plate, it's very hot,' she warned. 'Take some bread and butter to eat with it. I'm sure you must be hungry after being out in the fresh air all day.'

Benjamin obediently took a piece of bread and butter and dipped it into the melted cheese. Merry watched him for a minute before starting her own meal. She was happier than she had been in years despite the fact that every single day she still thought of Alice, her little girl. When she could she went to the tiny grave and sat for a short while there, but she was always nervous in case she should bump into Robbie or his mother. Her father-in-law didn't worry her – on the one occasion she had bumped into him unexpectedly in Newgate Street, he had simply smiled and walked on.

'Can I, Mam?'

'Can you what?' she replied absently. The cheese was rich and gooey in her mouth and she savoured it, eating slowly.

'Mam, I asked you, please, Mam, can I have a paint box. And proper brushes. Mrs Macready says you have to have the proper brushes.'

'Oh, Benny – Benjamin,' she corrected herself hastily. 'I can't afford anything extra just now.' She didn't get a big wage from the doctor and most of her money went on necessities. This week she had had to buy new shoes for him to start the new school year this coming Monday.

Benjamin said nothing, just looked down at his plate and began pushing his food about.

'Eat it,' Benjamin,' she said gently. 'Maybe at Christmas eh?'

Chapter Twenty-four

Tom decided to take the train into Bishop Auckland when he at last had a Saturday free. It had been weeks since he had seen his father and stepmother because of the diphtheria epidemic, and he had had to put Miles off visiting him earlier in the summer, as the disease was suddenly raging over most of the county.

At least it had eased now the cooler weather had arrived, he thought, as he cycled in to Durham Station with the wind chill in his face. Soon it would be winter and that would bring its own plagues of colds, influenza and chest complaints.

'A third-class return to Bishop Auckland, please,' he said to the man in the ticket office. No sense in wasting money on a first-class ticket for such a short journey, he reckoned. The wind whistled down the platform as he stood waiting after seeing his bicycle onto the guards van. Fortunately the small local train came in on time and he took a seat by the window. As he always did he watched out for a glimpse of the cathedral and castle as the train chugged out of the station. How many children's epidemics had it seen in the hundreds of years it had stood there, he wondered idly, and stretched his legs out before him. It was good to relax; this was the first full day he had had free for weeks. His thoughts turned to his father as he wondered if he was any happier in his marriage. Why on earth had he married Bertha Porritt in the first place?

Tom had to admit to himself that he knew why, really. It was the chance of owning his own mine, or even more than one, that drove his father. But perhaps he was being unfair to him; perhaps Miles really was in love with his wife. He shifted uncomfortably on the hard seat. The only other person in with him was a housewife with a large covered basket on her lap. She smiled as he glanced over to her, showing crooked teeth; he nodded and turned back to the window. They were pulling out of Coundon Station, just one stop before Bishop Auckland.

Tom's thoughts wandered to Jane Hall. At one time he had thought the two of them might make a go of it but she had made it plain that the life of a doctor's wife was not for her.

'A girl would have to be a saint to marry a family doctor,' she remarked after Tom had had to cancel a date for the third time in a row. He hadn't asked her, he said to himself but not to her. Later she had become engaged to a lecturer at the university and was getting married in November. He had to admit that his heart was not broken.

The train went into the tunnel by Canney Hill and out into the daylight on the outskirts of the town. They were there. He waited as the housewife got out then followed her onto the platform. Soon he had his bicycle and was cycling the short distance back out to Canney Hill and his father's house.

'It's good to see you, Tom,' Bertha said primly and offered her cheek for him to kiss. 'It certainly is quite a while since you visited us.'

'I'm sorry. It has been a busy summer, what with—'

'Yes, I'm sure,' she interrupted him. 'You are so like your father – always too busy for his family.'

Tom let that pass and moved to shake his father's hand. Miles was looking older, he thought, and slightly harassed which was not like him.

'Why didn't you bring the trap?' asked Bertha and wrinkled her nose. 'You smell of smoke.'

204

'I enjoy a train ride,' he replied.

They sat down to a lunch of vegetable soup and salad with pressed tongue, a meat that Tom knew his father disliked. Bertha made most of the conversation; his father ate his food and answered when spoken to. Afterwards the two men went out into the conservatory that Bertha had had added, while Miles smoked his pipe. Bertha had announced her intention of slipping into town for a few odds and ends as she called them.

'It is not often I can use the trap,' she said to Tom, though she was watching her husband coldly as she spoke. 'Miles insists on living here and he needs the trap, he says. Though why we can't have a carriage—'. She had shrugged. Miles did not rise to this.

'How are you, really, Father?' Tom asked when the pipe was going well and Bertha had gone off down the driveway.

Miles laughed shortly. 'I'm well enough,' he replied. 'Don't worry about your stepmother and I. She talks a lot but I have learned to let it wash over me. She has her good points.'

After the tedious hour at lunch Tom had some difficulty in thinking what they might be but he did not comment.

'It has been a bad summer of diphtheria and scarlet fever,' he remarked. 'I understand it has been the same in Winton and Eden Hope.'

'Yes,' his father said. 'These people have no sense of hygiene, that's the problem.'

'How can you say that? What can you expect when the only water tap for a whole row is in the street; when there is no proper drainage or sanitation? This hot summer we were lucky to escape cholera. This is the twentieth century, surely we can do better.'

Miles took his pipe out to reply. 'For God's sake, Tom,' he snapped. 'Can't you talk about anything else? I haven't seen you for months. Haven't you got a nice girl yet? When are you going to give me any grandchildren?' He was going red in the face.

'Calm down, Father,' said Tom. 'You'll have an attack of apoplexy if you're not careful. I'm sorry, you're right, I shouldn't talk about work.'

Miles grunted and drew on his pipe causing acrid fumes to swirl and rise to the glass roof of the conservatory.

'I asked you a question.'

'Yes, sorry,' Tom said again. 'No, I haven't got a future wife in mind at the moment. I don't have much spare time, you know, and women don't like having to take second place to a job of work.' For some reason his father's question had brought to mind not Jane Hall but a picture of Old Pit in a snowstorm and the young girl who had wanted to be a nurse. She was married now, had been for years. She probably had half a dozen children and was middle-aged and careworn before her time, like some of the miners' wives that were his patients at Burdon.

Miles talked a little about his work: how one seam in Winton was petering out; how they had decided to sink a shaft to try to reach Busty seam but their efforts were hampered by water which they were pumping out into a new reservoir. The chances of actually making a profit after all this capital expenditure were poor and they would likely have to reduce the men's wages further. The chance of unrest if this was done was very real – the miners' Union was becoming too powerful, that was the trouble.

Tom thought of the miners and their families and bit his lip. Since the end of the Boer War coal and steel were not in such high demand and the wages bill was the easiest thing to cut down in spite of the Union.

'There will be hard times ahead for the families here then,' he said.

'Nonsense,' Miles replied tersely. 'If the men drank a bit less and stayed away from the pitch and toss schools behind the slag heaps, their families would do well enough.'

Tom didn't answer, for there was no point. Sadly he felt he had grown even further away from his father than he had been. They would never think alike. Miles rose to his feet.

'I have to reply to a letter from Bolton – the owner, you know. Best do it while Bertha is out of the house and it is quiet, I think. You can amuse yourself for a while, Tom?'

It was a crisp October afternoon and the sun still shone, though there was little heat in it. Tom fancied looking round his old haunts.

'I might go for a short ride out if you don't mind, Father,' he said as Miles knocked out his pipe in a large plant pot containing a sorry looking spider plant and went back into the house.

It was good freewheeling down the bank to Winton Colliery. He cycled by the miners' rows then took the road to Eden Hope. He considered calling in on Dr Macready then changed his mind as the house looked so peaceful and no one was in sight. It was a shame to disturb his colleague if he was having a rest. It was fairly quiet being Saturday afternoon. Bishop Auckland was playing a football match against Shildon and most of the men and boys who could afford tickets were probably there, he guessed. Most of the women were likely to be looking for bargains at the market in the town.

The place looked just the same apart from that. Two or three urchins playing 'kicky off chock' with an old tin can on the end of the rows. Tom turned on to the road leading up to Coundon, intending to do a circular tour that would bring him back to Canney Hill. At the top of the bank he paused to catch his breath and looked out over the valley with its mixture of green farms and woodland, and pockets of industry with pit winding wheels and chimneys sticking up against the hillside opposite. He glanced along the farm track that intersected the road. To the left, the track would bring him back to Canney Hill. To the right it led past the stile and path leading down past Parkin's Farm to Old Pit. He climbed back on his bicycle and pedalled along the track. At the stile he lifted the machine over and freewheeled down the grass to the waggon way then the path that ran alongside.

It was slow going and he had to watch out for stones and patches of gravel or oil but eventually he came to where the waggon way divided. He took the branch that led to Old Pit, having to dismount and walk now for the way was neglected and overgrown. Great beds of nettles and rosebay willow herb and long strands of bramble stuck out from the side. The waggon rails were rusty and some of the sleepers displaced so that there were gaps between some joints.

The sun had gone in when he reached the houses of Old Pit. There was no wind and a chill silence hung over the place. Grass grew among the cobbles. Yet some of the cottages still had doors and there was the glint of glass from a few of the windows. Tom left his bicycle and walked up the road in the middle. There were patches of weeds growing there too, between the patches of stone and brick that the old miners had once formed into a surface that would not turn into mud every time it rained. The pump was still there and what's more it seemed to be still in working order for there was a trickle of water from its spout.

Tom looked through the window of the end house and was surprised to see signs that someone had been there and not too long ago either – there was straw in the corner, straw that looked fresh. And there were ashes and cinders in the grate and an old chair by it. He went in and felt the bar; it was still warm. Probably some tramp, he thought. Or perhaps some children from round about played here, playing house. He smiled and went out, closing the rickety door after him. He turned, frowning and looked across at the houses opposite – for a moment he had thought someone was watching him. But there were only the blank holes where most of the windows had been and dirty glass in one or two, black now and reflecting nothing for the sun had gone.

Tom went to the pump and worked the handle a few times – sure enough water came out in a trickle at first and then a steady stream splashing out over the square of bricks

208

beneath. He cupped his hand and took a drink; the water was cold and tasted faintly of minerals but seemed pure.

Standing up straight he looked again at the houses opposite, even considered going over to look closer but in the end changed his mind. His imagination was working overtime, he told himself, and walked up the length of the street to where he had left his bicycle.

He had to walk his machine up the bank to the track then cycle along its length to where it met the road just below Canney Hill. The day was darkening as the early October dusk came in. He could see patches of white fog swirling at the bottom of the valley and the air had turned bitterly cold.

'Where have you been?' Miles demanded as he entered the house and stood to take off the bicycle clamps around his trouser bottoms. 'I've been waiting for my tea.'

'Oh, just around,' Tom answered.

'Well, come on in now and I'll ring for Polly,' said Miles. 'I'm surprised you stayed out so long when it has turned cold. Now we have hardly any time left to talk before you will have to go back.'

As Tom drank tea and ate toasted pikelets oozing with butter he was listening to his father with only half an ear. After a while Miles fell silent too. Tom was still thinking with regret of Merry. He should not have gone to Old Pit, it merely stirred up bittersweet memories. Yet he hadn't known her well, he told himself. Apart from that one night all he saw of her was at the hospital, a small hard-working little girl being bossed around by Sister Harrison.

The telephone rang in the hall and after a moment Polly came in. 'It's the mistress, sir, she wants to speak to you,' she told Miles and he got up with a heavy sigh and went out.

'She's staying at her father's house,' he reported when he came back. 'She left it too late to come back. She doesn't want to travel in the dark. She has more sense than you – you shouldn't be travelling in the dark either.'

Tom reflected that his father seemed happy enough about

209

his wife staying away for the night but merely remarked that it wasn't far to the station and he did have lights.

'I'll have to go now to catch the train,' he said and Miles grunted what could have been a goodbye. As he rode down the hill and up the other side into the market place Tom thought his father seemed to be thinking of something else. Perhaps he should have taken more interest when Miles was talking about his work; perhaps his father was worried about something there. He would have to come home more often, he thought.

Miles had been thinking of something else but not what Tom had supposed. A plan was forming in his mind, a plan that might achieve his ends. He spent the evening sitting before the fire working the plan out in his mind; he would have to be very careful and take plenty of time to work it out, for he couldn't afford a mistake.

Chapter Twenty-five

Christmas Eve 1902

'Is it time to go to the carol service, Mam?' asked Benjamin as he had already done half a dozen times in the last hour.

'Not yet, pet, we'll go at five o'clock,' Merry answered. 'That gives us half an hour to walk to Bondgate and half an hour for you to get ready. It's only half-past four now, come and have something to eat. If you don't you'll get hungry halfway through and not be able to sing.'

'I will,' Benjamin asserted but he came to the table and picked up a sandwich. He ate a couple of bites and put it down. 'I'm not hungry, Mam,' he said.

'You're too excited to eat, that's the trouble,' said Merry. She gazed at him fondly. At seven years Benjamin was beginning to look more and more like his uncle Ben; although his hair was slightly darker his eyes were the same piercing blue. Sometimes she almost felt as though she had her brother back again when she saw him and her heart lurched. Sometimes she saw his father in him, for he had Tom's gentle, kind smile, but it was Ben, the lost brother she had named him for, that he resembled the most.

The time she had had living over the surgery where she worked with Dr Macready was the happiest in her life. After that once, Doris Wright didn't bother her and she understood the family had moved to Dr Moody's panel. At first she had expected her husband to come looking for

211

trouble but he had not and she hadn't seen him since she left. Of course she tried her level best to keep out of his way, nevertheless she was surprised he left her in peace.

Benjamin was a changed boy, no longer nervous and clinging. There was colour in his cheeks, a few freckles across his nose and he smiled almost all the time. He had left the school at Eden Hope for the one in Coundon. It had been Merry's idea really, for she was terrified Robbie would grab him and hurt him.

Benjamin had joined the Sunday school, and that was how they had discovered he could sing. Tonight all the chapels in the circuit were together in Bondgate for the carol service and Benjamin was singing a solo. As she gazed at him she was filled with pride and love.

The Wesleyan Chapel was full when they got there but Merry found a seat near the front, squeezed in on the end of a pew. The children were assembling at the front, all the boys dressed in their Sunday best suits and the girls with fancy white pinafores over their dresses, all looking like angels as they began to sing 'In The Deep Mid-Winter'. When it came to Benjamin's turn to sing and his true, treble rang out over the congregation, never faltering, never a sign of nervousness, she couldn't help whispering to her neighbour that it was her son up there. Oh, it was indeed a night to remember and she thanked God for it.

Later, after the service, they all filed out of the chapel into Bondgate, she holding on to Benjamin's hand for it was dark out on the street, apart from the light spilling out from the open doors and the lanterns some folk carried as they all hurried away. In a minute or two the street would be deserted, the only light from the public house further down towards the market place. Merry had intended to bring a candle lamp but somehow had forgotten. Still, she told herself, it wasn't so far and she could keep to the main Durham Road.

Then they met the contingent from Eden Hope. Merry's heart fell to her boots for Robbie was walking across the

212

road to them, a woman on his arm. He must have come from one of the pubs on the other side for he was smiling broadly and fondling the woman as he came. Merry could see plainly for there was a pool of light there from lanterns in the group. She shrank back against the wall of the chapel, pulling Benjamin with her but it was no good, Robbie had seen her. He pushed the woman's hand from his arm and strode towards her. She couldn't actually see the expression on his face but his very stance was aggressive as he stood before her, legs astride.

Merry looked from left to right desperately. The people were beginning to disperse and there wasn't a man she could see she could call upon for help. She glanced behind her, thinking she could appeal to the steward at the door but he was in the act of closing it and pushing the bolt in at the top, anxious to get home to the warm.

'You have a nerve, do you know that? Going into a chapel with decent folk and letting your bastard make a show of himself? Call it singing? It was more like a cat screeching.'

'Watch your language, man,' someone said, a man's voice. It was the steward.

'Keep your neb out,' Robbie snarled. 'Any road, what are you going to do about it?' He stepped into the gloom to confront the man who had spoken.

'The police station is just over the road,' the man answered. 'I'll call a polis.' But he was backing away, drawn by his wife who was muttering about not interfering.

'Robbie, howay, man, I want to go now,' the woman he was with called.

'I won't be a minute, I'm just giving the whore a piece of my mind,' Robbie growled. He leaned forward and grabbed her coat and blouse at the front and Benjamin jumped forward.

'Leave me mam alone, you big bully!' He put his small body between his mother and his stepfather, and Robbie laughed. He grabbed at the boy's chest, catching a handful

213

of shirt and jacket and lifting Benjamin to his toes.

'Don't you touch him!' cried Merry and threw herself between them, trying to push Benjamin away. The woman with Robbie started forward as though to join in.

'What's this? What's this?' Without them noticing a pony and trap had pulled up on the road before the chapel and Dr Macready jumped down. 'If you don't stop that this instant I will put you in charge!'

Surprised at the authoritative tone, Robbie loosed his hold and took a step back before he realised it was the doctor, then he growled. 'It's you, is it? Well—'

'Howay, Robbie, here's the polis,' the woman with him hissed and sure enough the door of the police station across the road had opened and a policeman was coming out and over to them. Robbie took hold of her arm and strode off into the dark of Fore Bondgate.

'Is there some trouble here?' the officer asked Dr Macready.

'Not now, officer, thank you. I'm just picking up our friends. Come along, Mrs Wright, get in the trap and we'll be on our way.'

Merry had been standing with an arm around Benjamin. She could feel him trembling beneath her arm and she herself was trembling almost as badly. She hurried over to the trap and got in beside Kirsty who fussed over her and drew the rug over both their knees.

'Goodnight, Constable,' the doctor was saying. 'Merry Christmas.'

'Merry Christmas. Merry Christmas.' The sentiment echoed around them as they drove off into the market place and on towards home.

Kirsty chatted about the carol service they had had at St Anne's, the Church of England, which stood next to the Town Hall.

'We thought we would pick you up as we were so near,' she said and asked how Benjamin had done and Merry answered normally, saying how beautiful he had sounded

214

singing 'Away In A Manger'. Kirsty said he should sing it tomorrow for them and she would play the piano for him and by the time they reached the house Benjamin had stopped trembling and was glowing with all the praise.

Merry realised properly then that she and Benjamin were not on their own against the world as she had always been. The Macreadys were so kind and caring and it was a lovely feeling. A feeling she could not remember having since she was small and there was Gran and Ben and her living in the deserted village of Old Pit.

The next day they were invited to the Macready's house for Christmas dinner. Merry helped Maisie with the cooking and Kirsty wandered in and out of the kitchen getting in the way, but in the end the feast was prepared and was everything Merry had read about but had never been able to afford.

After the Christmas pudding had been flamed and 'oohed' and 'aahed' over, with Benjamin's eyes as big as saucers before it was demolished, Kirsty insisted that they sit in the drawing room for a while before the dishes were attended too. There was a decorated Christmas tree such as Merry had never seen except in the magazines in Jos Turner's shop, and crackers and paper hats. And for tea, there were mince pies and cake. But best of all, Kirsty had bought a proper sketchpad for Benjamin and a paint box. Not a small, children's paint box but a large one, with squares of watercolour and a palette and little jars of brilliant colours and assorted brushes.

Benjamin was starry-eyed and reluctant to go next door to the flat when the time came. But he was sleepy and went to bed with little demur.

'It was grand, Mam, wasn't it grand, Mam?' he said even as his eyes were closing.

Later, sitting by herself in the living room, Merry couldn't settle to the jersey she was knitting for Benjamin. She worked on a few rows then put it aside and wandered over to the window looking out onto Eden Hope below. A moon had risen and the frost on the slate roofs of the houses glinted. There was a ring round the moon and Merry gazed at it, remembering when she and Ben were small. Gran had said they were in for hard weather when that happened. As she was standing there, something flitted across the path outside, a shadow, that was all. She could not tell what it was. She stared out for a few minutes but there was nothing else, no movement at all. Most people were at home celebrating Christmas with their families. It must have been her imagination. Merry sighed and closed the curtains and sat down again by the fire.

She had saved and bought a child's box of watercolours from Turner's shop for Benjamin, giving him it that morning in the stocking he had hung on the mantelpiece for Father Christmas to fill. The nuts and orange and bar of chocolate she had put in the stocking along with the water-colours were all she could afford but she had been so looking forward to seeing Benjamin's face when he saw the paint box. And his face had been a picture, a picture of a small boy trying to hide his disappointment.

Kirsty's gift on the other hand had filled him with joy. It was a real, grown-up set and must have cost a lot of money in an artist's supply shop in Darlington or Durham City.

All Benjamin's talk now was of Kirsty and the doctor: how Kirsty had shown him how to mix colours properly to get the right shade of green for the fields; how most tree trunks were not really brown but a variety of colours.

'I'm going to be a painter when I grow up,' he declared. And Dr Macready had taken him fishing in the Wear and he had come home proudly carrying two brown trout.

I'm jealous, Merry thought. Jealous because they can give him more than I can. I should be pleased, and I am in a way, but I'm jealous. At least he's safe here from Robbie Wright and his mother. That is the important thing.

Merry wrapped up her knitting and went to get ready for bed. But once there she lay on her pillow still feeling restless and unable to sleep. Her thoughts wandered to Tom Gallagher, Benjamin's father. Even after all this time she could picture his face vividly in her mind's eye. The thought of him brought a yearning to her, which was silly for hadn't he made it plain that he didn't want her, had never wanted her? Benjamin had been the result of a man and woman being thrown together in a storm and it was plain that he must have regretted it for he had not come near her afterwards. He had probably forgotten all about her.

How could she forget him though, when Benjamin looked so much like him? She had tried to tell herself he looked like her brother and he did, but sometimes, especially as he grew older, she could see Tom's very smile in him, his gestures.

Merry turned over onto her other side and pummelled the pillow. In the night, lying on her own in the dark, the same thoughts returned to her quite often, though she tried to dismiss them as just coincidence. There was no doubt that Tom and her brother Ben had looked alike and now Benjamin too. Could there possibly have been a connection between Ben and Tom? It was a puzzle that had been staring her in the face forever but with all her family gone she had no one to ask, and if Gran had been alive today, could she have asked?

Merry turned again and lay on her back, telling herself she had built all this up in her mind and it was downright silly. Of course there was no connection. She closed her eyes and at last felt herself drifting off into sleep.

Almost the next minute, or so it seemed to her she heard the patter of gravel against her window. Her eyes flew open and she lay perfectly still listening, poised to run to the house to alert the doctor. Was someone trying to break in to the surgery? No, they would not have thrown anything at an upstairs window, of course not.

'Merry!'

The call was low, so she only just heard it but then it

came again. She got out of bed and went to the window, moving only a corner of the curtain to look out. On the moonlit path below there was the figure of a man standing, legs astride and looking up at her. She dropped the curtain. No, it couldn't be, she told herself. But then he called again and this time there was something familiar in the voice.

'Merry! Let me in, it's me, Ben.'

Ben? A wild hope whirled within her, but no, it couldn't be could it? She had to force herself to open the curtain and look out properly. Ben looked up at her. Oh yes, it was Ben's face and it was Ben's voice – even though it was so many years since she had seen him, it was him.

She didn't think any more, but rushed downstairs, through the surgery and opened the door – and there he was, her brother Ben.

Chapter Twenty-six

Merry put a Lucifer to the gas mantle that hung from the ceiling in the living room and blinked as light flooded the room. It was all a dream, it had to be, she told herself, and stood absolutely still for a couple of seconds. If she turned she would wake up and she didn't want to wake up from this dream. At last, she did turn and he was still there looking at her with a sort of half smile on his face. She stared at him; he had a deep tan and his hair was lighter than she remembered, bleached almost white.

'You're taller than you were,' she said stupidly. He laughed and stepped forward, and then she knew that he was real – he was there and she could feel his arms around her as he kissed her on both cheeks before stepping back.

'It would be a bad job if I wasn't,' he said. 'I'm a man now, Merry. Aren't you going to ask me to sit down?' His accent was different somehow, his words clipped.

'Yes. Yes of course, sit down, sit down.' She was gabbling, she thought dimly and sat down herself before she fell down, she felt so strange.

'Oh Merry, Merry, I've dreamed of this day so many times,' he said as he took a seat in the chair opposite hers.

'But where have you been?' she suddenly demanded, anger bursting through her elation at seeing him. 'I thought you were dead! It was cruel, Ben, why did you go?'

'I didn't just run away, Merry,' he said and the light in

his eyes died as he thought about that time when he was a young lad and Miles Gallagher had come upon him in the garden at Old Pit. A rage built up in him as it always did when he allowed himself to recall it. He looked down at his fists, which had curled into balls, the knuckles white.

'What then? What happened? Ben, I thought you were dead! Dead under that fall of stone in the entrance to the drift up in the woods beyond Old Pit. We searched, Ben. The lads from Eden Hope helped me. I found a rag from your trousers, Ben.' Reaction set in and tears sprang to her eyes. 'Where have you been?' she cried angrily.

'South Africa,' said Ben. 'I joined the army when the war began. And after the war I didn't come home with the rest, I worked my way round the world on a tramp steamer.'

'But why?'

'He put the fear of God into me,' Ben replied simply. 'I was only a young lad after all.'

'Who? Who did that? Why?'

The questions were crowding Merry's brain. All the anguish she had suffered since he went dimming her delight in seeing him again and realising her precious brother was not dead, he was here, real, alive. She rose to her feet and touched him, feeling the warm skin of his hand, his smooth blonde hair. He really was alive. 'Why?' she demanded again, sharply this time. Surely he could have got in touch, found some way to let her know where he was?

'I wrote. When I thought it was safe, I wrote. But I only had the address at Old Pit. And I was frightened *he* would find out and he would do something to hurt you. He's an evil man, Merry. He still is. He must not find out I'm back.'

'Who? Who, Ben?'

'Miles Gallagher. You know him? The mine agent?' He saw by her face that she did. 'He hasn't tried to hurt you, has he?' Ben started to his feet but Merry shook her head.

'No, no, of course he hasn't. Why should he?'

Miles Gallagher, she thought. Tom's father. Dear God,

Benjamin's grandfather. Did Ben know about her son, named for him? She couldn't ask, not yet, not now.

'Ben, I don't understand any of this.'

She had not accepted his death, not at first – after all they hadn't found him. The young miners had dug away at the newest fall in the entrance to the drift mine but they had been unable to shift the hundreds of tons of stone and shale that had fallen before that. Half the hill, it had looked like to her. And when she found the rag there had been the niggling thought that Ben was there, under some of that rubble. Yet without a body there had been hope. Oh, she was so muddled and mixed up.

'Make a cup of tea, lass, will you? I haven't had a decent cup of tea for I don't know how long.' Ben sounded weary and no wonder. Merry made the tea and came back to him. He was sprawled back in the chair, his legs stretched out, to the fire, his eyes closed. He looked so tired and so young though of course he was only a couple of years younger than she was. She had always felt older though, always looked after him when he was small. She felt a rush of tenderness towards him.

He heard her footsteps and opened his eyes and sat up. 'Sorry,' he said. 'I've been living at Old Pit. Hiding out really.' She handed him a pint pot of tea and he took a long swallow. 'Thanks, pet, I needed that. I only light a fire at night in case someone seems the smoke.'

'Tell me what happened that day at least,' she said.

Ben sat back and allowed himself to remember the day the man he found out later was Miles Gallagher had found him in the garden at Old Pit. The details were fixed firmly in his mind. He'd been apprehensive at first and his instincts had been right, he thought bitterly. Then when the man had said he would take him a ride on his horse he had reckoned he might not be so bad after all. But at the ventilation shaft along by the woods he had been scared. For a minute he had thought the man would tip him into the shaft and he was terrified of falling into the darkness below. He

221

would never get out, Merry would never know where he had gone.

Ben remembered falling, then nothing until he woke up – he was on a ship with other boys and they told him they were going to South Africa to become farmers. The other boys were all orphans, or so Harry told him. Harry was the boy in the next bunk to him in the stifling place between decks where they slept and spent a lot of their time. They were allowed on the lower deck once a day for an hour in the afternoon, emerging pale and blinking into the sunshine or shivering in the wind and rain.

'I'm going to be rich,' Harry asserted. 'Father Donovan said if we work hard and save our money we will be able to buy our own farms, they're dirt cheap there.'

Every day the ship's captain came to see Ben. He and another man would look at the wound on Ben's head and ask how he was.

'How did I get here?' Ben asked. His head ached and ached and he couldn't think straight. ('My brain felt scrambled,' he told Merry as he sat nursing his pot of tea in the snug room over the surgery.)

'Never you mind,' said the captain. He looked at the man with him who was a doctor, or so Harry told Ben. 'You're very lucky you're going out to a fine life in the colonies. A rich man you'll be, the lads at home will be jealous as hell.'

There was only Merry, he had to write to Merry as soon as he got to wherever he was going. Then he had to find his way back to Old Pit because Merry couldn't manage without him.

Ben told his tale in a quiet monotonous voice but there was a suppressed anger beneath it; Merry could sense it. Now he went quiet, staring into his pot of tea.

'I was past myself with worry about you,' said Merry. 'That wicked, wicked man. But why? Why did he do it?'

'That I don't know. What I do know is that when we landed the captain handed me an envelope with a note inside. It was from him, I knew, though it wasn't signed.

222

And he said that if I did come back or tell anyone it would be you who would suffer.'

Merry gasped. 'Are you sure it was the mine agent?'

'Miles Gallagher. Yes I am. I've been back a week now and I've seen him.' Suddenly he yawned. 'Sorry. I've had little sleep since I've been back at Old Pit.'

'Why don't you stay? I can make you a shakey-down bed in here.'

'No, I can't. I can't risk it. Not until I do something about *him*. I'll go now. I'll be back though. And Miles flaming Gallagher will get what's coming to him, I promise you.'

'Be careful, Ben, please.'

'Oh, I'll be careful, pet, never fear,' her brother replied.

He kissed her forehead and went to the door. After she had seen him out she went back upstairs and put out the gas and lit a candle to go into the bedroom. She undressed quickly, blew out the candle and climbed into bed but her head was too full of Ben and she lay awake until it was almost morning before dropping off to sleep through sheer exhaustion. Consequently she woke tired and with an aching head. But still, not even that could dim the joy of having Ben back and alive.

There were so many questions buzzing round in her head though. Questions about Tom's father, the thought of him was hanging over her joy menacingly. Why had he done what he had to Ben? Ben was just a young boy when it happened, how could be have hurt the mine agent? Then there was her own son, Ben hadn't asked about him, did he not know? In fact he hadn't asked anything about her, how she had managed, about her marriage, not anything. But then there hadn't been much time and perhaps he hadn't heard anything as he was in hiding and wouldn't have spoken to anyone from Winton Colliery or Eden Hope. She would go to Old Pit this afternoon, she decided, it was Boxing Day and she was free. Benjamin was spending the afternoon with Mrs Macready having a drawing lesson.

*

Merry didn't walk along the waggon way from the pit yard to get to Old Pit. She didn't want to meet anyone from the pit villages so she took a footpath through the fields to Coundon, turning off on the path that led down past Parkin's Farm. She hurried past the farm buildings but there was no one about. The day was rawly cold, already darkening and icy rain had started to fall. There was no one about at all; even the cattle were indoors at this time of the year and the only sounds were of rain dripping from the trees.

She climbed the sodden stile and her feet squelched in the puddle at the other side. Dirty water went over her shoes and her stockings were soaked. Gritting her teeth she plodded on until she came to the place where she had grown up but there was no sign of Ben and her heart lurched with disappointment. She stood by the pump and looked about her. Old Pit was much the same as she remembered it. Two of the houses had had their roof slates removed and there were other things missing but evidently there hadn't been much worth salvaging.

The door to the end house was open about an inch but it was warped with the rain and was stuck fast. She tried pushing it but it was hopeless. She walked round the side to the back door and found that it opened with a screech of wood on the flagstone when she pushed hard enough. There were no stairs to the upper floor – where they had been short pieces of metal jutted out from the wall.

Merry felt a surge of sadness as she remembered how her grandmother had struggled to keep the place clean and neat and tidy, and now it was simply a ruin. Leaves swirled in the corner with the draught and the iron range was red with rust instead of polished and shining from black lead.

Ben had covered his tracks well; she could see no sign of him, though there were ashes in the grate and a few cinders even. Merry went closer and saw a faint glow of red just dying. She went beneath the hole of what had once been the top of the stairs and called softly.

'Ben?'

'Merry! Why have you come here? I told you it was dangerous. Are you sure no one saw you?'

'No, no they didn't,' said Merry. 'There's nobody about, Ben, nobody at all. It's Boxing Day, the pits are off and any road it's blooming awful weather.'

'Howay, come on up,' said Ben and let down a roughly knotted rope ladder. 'You can climb that, can't you?'

''Course I can,' she asserted, though in truth the ladder swayed alarmingly as she stood on the first rung and she clung to the rope. Eventually though, she reached the top and Ben helped her into what had once been the bedroom. He was wearing a dark-blue topcoat such as a seaman might wear with the collar turned up on his neck, yet when he had touched her his hand was icy. There were a couple of blankets on top of some dried bracken in a corner and a pile of rags that he had obviously been using as a pillow. A chair with a broken back was there too and a small stool – a cracket, the miners called them, when they were used in the pits in very low seams. She looked in horror at this evidence of how poorly he was living in this bitter weather. As if to emphasise it rain began pattering at the window, some getting in immediately through the ill-fitting frame.

'Heck, Ben, you can't live like this,' she said.

He shrugged. 'I've lived in worse places and when I was but a bairn an' all. When you toil in the gold mines and it's so hot you fancy your brains are frying, all that keeps you sane is the thought of an English winter.'

She gazed at her brother: his skin was burned dark bronze and showed no sign of fading; his eyes had become shuttered and cold and she guessed he was looking back to those days. Her heart ached for him.

'The mines? I thought you were going on the farms?'

'Aye, well we were sold off like cattle at the other end. Most of the lads were Catholics and some of them went to farms. Me, I went to a mine owner. I was in the mines three years before I got away.'

225

'You're home now,' she said softly.

'Aye, but I can't come out into the open until I've seen to *him.*' He shook his head as though clearing his mind, went to the window and peered out. 'You sure no one followed you?'

'No Ben, no one did.'

'Well, there's no one there, any road.' He turned back into the room, smiling self-consciously. 'I'm not worried, really, I can take care of myself now and you an' all. This Gallagher chap is only a man after all.'

'Still, best be careful, Ben,' said Merry.

'Oh, I will, believe me, I will,' he assured her. 'Now, come and sit down and tell me what's been happening to you in all these years.' He squatted on his hunkers against the wall in the age-old way of miners, and Merry took a seat. This was the moment she had been dreading. She wondered how to tell him about Benjamin and about her failed marriage. About the fact that Miles Gallagher's son was Benjamin's father. He was looking up at her expectantly but she was hesitant about where to begin. In the end he helped her.

'I know you have a son, that you must have been married,' he said. 'What happened? Did your man die?'

'No, he's not dead, no,' she replied. Once she started on the story of her marriage she told it as it had happened, right until the day when Robbie had locked her out.

'The rotten sod!'

Ben had listened with only the occasional ejaculation of anger or surprise. She stumbled over the telling how the diphtheria epidemic had taken little Alice, almost taken Benjamin.

'Oh my God, I'm sorry, Merry,' he murmured and she looked down at her hands clasped tightly in her lap as the pain of it came back in full force. Still, she went on, glossing over the times Robbie had hit her, but not about the way he had treated Benjamin. When she came to tell him of the day her husband had put her out of the house he jumped to his feet and paced the room.

226

'I'll kill him, I will, I'll flaming well kill him!' he said savagely.

'No, Ben, don't, just leave it. He did Benjamin and me a favour, really. We're both of us happier where we are.'

Merry got to her feet and looked around the room again.

'You can't stay here, Ben, of course you can't. You will have to find somewhere else.'

'I will, don't worry about me, Merry,' he replied. 'I'll be all right.'

Walking home she pondered on the fact that he had hardly mentioned Benjamin; asked not a single question about him. But it would come out; it had to, she thought. And what would he think when he found out who Benjamin's father was?

227

Chapter Twenty-seven

Merry looked around the flat when she got home, seeing anew how comfortable it was, especially in comparison to the conditions at Old Pit where Ben was living. She was so glad to see him, to know he was not dead and yet ... already she was worrying about him, worrying what he was going to do. For he must have a plan, he had probably been thinking of a plan all the years he was exiled.

The questions whirled around in her head until it ached. Why had Mr Gallagher done what he had done to a lad as young as Ben had been? He had gone to such extraordinary lengths to get Ben away, he must have bribed the captain of that ship taking orphans to the colonies. Yet it would have been so easy to get rid of Ben in that drift mine or down the old ventilation shaft. But he had stopped short of killing the boy. Why?

Ben could sleep here sometimes, she decided as she dusted the waiting and consulting rooms ready for morning surgery – providing he came secretly after Benjamin had gone to sleep and left early in the morning. Benjamin was a good sleeper, rarely waking once he was settled for the night. She would insist on it next time she saw him, otherwise he would end up with pneumonia. Tomorrow she would somehow manage to take him a basket of food, a pie perhaps, soup to heat up.

She gave a last glance around the surgery and went

upstairs to prepare Benjamin's supper, feeling a little better about Ben now she could do something for him. Yet still she was worried about him for she knew he was determined to get revenge on Tom's father and Miles Gallagher was a powerful man in the area.

Merry refused to think about how she was going to tell Ben about her son, his namesake. She would have to, of course, and yet again wondered what he would do when he found out the boy's father was Miles Gallagher's son.

Tom was just ending surgery when the telephone rang. He sighed heavily as he picked up the receiver. He had had an interrupted night, being called out to a minor accident at the mine. Then the surgery had been full after being closed for the Christmas holidays and he had a full list of house calls to start – now this was probably yet another.

'Dr Gallagher,' he said even as he was finishing writing up the last patient's notes. If it wasn't too urgent he would be able to snatch a cup of coffee before he set off. Lunch was likely to be very late.

'Tom!'

He sat forward, leaning his elbow on the desk. It was his stepmother and she sounded almost hysterical.

'Yes? What is it? Is something wrong, Bertha?'

Bertha gave a strangled sound that could have been a laugh or a cry. 'Wrong? Wrong? Tom, there has been an accident.'

'Father? Is it Father?'

'My father and yours, Tom, both of them, the fools went down the Winnipeg! Oh, I don't know what to do, Tom, I don't. How could they do this to me?'

'He's not dead, is he?' Tom was having trouble making his stunned brain take in what she was saying.

'Dead? Of course he's dead, what do you think? He's—'

'I'll be right over,' he said and put down the receiver so he didn't hear the end of the sentence as she went on about him being an old man and Miles should never have allowed it to happen.

Within half an hour Tom had arranged for the neighbouring practice to take over his day's work for him and was driving out towards Willington which was north of the river and the sharpest way to get to Winnipeg Colliery. He was thankful that he had recently bought a car, a Wolsey, which he had second-hand from a colleague who had bought it on impulse but couldn't get the hang of driving it, and whose wife hated it. Otherwise he would not have been able to afford an automobile, not yet – after all, a new car of the same type cost £260. As it was it cost him less than £200 and had taken all his savings. He judged it well worth it, however; it saved him time, being all of five-horse power. It was a two-seater but after all, he hadn't a family to consider.

Bertha was in the sitting-cum-drawing room of her father's house, not sitting down but striding up and down in agitation.

'Oh, you're here,' she greeted Tom. 'He's not back yet; he's arranging for the ... body to be brought home. Though probably there will be a post-mortem, won't there? Oh, I don't know what is happening, we women just have to wait, that's what men expect, isn't it?'

Tom looked at her in perplexity. 'Who?' he asked. His mind had gone completely blank.

Bertha looked at him impatiently. 'Who what? Miles, of course. He didn't even come to tell me himself, sent an overman would you believe.'

'My father? You mean he's all right?'

Bertha sighed impatiently. 'I said so, didn't I?'

She had not, Tom thought but didn't say. 'And your father, what happened?'

'The old fool went down the mine with Miles and slipped into a hole or something, I don't know. Now look how he's left me.'

'I'm sorry,' said Tom. 'Sit down, do. This has been an awful shock to you. I'll ring for some tea, shall I?' He went to the bell pull by the side of the fireplace and tugged the cord.

230

'Sorry. Yes of course.' Bertha sat down by the fire but within a couple of minutes was up again and striding to the window, looking out, then coming back. When the maid brought in tea, Tom poured her a cup, added milk and two spoonfuls of sugar and took it to her. He sat down opposite her chair with his own cup and watched her as he sipped. He could give her a sedative but really he should call the family physician. She was bursting with nervous energy and would be totally exhausted if she didn't slow down.

'Here he is now,' she said from the window where she had carried her tea. 'Now we'll find out what happened.' She put her cup down on the windowsill and turned to face the door, her demeanour showing how she was bracing herself.

Miles was very pale and there was a small cut on his cheek that was blue-black with the coal. He also had a bandage on his hand but as far as Tom could see that was the extent of his father's injuries and he sighed with relief.

'Father!' he said, 'I was worried about you.'

'I'm all right,' Miles said briefly, crossed over to where Bertha was standing by the window and took her hand.

'I'm sorry, Bertha,' he said.

'It's true then?' she asked and he nodded.

Bertha shook off his hand and strode to the fire where she turned and stood, legs apart and with her hands on her hips. Her face twisted with anger, not grief. Tom, watching, though she must be holding off her grief by whipping herself into a rage and he bit his lip.

'How could you do it?' she screamed at Miles. 'Why did you take him down the mine? Why?'

'I–I couldn't stop him, it was his idea, he—'

'Rubbish, you could have stopped him, he's an old man!' She was glaring at him, her face suffused with colour and her eyes bulging.

'Bertha,' said Tom, moving towards her and laying his hand on her arm. 'Sit down, Bertha, please. You've had a terrible shock.'

231

'A shock is it? My husband leads my father to his death and then hasn't the nerve to come and tell me himself? He sent an overman for God's sake, an overman from the pit.' She shook off Tom's arm in the manner she had shaken off his father's. Her whole body was trembling with the depth of her feeling. 'Well? Have you nothing more to say to me?' she shouted.

'I'm sorry, Bertha, I really am,' said Miles. Tom looked at him.

'I think you had better sit down, both of you in fact,' he said and Miles made to sit but Bertha screeched at him again.

'Don't you dare sit on any of my chairs, Miles Gallagher, you've been down the pit, haven't you? Look at you, you're filthy. Go and clean yourself up. Go on, I can't bear the sight of you.'

Miles shrugged and glanced at Tom, then walked to the door like an old man. It was the first time Tom had seen him like that so he strode quickly to the door himself and opened it.

'Will you be all right?' he asked in a low voice as his father went out. 'Shall I come with you? She doesn't mean any of this, you know. Shock takes people in different ways.'

Miles shook his head and headed towards the stairs. Tom glanced back into the room and seeing Bertha's figure beginning to slump decided he had better see to her first. He was just in time to catch her as she fell and laid her on the chaise-longue. The faint lasted only seconds though and she sat up and looked at him with pain-filled eyes.

'Keep still,' he ordered. 'It was just the shock.'

Bertha began to cry as at last the grief for her father hit with full force. She lay back against the raised end of the chaise-longue and sobbed. Tom got her fresh tea, adding brandy and sugar, and she sipped at it between hiccuping and dabbing at her eyes. After a while she became quiet.

'Are you all right?' he asked and she nodded. 'I'll just go

232

up and see how my father is,' he added. 'Shall I call the maid?'

'No.'

Tom gazed at her with concern until she said, 'Oh for goodness sake, leave me alone and go and see to your precious father.' He nodded and went out and up the stairs. Miles was in the bathroom looking at the cut on his face in the mirror over the basin.

'I must get rid of the coal mark,' he said to Tom.

'I doubt you can, but we can try,' Tom replied.

He dabbed at the small cut with cotton wool soaked in a solution of hydrogen peroxide. 'It could put a dressing on it but really it is better open to the air,' he said. 'How do you feel now? I could give you something—'

'No, I don't want anything, I told that Doctor whatshis-name at the pit.'

'Sure?'

'I'm sure,' Miles said shortly. 'For God's sake don't fuss.'

Tom shrugged. 'All right. But take it easy, please. Have a warm bath, not too hot, and a rest. I'll stay and attend to whatever has to be done.'

Tom was at the door when Miles said suddenly, 'Were you up at the pit yard this morning, Tom?'

'No, of course not, I was at home. I had just come not long before you came in, Bertha telephoned me. Why?'

'Nothing, I just thought I caught a glimpse – no, it was nothing.' Tom nodded and went out. No doubt his father had been suffering from the effects of the accident and then the sudden emergence into the light as he came to bank.

When he went out Miles locked the bathroom door, ran the bath and climbed in. He had been going to anyway. He stretched out on the deep iron-enamelled tub and let his thoughts wander back over the happenings of the day. Bertha he didn't give a second thought to. Oh, he had said he was sorry and he was, but not for what had happened to her father. The old sod was past it anyway, so he was better

233

out of the road. Now he could put the next stage of his plan into action.

No, what he was sorry about was that it hadn't turned out the way he had planned. And he had planned it meticulously, prodding the old man to go down to the second level with him and without the manager, on a day and at a time when there were few men in the mine, so it was easier to make sure there were no witnesses.

'I think it is important to keep a thorough watch on the way the seam is being worked out,' he had said to old Porritt. That was how he thought of him, always old Porritt. 'Carney is as trustworthy and efficient as most managers but after all, he is just an employee. Employees haven't got your interests at heart, of course they haven't. No, I think we should go down ourselves and then we'll know exactly what he's talking about.'

Carney, the manager had reported that the pit props all needed replacing as the roof was showing signs of sagging in one particular area. Near where they were thinking of going down a level, it was. He wanted good Norwegian spruce pit props and a more efficient ventilation engine than the ancient one in use.

'It works perfectly adequately,' old Porritt had protested and sent Miles down to look at it. It was a long time since he himself had ventured down the mine. For Miles it was the perfect opportunity to put his plan in motion.

'You must come and see for yourself,' he had told the old man. 'It is not too far from the shaft bottom, so you won't find the walk taxing. In any case, I'll be with you.'

It would be easy, he had thought. All he had to do was walk behind old Porritt and hit him with a lump of stone when he wasn't looking. It would look as though the stone had fallen from the badly supported roof. But in the event, part of the roof *had* fallen as a pit prop cracked and sagged, and stone had fallen on Porritt's prone body.

He had had a bad fright, Miles told himself as he stretched out in the warm water. He had actually been hit

234

himself by flying debris and had had to jump back and run for the main way, stumbling over the rails and falling, hitting his head on a rail. By, that was a bad moment.

Still, it had lent his story credence. Miles reached to the side for the loofah and soap and scrubbed at his arms. Gingerly he felt the small wound on his cheek. He hoped Tom had got rid of the blue coal scar, he thought. Such scars were the marks of the common pitmen and not suited to someone of his status, for he was now an owner besides being the agent for Arthur Bolton and Co. Or he soon would be – there was only Bertha in the way now.

It was as he was pulling on his robe that he remembered the man he had seen in the pit yard. It was funny that – for a minute he had been sure it was Tom. But Tom hadn't been there, so it must have been his imagination or a trick his eyes played on coming out of the pit into the bright light on top.

For the first time in years he thought about the boy he had put on the boat at Hartlepool. With hindsight it had been a daft thing to do, he reckoned. Much better to have done what he intended to do in the first place – put him in the old ventilation shaft or throw him over the roof fall in the drift mine. Yet somehow he hadn't found himself able to do it.

He was letting his imagination run away with him, he decided as he reached for the bath towel on the rail above the bath. It must have been another fair-haired man he had seen, he told himself. The other one would likely be dead by now and if he wasn't he wouldn't have the means to come back and seek revenge. He was half-dead when he last saw him.

He stood up and wrapped the towel round himself and climbed out of the bath before rubbing himself dry. He felt strangely lethargic yet exhilarated. No doubt it was something to do with the brush with death he had experienced. He went into the bedroom and climbed into bed. No need to face Bertha again today. Tom would look after her. That lad was altogether too much like his soft-hearted mother.

When Tom looked in the bedroom a few minutes later Miles was fast asleep and snoring. He stood and gazed down at his father for a few minutes; felt for the pulse at his temple. It was a little fast but quite strong and steady. He pulled the eiderdown up round his father's shoulders and went out, closing the door quietly after him. The rest would do him good and besides there would be things to see to tomorrow.

Downstairs Bertha was also asleep, lying on the chaise-longue and making small bubbly noises through her rather thin lips. Tom pondered what to do, then went to the telephone in the hall and rang his deputy in Borden and asked if he minded taking over for another day or so.

'Of course not,' his colleague replied. 'And please offer my most sincere condolences to your stepmother.'

Tom went in search of a pot of tea in the kitchen. Goodness knows what state Bertha might be in when she awoke.

Chapter Twenty-eight

Merry was tidying up after morning surgery when she saw the news article in the *Chronicle*. Dr Macready liked her to do the cleaning in the surgery rather than leave it to Maisie, who was all right, and was good at cleaning but he still wasn't sure she understood about asepsis or things being surgically clean or simply clean. And she had a habit of polishing everything in sight.

'Of course I don't mind doing it, Doctor,' Merry had said when he mentioned it to her. 'I'll do anything at all, anything you think I should.'

So she was putting the things on his desk straight when she happened to glance at the article in the newspaper he had been reading while he drank the cup of tea she always made for him when surgery was over and before he started his rounds.

The article was on the front page which was enough to attract Merry's attention. The headline was: 'Accident at Winnipeg Colliery. Owner dead and local mine agent injured.'

Most pit accidents where only one man was killed usually rated little more than a few lines in the local paper but of course this was an owner, a gentleman, not an ordinary miner.

What she read next made Merry sit down hurriedly in Dr Macready's chair.

Mr Frederick Porritt, the well-known businessman and mine owner, was tragically killed on Sunday morning while he and his son-in-law, Mr Miles Gallagher were down Winnipeg Colliery on an inspection tour. Mr Gallagher was slightly hurt when a roof support sagged and there was a slight fall of stone. Unfortunately his father-in-law was killed outright. Mr Porritt leaves a daughter but no other issue. Mr Gallagher is the mine agent for Arthur Bolton and Company, the ironworks in Middlesbrough. Both men were very experienced in mine-working.

Unfortunately, it was a public holiday and the mine was not working. However there was a group of safety men working nearby and they reached the injured man and brought both to bank.

Ben couldn't have had anything to do with it. It was crazy to even think it. How would he have got down Winnipeg pit anyway? And it was Miles's father-in-law who had been killed, not Miles. She was being silly, thinking such wild thoughts, she told herself. Ben wasn't like that, he had been a gentle child. No, it was wicked of her even to think such a thing.

Merry got to her feet and cast a last look around the surgery before going upstairs to her own flat. Benjamin was lying on the clippie mat on the living-room floor, a large pad of paper in front of him, drawing. He was concentrating so hard, the tip of his tongue peeping out from the corner of his mouth, that he didn't even hear her come in. She looked down to see what he was drawing and he glanced up quickly before putting a protective arm around his work.

'Don't look,' he said. 'It's not finished yet. I don't want you to see it until it's finished.'

'All right, all right,' Merry said. 'How about a cup of cocoa? It'll warm you up.'

'I'm not cold,' Benjamin replied and watched her until

she walked away towards the kitchen. She had meat already stewed for a pie and she began to make pastry, including some extra so there would be enough for Ben if he came. Surely he would come tonight. She needed to see him, to reassure herself that he had had nothing to do with the accident even though common sense told her he couldn't have.

She spooned meat into the oven dish before inserting an upside down eggcup in the centre of the dish, then she covered it with a thick layer of shortcrust pastry. The oven at the side of the range was hot and she slipped the pie inside to cook.

She worked automatically, slicing apples for an apple pie, peeling turnips and potatoes to go with the meat pie and putting them on to boil; meanwhile her thoughts were busy elsewhere – not with her brother or her son but with Tom. It wasn't often she allowed herself to think about Tom. Long ago she had decided it was a waste of time yearning for him. He simply must not want her; what had happened between them should not have happened. He must have regretted it almost at once, otherwise why hadn't he got in touch with her? He didn't want her, she just wasn't good enough for him. Well, she had managed without him all these years.

Still, whenever she did think of him there was a place inside her that seemed to melt. Suppose he had lost his father in the Winnipeg mine and suppose Ben had had a hand in it. Merry was horrified at the turn her thoughts had taken. It hadn't happened and it wouldn't happen either. Ben was not like that no matter how much he hated Miles Gallagher for what he had done. She would tell him what had happened, or perhaps he already knew.

Merry put the apple pie on the oven shelf above the meat pie and closed the oven door. She picked up the poker and poked the fire closer to the vent that sent hot air round the oven, and raked more coal onto the fire.

'Is the dinner ready yet? Mrs Macready is taking me out

239

to the dam head; she's going to show me how to sketch the water. She said half-past one and I can't be late, Mam.' Benjamin put his head round the kitchen door and Merry was so lost in her own thoughts she jumped.

'Lay the table then, it'll be ready in twenty minutes,' she replied. It was Mrs Macready this and Mrs Macready that, she thought grumpily. Sometimes it felt as though the boy was no longer her own. But the doctor and his wife had been so good to them that Merry felt a twinge of guilt at even thinking such a jealous thought.

'Why are you in such a hurry?' Merry asked Benjamin. He was spooning his meal into his mouth so hastily he couldn't possibly be chewing it properly.

'I told you, Mam, me and Kirsty are going out to the dam head.'

'Mrs Macready and I,' Merry corrected him. 'Anyway, she'll wait for you, I'm sure.' But Benjamin had finished his dinner. He drank his milk and looked expectantly at his mother for permission to go.

'Go on then, have a good time,' she said. 'Behave yourself, mind.'

That afternoon Merry was busy in the surgery making up bottles of cough mixture from the large demi-john which had just been delivered. She would have liked to have gone to Old Pit to see if Ben was there but she had to man the telephone for Dr Macready. Her thoughts went from Ben to Tom and from Tom to Ben; vague unformed worries about them both dimming her normally good spirits.

It was midnight when she heard the rattle of gravel against her window and hurried down to let Ben in. She was filled to overflowing with questions but first she put the pie in the oven for him and made tea from the kettle that was simmering on the hob.

He stretched his feet out on the fender and sighed. 'By, it's good to be here, our Merry,' he said. She had brought up Dr Macready's discarded *Auckland Chronicle* and now

240

she handed it to him, pointing out the article about the mine accident.

'Mr Gallagher was lucky,' he observed after having read it. 'A shame about the other fellow though.'

Merry gazed at him as he seemed to know already about it and her anxiety deepened. He frowned as he saw her expression.

'What?'

'Did you know about it? Was it anything to do with you?'

The meat pie in the oven was beginning to smell deliciously and he sniffed the air. 'By, I'm starving,' he said. 'Is it ready?'

Merry took a cloth from the line and lifted the pie from the oven to the table. She said nothing.

Ben sat down and began to eat. It was very quiet in the room, and Merry became very aware of the ticking of the wall clock. Ben finished his meal, picked up his pot of tea and took a long swallow.

'Well?' Merry asked.

'Well what? Do you think I found a way to sneak down Winnipeg pit and tamper with a pit prop or something? Did you?'

'No, no, I'm sorry, of course not.' Put like that it did sound ridiculous, she thought.

'Mind, if I had done it I would have made sure it was bloody Miles Gallagher that was under the stone, not the poor old gaffer.'

'Ben, you wouldn't.'

Ben laughed, a hard bitter laugh. 'I dreamed about it often enough – never think I haven't. I thought about it most in the early days when I was slaving in the heat and dust of that hell in South Africa. I plotted and planned what I would do if I ever got the chance, but that was when I was only a lad. Now, I don't think he's worth making myself a murderer for. No, no indeed.'

Ben drank from his pot, swallowing until it was empty

241

before putting it back on the table by his empty plate.

'That was grand,' he said by way of thanks and went back to his seat by the fire. He stared into the glowing embers for a few minutes, lost in thought. Merry cleared the table in case Benjamin should get up in the morning and wonder who had been in, then sat down opposite him. It was getting on for a quarter to one and she had to be up early in the morning to open the surgery, but she still didn't want Ben to go. She had things to tell him first and she had to get it over with, although it was Ben who started talking first.

'I worried about you, Merry,' he said. 'But when I could write I didn't know where to write to and besides, I was always afraid Miles Gallagher would do something to you. So what could I do? Then later there was the war an' all, but I never forgot you and I took the first chance I got.'

'It's all right, Ben. I was all right.'

Ben gazed at her. 'What about your husband, Merry? I found out who it was but I don't know what happened, why you split up.'

Merry bit her lip. 'He's a violent man, Ben. I should never have married him. But there was the bairn, I was carrying a bairn.' She looked down at her hands, twisting on her lap and blushed. What would he think of her?'

'I should have been here,' said Ben.

'Well, you couldn't help that,' said Merry. She rose to her feet and began to pace up and down the room as she tried to think of the best way of telling him the rest. It was no good, she would just have to come out with it, she thought.

'Ben, there's more. Robbie wasn't altogether to blame. The bairn wasn't his.'

'Did someone take you down? I'll kill the bastard—'

'No, no, it wasn't like that,' she cried.

'Who was it?'

'It was a doctor. I loved him. He was good to me when I worked at the workhouse hospital.'

'Who?' Ben was shouting now.

'Sssh! Don't wake the lad,' she begged. 'It was Tom Gallagher, Ben.'

'Why didn't he marry you?'

Merry shook her head dumbly.

'You weren't good enough for him, was that it? Wait a minute, who did you say? Tom *Gallagher*?'

'He's a good man, Ben,' Merry said but Ben wasn't listening. 'Tom bloody Gallagher? That man's son?' he persisted.

Merry nodded. 'I was still at Old Pit, Ben. I had hurt ankle and there was a snowstorm—'

'Mam? Mam?' Benjamin interrupted her attempt at an explanation of what had happened. He came in in his night-shirt, rubbing the sleep from his eyes. When he saw the angry-looking man standing over his mother he ran to her and turned to face Ben, scowling.

'Don't you hit my mam!' he shouted. 'Don't you dare!'

Merry put her arms round him. 'He's not going to hit me, pet,' she said. 'It's all right.' The boy was trembling and she realised it must have brought back memories of the violent rages his stepfather used to get into, especially when he had been drinking. She tried to soothe him but he stepped away from her and confronted Ben.

'You're a nasty man!' he shouted at him.

Ben was staring at the boy, his fair hair tousled and his cheeks red, his eyes bright blue. 'Dear God,' he said, 'he looks just like the Gallaghers.'

'He doesn't, he looks like you,' said Merry, her voice rising. Ben looked at her holding on to the boy but he was resisting, trying to pull away.

Ben sighed and squatted on his haunches so that his face was in line with Benjamin's. Benjamin's lip quivered but he stood his ground.

'Don't you hit me neither!' he shouted.

'I'm not going to hit you or your mother, Benjamin,' he said and his voice had changed, become gentle. 'We were just having an argument, that's all. I love your mother. She is my sister. Do you know what that makes me, Benjamin?'

Benjamin was still glaring at him but gradually he relaxed, beginning to recognise that there was no threat to his mother or him.

'My uncle. But you're not my uncle, I haven't got an uncle.'

'Yes you have Benjamin. You have me,' said Ben. 'You were called after me, do you see?'

'Where've you been then?' asked the boy. 'Where were you?'

'Ah, that's a long story I'll have to tell you another time. Now I have to go,' his uncle replied. 'I'll tell you all about it another time.'

Chapter Twenty-nine

It was an afternoon in March when Merry met Tom again and the unexpectedness of it took her breath away. For a minute she couldn't think of anything except the pleasure that ran through her as she gazed up at him.

'Merry,' he said and stopped in front of her as Benjamin, standing beside her, looked from his mother to the strange man and back again, his brow knitting. For the minute Tom had eyes for no one but the boy's mother.

'Hello, Doctor Gallagher,' said Merry.

They were outside the Co-op Store in Newgate Street and Merry was about to go in. He looks just the same, she thought, he hasn't changed at all. Oh God, why had he left her, forgotten about her? He took off his hat and his light blonde hair waved back from the sides of his head in just the way Benjamin's did. His eyes were as vivid a blue, his lips ... Benjamin! She moved slightly in a daft attempt to hide Benjamin from him. He looked more like Tom than Ben, she thought in a panic.

'Mam? Mam? I thought we were going for my new trousers for school,' Benjamin said and as Tom looked down at him his eyes widened. It was plain to see what was racing through his mind.

'He takes after my brother,' Merry said quickly. Tom said nothing to this, but looked from Merry to the boy.

'Does he indeed?' Tom smiled and transferred his

attention to the boy. 'What's your name, lad?' he asked him.

'Benjamin Wright.'

'Well, Benjamin, would you like to go in to the teashop? They sell good cakes there and your mother and I need to talk.'

'Yes please,' Benjamin breathed, his eyes lighting up. He loved eating in cafes and he didn't often get the chance to.

'Emm, we haven't got time,' Merry demurred weakly. She felt as though she was being drawn along with no will of her own. 'I have messages to get and then—'

'Mam!' cried Benjamin.

'We needn't be too long, Merry,' said Tom and held open the door for them. Benjamin raced through and Merry had to follow.

They walked through the haberdashery department to the teashop. Being Saturday afternoon the place was crowded, yet somehow within a minute or two Tom had them installed at a table in an alcove away from the main floor and a waitress was hovering to take their order.

'Tea and cakes, please,' said Tom. When she had gone he turned to Merry. 'Is he mine?' he asked baldly. Benjamin was watching the bustle around him, happy and wide eyed as if it was Christmas all over again. Though she glanced quickly at him she didn't think he had heard the direct question.

'Why would you want to know now after all this time?' she asked. The old hurt when he had walked away and forgotten her still smarted; in fact it swelled within her now.

'Of course I want to know,' said Tom shortly. 'If he is, I want to know the answers to some more questions too. Why didn't you tell me?' His voice was beginning to rise and Benjamin looked from him to his mother, his happy grin slipping slightly.

'Sssh, you're worrying him,' Merry cautioned. Tom

glanced at the boy and smiled, though it obviously took some effort.

'Here's the waitress coming with a plate of cakes,' he said. 'You can have first choice, Benjamin.'

'Can I? Really?' The waitress put the cakes down on the table together with the tray of tea and Benjamin deliberated over them, all his attention now on what to choose. In the end he picked a large meringue with cream and angelica pieces and was soon absorbed in savouring every mouthful.

Merry poured the tea and handed a cup to Tom. He watched her broodingly as she offered the cakes.

'No thanks,' he said in a more normal tone. 'Are you going to answer my question?'

'Yes.'

'Yes what? You're going to answer or yes, he is mine?'

'Benjamin takes after my brother, I told you.'

'Oh yes? But that wasn't my question was it? You don't think he looks just a little bit like me?'

'A bit, but he also looks like my brother Ben,' she insisted stubbornly. She picked up her teaspoon and put a spoonful of sugar in her tea.

'Merry?'

'All right, he looks like you,' Merry said in an angry whisper. 'Yes, he is yours.' She was defeated.

'And you never thought to tell me?'

'Do you think I didn't try? I couldn't find you to tell you! You disappeared, so I thought you were keeping out of my way. I thought you were ashamed, you—'

'Ashamed? Ashamed of what?'

'Of me, I wasn't good enough for you. You didn't want to know. I went to your house and I saw your father but he told me to be off. What was I to think?'

Tom bit his lip as he studied her expression. He could see there was anger there and hurt too. He thought back to the time just after the big snowstorm that winter. Not that he could remember a lot about it after the time with Merry

247

and how sweet it had been despite the conditions. The time after that, the time he had struggled to get back to Winton Colliery and tell the men about her injury was like the memory of a nightmare – there were great gaps in it. And afterwards he could just remember sitting in the trap with the snow driving in his face, but no more. He had been ill for such a long time too.

'I was ill,' he said now. 'I had pneumonia. My father should not have sent you away.' Anger against his father was rising in him.

'Well, of course he would,' said Merry. 'I was from a pit family, wasn't I? Destitute, a down and out. He didn't want me dirtying his drive, did he?' She could not help the bitterness showing in her voice. Oh yes, she had been badly hurt and Tom's heart ached for her.

He glanced quickly at the boy but he was eating a chunk of meringue, a moustache of cream on his upper lip. He was taking no notice of the strange doctor and his mam, having decided that the man posed no threat.

'It wouldn't be like that,' he said lamely but he knew it would. That was exactly how his father thought about the pit folk, with contempt. 'I'm sorry, Merry. I'm sorry you were hurt. Oh, what a mess we've made of everything!'

Merry stared at the cooling tea in her cup. There were so many questions left unanswered and yet just at this minute she couldn't think of one of them.

'I have to go,' she murmured, for suddenly it felt very stuffy in the teashop and anyway Benjamin had finished his cake and glass of milk and was getting restless.

'Come for a walk,' said Tom. 'Come down the park or along by the river to the dam head. The fresh air will be good for Benjamin.' He had the feeling that if he let her go now he might not see her again, or at least not for years.

'I can't. We have to buy trousers and shirts for Benjamin. That's why we are here.'

'Oh Mam, I want to go to the park,' the boy cried.

'We haven't time, you know I have to be back to answer the telephone,' she replied.

'I will come with you then,' Tom put in quickly. 'I haven't to be back in Durham until tonight. You can do your shopping and then I'll take you home. I have the car and I'll drive you.'

Benjamin's face lit up. 'You've got a motor? Can I sit next to you? Please?'

'We have return tickets on the horse bus,' said Merry.

'Mam!' Benjamin looked shocked that she could deny him a ride in a real motor car. Dr Macready just had a horse and trap, and Mrs Macready a governess cart and an ancient pony.

Tom smiled; he knew by the weakening expression on Merry's face that he had won. He paid the bill at the desk and they went up the stairs to the drapery department. All the time Benjamin chatted, even when he was being fitted for trousers for his new school.

'I'm going to the Friends' School at Great Ayton next term,' he said proudly. 'I'm going a term early, aren't I, Mam? I've got a scholarship.'

'The Friends' School, eh? Gosh, you must be very clever,' said Tom, sounding awed and Benjamin grinned happily.

'He wouldn't have been able to go if it hadn't been for Dr Macready,' said Merry. 'Well, actually it was Mrs Macready who showed me how to go about it. She says he is very clever and will be a talented artist one day if he works hard.' Merry still couldn't believe it was happening. Not so long ago it would have been unthinkable for Benjamin to go to such a school – even if he had a scholarship she would never have been able to afford the uniform. However the Macreadys had offered to help out and how could she refuse when it was such a good chance for the boy? But Merry said none of this to Tom.

After they had finished the shopping Tom led the way out

to where the Wolsey was parked. He was full of questions he needed answers to, the most important to his mind being the one concerning her husband.

'Where do you live now?' he asked as he picked up the starting handle ready to crank up the engine. 'Eden Hope, isn't it?'

'No, just outside Winton Colliery. We live in the flat above Dr Macready's surgery. I work for him, as a nurse really. I help him in the surgery.'

Tom had to ask whether the boy was there or not. 'What about your husband? You married Robert Wright, didn't you?'

Merry glanced swiftly at Benjamin but he was so absorbed in looking at everything about the car that he was taking no interest in what the grown-ups were saying.

'I left him,' she said tersely. 'And I don't want to talk about it as it upsets him.' She nodded at Benjamin.

'All right, we won't,' said Tom, his tone bright and conversational. He turned to the boy and began to explain and demonstrate to him how he used the handle to start the engine; Benjamin listened with his head on one side. He explained how the brake worked and the hand lever that changed the gears; Benjamin kept very quiet, taking everything in.

Eventually they drove down Newgate Street and on to Durham Road. When Tom said it was important to go slowly and as quietly as possible past any horses on the road for fear of alarming them, Benjamin nodded sagely.

'I *was* ill, you know,' said Tom as though he thought she wouldn't believe him. They had left the town and were bowling along the country road which led to the village. 'I wasn't myself for weeks. Then when I recovered and looked for you I discovered you were married.'

Merry closed her eyes for a moment in anguish. If only she had known, if only she had waited. All she and Benjamin had gone through could have been avoided if

250

she had had the courage to have him on her own. But she hadn't and she had paid the price all right.

Benjamin was sitting there in his father's car if he but knew it, delirious with pride and happiness at the unexpected treat. And he looked so like Tom that everyone would know when they were seen together. After all, it was years since Ben had been seen around here, so no one would think the boy took after him. This should have rung warning bells in her mind as they were approaching Winton Colliery, but it didn't for she was in such a bemused state of mind herself. Despite the fact that Benjamin was sitting between them there was something there, connecting them. Something warm and heady and electric and it was clouding her brain. She had to hold it at bay, so she turned and stared out at the passing countryside.

They drove past the end of the rows and up the gentle incline beyond the pit yard. There were few people about anyway though unluckily the horse bus from Eden Hope passed them just beyond the colliery and everyone on it stared out of the windows at the motor car and its occupants.

Doris Wright and Annie Suggett were sitting halfway down the bus and they both turned and watched the car as it chugged along.

'Did you see that?' gasped Doris.

'I did,' Annie replied.

'Not the car,' said Doris. 'That was Merry and her by-blow with Dr Gallagher! You remember, he was doctor at Winton before Dr Macready.'

'Yes, I know,' said Annie.

'Aye, but did you see how like he is to that lad of hers?' demanded Doris. 'Do you know, I thought he looked familiar somehow.'

Meanwhile, Tom was drawing up in front of Dr Macready's house. 'We have a lot to talk about, Merry,' he said. 'I want to know everything that has happened.'

251

'Well, you should have come sooner!' It burst out of her as she fumbled with the door catch, unable to open it.

Tom got out, walked round to her side and opened it for her and the boy to alight. 'Your mother and I have to talk,' he said to Benjamin who was hovering round the car, unwilling to leave it.

'I have to man the telephone,' said Merry.

'Then may I come in?'

Benjamin had run off around the back of the surgery to see if Kirsty was in, bursting to tell her about his ride in the motor car. Reluctantly Merry allowed Tom to carry her parcels and led the way up the stairs to her flat. He dumped the parcels on the table and came to her and she took a step back.

'Listen, Merry, I can explain everything,' he said. 'I did come looking for you when I was well enough but you were gone from Old Pit. And then I found out you were living at Eden Hope, and had married Robbie Wright. What could I do? I moved to—' He was interrupted by the telephone ringing.

'I have to answer that,' said Merry and went out to the landing where the telephone extension from the surgery was. Tom could hear her talking in a low voice and fumed impatiently.

'I have to tell Dr Macready, there's an urgent callout. I'm sorry but you'll have to go.'

'But—' Tom began but she was already turning for the stairs and so he hurried after her.

'All right,' he said. 'I have to go too as I must get back to my practice. But I'll be back, I promise you I'll be back, first chance I get.'

'Will you?' said Merry and it was not a question.

'I will.'

She watched as he cranked the motor and climbed in. Then she turned and went to the house to call Dr Macready. For all her bitterness she knew there was still

a powerful attraction between them – she couldn't bear
the thought of all the heartache if he were to let her
down.

Chapter Thirty

'Why don't you give in your notice to Arthur Bolton?'
Bertha demanded. They had been sitting at breakfast in
what had been her father's house and was now hers. The
coroner's verdict upon her father had been accidental death
and he had been buried the day before. In the afternoon his
will had been read and, as expected he had left everything
to his daughter with the proviso that Miles should have
control of the mine.

'Notice? Why on earth should I give notice?'

Miles looked up from his perusal of *The Times* with an
expression of astonishment, though in fact he had been
expecting it.

'Because we have this place now,' said Bertha with
uncharacteristic patience. 'Why should we live over by
Winton when we have this lovely house here?'

'You can keep on this house anyway.'

'Miles, what is the point in keeping two houses?'

Miles folded his paper and put it on the table. 'I don't want
to discuss this now. I have to go to Eden Hope as I have business with the manager. After that I have an appointment in
Durham City. If it gets too late in the day I will stay at
Tom's.' He paused for a moment and considered his wife.
She was pale, the only colour on her face was the tip of her
bright red nose. 'Besides, it is too soon to come to any decisions – you are still overwrought my dear,' he added.

254

Bertha erupted. 'We'll talk about it now! This is my house and I won't be told to shut up, do you hear me?'

'I should think they could hear you in the kitchen,' said Miles. He rose to his feet and walked to the door. 'I'll send Rose in to you. I told you that you were overwrought.'

Bertha, even more infuriated, was left shouting after him but he wasn't in the mood to listen.

'I'll take the trap, John,' he said to the stableman. 'The mistress might want the carriage.'

'Yes sir.'

John, who had been Mr Porritt's stableman, backed the pony between the shafts and saw to the traces. There was something about Miles he didn't like – he had been too eager to take over from the master in John's opinion.

Mr Porritt might have been an old man but he had been a working mine owner for a lot of years and before that he had been fond of telling folk that he had started down the pit as a boy of six. The miners John met in the Pit Laddie tavern in the village had shaken their heads when they heard of the accident. Of course accidents happened – they were acts of God or the result of carelessness – but there had been something not right about that one.

Old Porritt was well able to read the coal face, aye, and listen to it to, at least as well as any of the old men who had spent their lives underground. And he would be very aware of outworn pit props.

> Jowl, jowl and listen lad
> And hear the coal face working.

One of the aged miners had quoted from the rhyme that every pitman learned as a young lad.

Still, when did coroners take notice of the likes of pitmen? John thought about it as he watched Miles drive out of the gates and take the road to Bishop Auckland. But there was nothing he or the miners could do anyway, no

255

matter what they thought. Even so, Miles Gallagher should have looked out for the old man, at least.

Miles took the train to Durham, leaving his pony and trap in the station stables at Auckland. He was quite happy and confident for his master plan was going well so far, the worst part already over. Now he felt he had earned himself some relaxation. He left the train at Durham and took a cab to Silver Street. Once there he walked the rest of the way to his destination, which was down one of the streets leading down from the other side of the market place – a small house with nothing about its outward appearance to show what it was.

His discreet knock was answered almost immediately and he was drawn inside by a maid in white cap and apron who dropped a quick curtsey.

'Good afternoon, sir,' she said as she closed the door after him. 'Who do you wish me to call?'

'Er, Lysette, I think,' he replied.

It was almost five o'clock when Miles emerged from the house and walked back towards the market place. Ben was sitting in a teashop close by the town hall waiting patiently. He had been shadowing Miles since he had returned to the country and by now he had worked out some sort of pattern. Miles strolled along over the cobbles and passed by on the opposite side of the statue of Lord Londonderry that stood in the centre of the wide square. Ben took the opportunity to throw a florin on the table for the startled waitress and slip out behind a couple of housewives and their children.

Miles was oblivious to Ben's presence as he hailed a cab from the rank before the town hall but Ben heard him call up to the driver, 'Borden Colliery.'

Ben nodded to himself. He had already established that Borden Colliery was where Tom Gallagher lived, the same Tom Gallagher who had shamed his sister. Merry swore he

256

was not a bad man, not like his father, but then she was a woman and obviously still had a soft spot for Tom in spite of the fact that he had deserted her. That was another score he had to settle with the Gallaghers' but for the time being it would have to wait until the main job was finished.

Ben paused for a moment considering his next move and then strode off towards Jennings and Co., an estate agents in Elvet.

'I am interested in buying a house somewhere in the Neville's Cross area,' he told the young man who came forward to meet him.

It showed how different he looked compared to when he had been living rough in the deserted village, that the young man gave him his undivided attention. Ben was dressed in an impeccable singlebreasted suit with cutaway coat and narrow trousers that was the epitome of the well-dressed gentleman in 1903.

He made appointments to view a number of properties in the coming week before returning to his motor car, which was parked in the yard of Elvet railway station, a small station on the outskirts of the city. He drove back as far as Coundon, only a mile or two from Winton and Bishop Auckland, where he had rented a room in a back street lodging house that catered for working men. It was bare of comforts but he at least had a room to himself and it was clean. Above all, the woman who ran it was totally uninterested in what her lodgers did or did not do so long as they paid their rent every Friday.

Once in his room, Ben changed into clothes more suited to a workman. He took a file from under his mattress and sat down at the window as he reviewed what he had gleaned that day. After a moment or two he took a pencil from his waistcoat pocket and began writing. Half an hour later the file was up to date and he read it through before closing it and replacing it under his mattress.

'I must go to see Merry tonight,' he murmured to himself. He ran his fingers through his hair before rising to

257

his feet and taking a bottle and glass from the clothes cupboard in the corner. He poured himself a tot and took it back to the window where he sipped the single malt in appreciation. Sometimes in this shabby, bare, little room, he missed the little luxuries he had become used to over the last year or two. But this style of living wouldn't last much longer now, he thought, not if things worked out as he had planned.

'Ben! I wasn't expecting you tonight,' said Merry. She closed the door quickly after him and led the way into the cosy sitting room. 'Are you hungry? I have some panack-elty left from our supper, or I could cook bacon and eggs if you liked?'

'No, I'm not hungry, thanks Merry. I had something in Coundon.' In fact he had eaten pie and peas in The Durham Ox and the food was lying heavily on his stomach. 'A touch of bicarbonate of soda would be welcome though,' he went on, smiling ruefully.

Merry mixed him a teaspoonful with a little water and he drank it in one gulp. Taking the glass from him she asked, 'Are you all right? You shouldn't be living as you do, really you shouldn't.'

'I'm not.'

Ben explained about his lodging in Coundon. 'I won't be there long either. I have decided to take a house in Durham City, and have been to the estate agents today. A house in Neville's Cross, I think. And I want you to move in with me, Merry, you and the boy.'

'Durham City? How can you do that? Afford it, I mean?' Merry was dumbfounded.

'I'm not destitute, Merry,' said Ben. 'In fact I am what you might call quite well off after my time in South Africa.'

'But, how?'

'It's a long story, pet. The fact is, though, I have enough to buy a decent house in the city, and enough left over to live on and keep you and the lad an' all.'

258

For all there was a faint foreign intonation to his speech, Ben still spoke in the idiom of the north-east of England, and Merry found it endearing. But leave here and go to Durham, live off her brother? She felt she couldn't do that.

'It's good of you to ask me and I'm truly grateful,' she said.

'Of course you can, there's no reason why you can't,' Ben argued. 'Go on, tell me a good reason.'

'I'm all right here,' Merry replied. 'I like it. And Dr Macready and Kirsty have been good to me; I couldn't let them down. And there's Benjamin – I can't move him yet again. He's set on going to the Friends' School and he loves Kirsty too. I know he'll only see her at the weekends but still—'

'But the boy can go to Durham School – it's a good school too. He'll have a good chance there. Merry, all the time I've been away I've dreamt of coming home and us being together as we used to be, looking out for one another. Merry, you have no reason really or the reasons you have don't matter much.'

Merry thought of the small grave in the cemetery at Eden Hope and knew she wasn't yet ready to abandon it. And besides, she told herself, here she was independent, she was useful to Dr Macready and was learning a lot about being his assistant, which was almost as good as being a nurse.

'They matter to me, Ben,' she said.

'Merry, listen to me, I want you and the bairn with me. I'm worried for you. Miles Gallagher has something against us both, I'm sure he has—'

He was interrupted by the opening of the sitting-room door. Neither of them had heard anyone coming up the stairs but a second later Dr Macready walked in. He looked from Ben to Merry and back again before speaking.

'What's going on? Who is this man, Merry?'

Dr Macready was standing there dressed but in his carpet slippers and looked very angry indeed. Merry stared at

259

him, colour staining her cheeks almost as though he had caught her entertaining a lover. As she hesitated Ben stepped forward and held out his hand.

'I'm so sorry we disturbed you, Doctor,' he said. 'I am Merry's brother and I'm very glad to meet you.'

Dr Macready looked at him sceptically. 'Her brother? I didn't know she had a brother.'

Merry found her voice. 'Well I have, Dr Macready. I didn't mention him before because I thought he was ... dead. Doctor, this is my brother Benjamin. I named the boy after him. Ben, this is Dr Macready, my employer.'

Dr Macready studied the face of the man before him and, evidently satisfied, shook his hand. 'How do you do?' he said formally. 'Now I look at you I can see who you are. Not that you look so much like Merry but the boy seems to take after you, in colouring at least.' He still looked a little puzzled though. Both Merry's brother and son reminded him of someone else, the brother in particular. He just couldn't put a name to whom it was though it hovered in the back of his mind. It would come back to him of course, he told himself, for he prided himself on his good memory.

'Well, Merry, it's nice to know you have some family. I always thought you and the boy were on your own,' he said.

'My brother has been in South Africa. I thought he was dead,' she replied.

'Well, that's great that he isn't. Look, it's very late, I'll go now and leave you in peace.' He turned to Ben. 'I'm sure we will meet again. I would love to hear about your travels.'

'I will look forward to it, Doctor,' said Ben as Dr Macready nodded and went back down the stairs.

'Damn,' said Ben. 'I didn't want anyone to know I was here. It might get back to Miles Gallagher. I didn't want to put you in any danger.'

'But surely I'm not,' said Merry, looking surprised.

Ben gave her an exasperated look. 'For goodness sake, Merry, haven't I told you it's dangerous for you?'

'But Miles Gallagher hasn't threatened me before. If he wanted to he could easily have found out where I am. I think you're worrying too much, Ben.'

'I'm not, believe me, I'm not.'

'Well,' said Merry. 'I don't think Dr Macready is a friend of Miles Gallagher. In fact I wouldn't be surprised if he even knows him.'

Ben had sat down beside the dying fire but now he got to his feet. 'I'm not going to argue now, Merry. It's time we were both in bed. But I'm not giving up on this either. I'll away now and let you get to bed.'

Chapter Thirty-one

Tom closed the surgery door after the last patient and breathed a sigh of relief. He picked up the pile of notes on his desk, took them over to the filing cabinet and began to file them away. Normally his assistant, an ex-miner who had been injured in an accident ten years ago and now had a limp, did the job for him but tonight being Friday, Walter was out collecting the panel pence in the rows. Walter had been a deputy and a safety-man and was proving to be very useful in the surgery, being trained as a St John Ambulance man.

Tom put the last file in place and banged the drawer shut, before sitting down behind his desk and leaning back in his chair for a rare moment of relaxation. As always his thoughts turned to Merry and the boy.

He would confront his father, he decided. He had not been through to Winnipeg Colliery since he learned about Benjamin – there just hadn't been the time to spare. Diphtheria had returned to the village, though thankfully not as virulent as the year before; still, it had been a busy few weeks. His father had been through to see him but unfortunately he had been out on a case, a difficult and protracted birth and Miles had gone by the time he got home.

He thought about his father, biting his lip and sighing as he did so. Miles was one of those men who thought that all a pitman was good for was to dig coal and their families little more than ignorant savages. Tom could quite see him sending Merry away and not even mentioning the incident but all the same, it filled him with rage.

He sighed again and got to his feet. He had arranged for a locum this weekend coming and he was determined to go to Winton and see Merry and his son, combining the visit with one to his father. It was well past the time he should be taking over responsibility for the boy, and his mother too. He bitterly regretted the years he had missed but the thought of seeing them gave him a pleasurable glow of anticipation as he went through to the house for supper.

Afterwards he telephoned his father at Canny Hill, the company house Tom had been raised in, to tell him he would be over at the weekend.

'Will you be at Winnipeg Colliery or Canny Hill?' he asked.

'Canny Hill,' Miles said tersely.

'Well, I thought Bertha might have managed to change your mind and got you to move in to her house, at least at weekends. I know she tries hard enough.'

'She won't succeed. You know it is one of the conditions of my employment by Bolton and Co. The agent must live in the company's house or at least make it his main residence.'

'I thought you might have decided to give the position up. After all—'

'Why should I?' Miles exploded. 'I can perfectly well see to my own colliery and see to the company's. After all, I have good managers. I like my position with Bolton's. It suits me.'

'You're not getting any younger,' Tom reminded him.

'For God's sake, if you have nothing of interest to say get off the telephone!' Miles said and Tom wisely did as he was told. His father sounded as though he might just have an apoplectic fit, he thought. He must check him over when

263

he went to Bishop Auckland – before he demanded to know why he had sent Merry away.

It was Friday evening when Merry was shocked awake by a commotion beneath her window. Her first thought was that Ben had come but of course it couldn't be him – since Dr Macready had met him he didn't need to use stealth, though he was still careful that as few people as possible knew he was about. She put a match to the gas mantle, which was set in the wall above the fireplace in her bedroom, and saw by the clock on the mantelpiece that it was only ten-thirty. She must have been asleep for less than half an hour.

The racket below the window got louder, the banging and shouting loud on the night air. Merry went to the window and opened it, poking her head out cautiously.

'Aye, I knew you were in there somewhere!'

Her heart sank as her fears were confirmed – it was Robbie and he was with a young girl she recognised as the youngest of Jim Hawthorne's daughters, Bessie, named after her mother. The girl was rolling about, unable to stand up but for the fact that she was hanging on to Robbie's arm.

'Bessie! What are you doing? You've been drinking!' Merry gazed at the girl in horror, for she was barely seventeen. Bessie grinned back, her mouth hanging open, her shirtwaist grubby and with a wet stain that gleamed darkly in the moonlight.

Bessie laughed and staggered against Robbie who put an arm round her waist. 'I'm going to marry your man,' she said. At least that was what Merry thought she said, though her words were slurred together.

'Bessie, you can't, you're just a bairn, get away home to your mam,' Merry replied. 'She must be looking for you.' Mrs Hawthorne was a decent, chapel-going woman, who must be frantic that Bessie was out so late, especially if she knew she was with an older man such as Robbie Wright.

'Never you mind, you slut!' Robbie shouted. 'It's none of your business, any road. I've come to tell you I'm going to divorce you. I'm going to marry Bessie, aren't I, pet?' He moved his hand from the girl's waist to cover her breast and she squirmed.

'Take the lass home, Robbie, go on,' Merry implored. 'Her dad will be mad, her brothers an' all; they'll come after you.'

'You don't think I'm frightened of Jim Hawthorne, do you? Nor his bloody sons. Let them come, me an' Bessie are going to get wed. I've promised her.'

Merry could imagine why. She hesitated – any minute now Dr Macready would hear the commotion and would come to find out what was causing it, and she didn't want that.

'Go home, take the lass, go on,' she urged again.

'An' you go to hell,' Robbie said calmly and laughed. 'Don't think I don't know what you're up to neither. I can easy get a divorce after I tell the judge what me mam told me. You riding about in a posh carriage with that sod of a doctor, son of the mining agent, for God's sake. Talk about selling your own folk out! An' me mam says that bastard of yours is the spit of him an' all. I reckon you were carrying on with him all the time you were living wi' me. Oh, aye, I'll have no trouble getting a divorce.'

'Please yourself what you do,' said Merry. 'Just get away from this house, will you? Have the decency to take Bessie home to her mam, man!'

'Don't you tell me what to do or I'll come up there and show you what for, aye an' your brat an' all,' Robbie shouted. He stepped forward, shrugging off the girl who staggered and fell into the bushes at the side of the path. She turned on her front and managed to get onto her hands and knees before vomiting on a cotoneaster bush. The stink of stale stout rose in the air, making Merry gag even at the height of her bedroom window.

'What's going on there?'

Merry closed her fists and gritted her teeth – they had woken Dr Macready just as she had dreaded they would. This was the second time he had been wakened up and he wouldn't stand for it, she knew he wouldn't; she and the bairn would have to go.

'Just go, Robbie, please. Take Bessie back to her mam, can you not see the lass isn't feeling well, man?'

Robbie turned and looked at the young girl who was just clambering to her feet. He shook his head. 'She can't hold her beer, that's the trouble with her,' he said. But he too had heard Dr Macready and he wasn't keen to meet up with him. He was sober enough by now to know it might mean a night in the cells if the doctor called the bobbies.

'Aye well, I'll go,' he said. 'I've said what I came to say. Mind my words, I'm lying idle come Monday an' I'm off to see the lawyers. I will get me divorce, see if I don't. Me mam told us it was a big mistake getting wed to you and by heck she was right.' He nodded his head a few times as he went over to Bessie and took her by the arm. 'By God, you stink summat awful for a young lass,' he said. 'Howay, then, babby, let's away.'

Dr Macready had come around the corner just as Robbie turned away. 'Just a minute,' he said with cold authority and Robbie halted. 'If I catch you on my property again I will call the law. Is that clear?'

'Yes, Doctor,' Robbie mumbled.

'Now take that child home and if I hear of anything happening to her I will know who is to blame. Do you understand me?'

'Yes, Doctor.'

The doctor watched the pair until they were out into the road, then turned and looked up at Merry. 'Just a moment, Merry,' he said. 'I'm coming up.'

She threw a large shawl round her shoulders and crossed it over her breasts before going into the sitting room. Was he going to tell her to go, she wondered, her heart beating

266

fast – he had every right after being disturbed twice like this. Doctors were disturbed often enough in the middle of the night by their patients so needed their sleep when they could get it.

'They didn't wake the boy?' Dr Macready asked when he came in, and Merry shook her head. 'Just as well,' he said as he went over to the fireplace and stood before the almost dead fire. 'Merry, something will have to be done. I won't have these disturbances going on.'

'I know, Doctor. I'm sorry. He's drunk. He wants a divorce.'

'Hmm. I suppose he needs a bit of Dutch courage to come and tell you. Well, let him have it, you will be well shot of him. But you might have to suffer a bit, you know. Have your name in the *Auckland Chronicle* and maybe even the *Northern Echo*. There's bound to be some notoriety. It's the boy I'm thinking of. Perhaps you should let him go to the Friends' School earlier than we thought.'

Almost on cue, Benjamin appeared in the doorway of the sitting room. Tears were streaming down his face yet he hadn't made a sound until now.

'That was *him*, wasn't it?' he cried. 'Mam, we haven't got to go back and live with him, have we?' The boy was shaking with terror. Merry held out her arms to him and he ran to her. His nightshirt was soaked with urine, she realised; it was the first time for ages.

'No, lad, we'll never go back to him. Don't worry, pet, everything will be all right, you'll see. Howay, son, I'll get you changed and back to bed,' she said and carried him through to his little bedroom. It didn't take her long to settle him and when she came back into the living room Dr Macready was still there standing before the fire.

'He soon settled down,' she said. 'Doctor, if you want us to go—'

'What? No of course I don't. But this is not doing the lad any good, is it?' asked the doctor.

267

'I don't think it'll happen again; I'm sure it won't. Robbie doesn't come round here usually. It was just he had a skinful.'

'Well, if Benjamin was over at Great Ayton—'

'My brother wants him to go to Durham School,' said Merry. The doctor looked astounded.

'Durham? But he has a scholarship to the Friends' School!'

'I know. But Ben is buying a house in Durham.'

'You're not leaving us, are you, Merry? Do you want to go? Kirsty will be very sorry to hear that and so would I.'

The doctor looked agitated as he took a few steps towards the window then back. Merry gazed at him. He and his wife had been so good to her and Benjamin it seemed like gross ingratitude to go against them. But these last few days she had been thinking of what Ben had said and was undecided about what to do. Sometimes though, she did have the feeling that the Macreadys were taking over and wanting to make decisions for her and Benjamin almost as though the boy belonged to them. To be honest, she thought, she didn't know what she wanted to do – one moment she was worried that the doctor would want her to go and was filled with anxiety, and the next she was toying with the idea of going to Durham.

Durham, near to where Tom lived and worked. The thought of it enticed her.

'Merry?'

She shook her head. 'No not really. I've been very happy here and so has the lad. You have been so good to us, both you and Mrs Macready and I love my job an' all. And even if we did go, we would always keep in touch with you both. You mean such a lot to us.'

If the doctor noticed the ambiguity of her answer he didn't comment on it. 'Well, Merry, I had better go back to bed before my wife comes looking for me,' he said and walked to the door. 'I don't think you'll hear any more from Robbie Wright, not tonight at any rate. If you did I would get the police without the slightest hesitation and he knows it.'

'Goodnight, Doctor and thank you,' said Merry and her thanks were heartfelt. She didn't know what she would have done without him, even tonight. She knew she would have had trouble getting rid of Robbie and young Bessie if the doctor hadn't come out.

She locked the door after him and went through to check on Benjamin. He was lying with one hand under his cheek, his eyelashes still wet, but he was sleeping peacefully enough.

These few months they had had with the Macreadys had been the happiest in his young life, she thought. In fact he had been transformed from a nervous youngster who had cowered behind her skirts, terrified of Robbie, to a self-confident little boy who was blooming more every day, intelligent and talented; self-confident enough to look forward to going away to boarding school, though he would be home for the weekends. It was a future she would never have hoped to be able to give him.

Merry pulled the bedclothes up over his shoulder and tucked them in. She dropped a kiss on his forehead and tiptoed out of the room. As she lay down in her own bed the thought of Tom came to her as she pictured him clearly in her mind's eye. And her heart ached for him.

She turned over restlessly in bed as her thoughts reverted to Robbie. Divorce was practically unheard of in the rows and she knew she would be in for a lot of stick if he managed to get one. He would say she hadn't told him Benjamin wasn't his, and would bring Tom into it too. Oh, she could imagine the lies he would tell – she would be the talk of the place, she was well aware of that. But if Benjamin was away at school it wouldn't affect him much. Or if they were living in Durham. No, the scandal would affect Tom, and she couldn't allow that. But how was she to stop it? That vindictive woman, Doris Wright, would tell everyone Tom was Benjamin's father and there would be a big scandal.

She had to stop thinking about it, Merry told herself. She was so tired, she needed her sleep. Everything looked worse at night-time, so Gran used to say. And she was right.

Chapter Thirty-two

Tom parked the Wolsey on the drive of the agent's house at Canney Hill and got out. It was a bright morning and he had decided to come here first to see his father before going on to Dr Macready's place in Winton. Dr Macready would have a Saturday morning surgery and no doubt both he and Merry would be busy there. It was only just gone ten o'clock as he paused and looked around him – at the house where he grew up, the sweep of the drive around the side of it to the stables and, as he turned and looked out over the valley, the view from the front of the house.

It was beautiful despite the fact that there was smoke from colliery stacks in two or three places, curling up into the blue of the sky. But from this height, even the slag heaps were distant and not out of place against the burgeoning green of the surrounding farms and woods. To the right, on the facing hill, lay the town, running along the ridge high over the Wear.

Tom smiled to himself, at the feeling of coming home, even though he lived only a few miles away. He was determined that before the weekend was over he would have matters resolved with Merry – she had said he was Benjamin's father, hadn't she? He felt a pleasurable thrill of anticipation at the thought of seeing her again. Everything would work out fine – he knew it would. But first he had to have a serious talk with his father and this time he wanted the truth about everything that had happened.

'Mr Gallagher is in the study, sir,' Polly said formally. 'Will I tell him you're here?'

'No, it's all right, you get on, Polly,' Tom replied and crossed the hall to the study door, opening and closing it behind him. Miles was sitting at his desk with a pile of papers in front of him. For a man in his sixties he was still erect, strong and alert, still ambitious.

'Tom!' he cried. 'It's good to see you, son.' He rose to his feet and walked forward a couple of steps, his bad temper on the telephone apparently forgotten, but his welcoming smile slipped away when he saw Tom's expression. 'What have I done now?' he asked.

Tom jumped straight in. 'Why did you not tell me Merry Trent was expecting my baby?'

'What? I don't know what you're talking about, Tom. I don't even know anyone called Trent.' Even as he said it the memory came to him of the broken-down old cottage in the deserted village of Jane Pit and the woman and little girl living there.

'Of course you do. You turned her away when she came looking for me, didn't you?'

'I told you—'

'Don't bother. I know you're lying.'

Miles shrugged. 'Oh, what the hell! So a miner's brat who'd got herself into trouble came crying to me saying it was you. I sent her away, of course I did. Of course she wanted to claim the father was someone better than those ruffians she had probably been with. Anyway, I had my hands full with you, in bed with pneumonia and likely to die. I couldn't be bothered with the lass, why should I? Even if you had been there it doesn't mean it was you, it could have been any number—'

'Shut your dirty mouth,' said Tom. 'I know the child is mine. I know Merry too – she was nursing at Oaklands when I was there. She is *not* promiscuous. And I intend to take responsibility for him. I will marry her and adopt the boy legally, that is if she'll have me. And there is not a thing you can do about it.'

'Tom! Think what you're about; you can't possibly know he's yours.'

'Have you seen him?'

'Seen him? Of course I haven't damn well seen him.'

'If you did you would know he was mine. There is a strong family likeness.'

'I don't care who he looks like, she can't prove a thing. Don't be a bloody fool, Tom!'

Tom walked to the door but before opening it he turned and gazed at his father. 'I'm going now. I don't want to hear another word from you. I will never forget you turned her away as you did. If it weren't for you we—'

Whatever Tom had been going to say he changed his mind abruptly and went out, ignoring Polly who was hovering in the hall and banging the front door behind him. Polly lost no time in running to the kitchen to regale the other servants with what she had heard from behind the closed door of the study.

'Aye well,' said Edna, nodding her head as though she had known all along, 'that lad didn't look like a Wright. I said so, didn't I, Cook?'

'It's none of our business. Now, howay, get on with your work instead of gossiping.'

Miles did not try to stop Tom from leaving, but sat down at his desk and stared unseeingly at the papers he had been studying before his son had interrupted him. He had other pressing things to see to, never mind Tom. He would come to his senses; he wasn't the type to hold a grudge and he was bound to see that it wouldn't do, anyway. The boy was too much like his mother; that was his problem. Soft he was, soft as clarts.

He tried to concentrate on the papers before him. They were records of the amount of coal won from the collieries belonging to Arthur Bolton and Co in the past month. Production at Eden Hope was up, so the ironworks would

273

not miss the amounts he intended to divert, he thought. He could easily falsify the documentation, but now was not the time – Tom had spoiled his concentration and he would need all of that to do what he intended to do. There could be no mistakes.

Miles sat back in his chair. The boy bore a strong family likeness, he had said. Just as that other boy had. It was a bloody nuisance that it should come out so strongly, especially the colouring, the silvery-fair hair.

Memories were crowding in on him, memories of that other boy. He could have been a full brother to Tom by the look of him, Miles reckoned. He was a fool for not putting an end to the brat instead of sending him to the colonies on that immigrant ship, but it had seemed a good idea at the time. The newspapers had been full of certain charities helping the boys to a new chance in life. The likelihood of him being able to return was practically nil. And yet, Miles could have sworn he had seen him or at least someone very like him, and not once but two or three times.

Not that he cared now if Bertha found out he had an illegitimate son, even one by a pitman's widow. She would do nothing about it, she couldn't. Even Tom couldn't say much; after all, he was in much the same position. But the lad himself, what would he do? He could create a hell of a fuss and spoil Miles's standing in the town altogether.

Miles sat back and threw his pen down on the desk. 'I'm becoming fanciful,' he said aloud. Of course it couldn't be the lad back from the colonies he had seen either of those times he thought he had done. It was just his imagination. He was getting fanciful in his old age. He rose to his feet and strode to the door.

'I'm going over to Winnipeg Colliery,' he said to Polly who was back in the hall polishing the bottom of the banister rail. 'Tell Cook I won't be in to dinner.' I might as well, he thought as he rode out of the drive on Marcus. The visit from Tom he had so looked forward to hadn't lasted five minutes, and Tom had been angry, talked to him as if

274

he was a small boy. He might as well go and see Bertha, keep her sweet. It wouldn't do for her to become suspicious when he hadn't yet worked out properly how to rid himself of her.

Tom parked the car before the surgery and went in. The waiting room was empty for surgery was finished and Merry was filing the patients' notes away in the cabinet in the corner. Dr Macready was sitting behind his desk writing a letter but he jumped to his feet when Tom knocked and walked in.

'Tom!' he cried. Merry dropped the notes she had in her hand and they spread across the linoleum by the filing cabinet.

'Good morning, Ian,' said Tom and they shook hands over the desk. 'I have been visiting my father so I thought I would call in to see you.' He smiled at Dr Macready but his eyes strayed to Merry who was kneeling in the corner picking up papers. She kept her head bent over to hide her flushed face but he could see the papers shake a little as she held them.

'Good morning, Merry,' he said softly.

'Hello, Doctor,' she replied as she stood up and turned to face him.

'You two know each other?' asked Dr Macready.

'We worked together at Oaklands,' said Tom. 'How are you, Nurse?'

'Well, thank you, Doctor,' said Merry and almost managed to keep the tremor out of her voice. She opened a filing drawer and leafed through the contents, barely seeing what they were.

Dr Macready looked from her to Tom. Tom was talking about the diphtheria epidemic, which, thankfully had not reached Winton this year and had not been quite so bad as last year at Borden.

'It's still too soon to relax though,' said Dr Macready. He was about to launch into an account of what he had told

275

the Council and Board of Health regarding the need for a proper sewerage system in the mining villages. 'Most have no provision at all,' he was saying when he realised that Tom was only half listening. His voice trailed into silence for a moment.

He'd been a bit dim, he thought, not to say slow. Things were beginning to click into place now, though, for there was something here he should have noticed much earlier. He looked again at Merry who was still leaning over the filing, though it should have been finished in a couple of minutes. Her face was hidden from him but he could see her agitation in the tremble of her fingers.

'Well, look, I'll leave you two to get re-acquainted,' he said. 'You don't mind, do you, Tom? Only I have things to do in the house. Do call in before you go, won't you? Kirsty would be sorry to miss you.'

'Yes of course,' Tom replied. He wrenched his eyes away from Merry to smile at his colleague.

'Yes. Well, I'll see what Kirsty and Benjamin are up to,' said Dr Macready as he moved towards the door at the back of the surgery that connected with the main house. He shook his head as he walked along the short corridor. It's a tangle and no mistake, he thought. And he must have been blind not to see the resemblance between Benjamin and Tom. But there had been Merry's brother – it was confusing to say the least. And then the girl was still married to that lout, Robbie Wright. He sighed. It was time it was all sorted out, he reckoned. Just as well her husband was after a divorce. The sooner the better, he would say.

There was a short silence in the surgery after the door closed behind Dr Macready. In the end it was broken by Tom.

'Aren't you glad to see me, Merry?'

'I thought you would have come to see me before now – I haven't heard from you since that day we met in Auckland. Not even a note, never mind a letter.'

276

Merry could hear the complaining in her voice – she hadn't meant to do that, it just came out. She stopped talking. Tom reached her in a couple of strides and put a finger under her chin, lifting it to look straight into her eyes. He had to get things straight between them, he had to.

'Aren't you glad to see me, Merry?' he asked again, softly.

Merry nodded her head slowly, hesitantly. Her thoughts were in turmoil. She had thought she was gaining control of them but his presence here, so close to her was making her forget all her resolve. Oh God, all she wanted, all she had ever wanted was bound up in him. She struggled to think of her son. He would be expecting her.

'Benjamin—'

'The Macreadys will see to him and keep him with them in the house, I think. Can we go upstairs?'

She led the way up to her flat and went into the kitchen where she checked the water in the kettle and put it on to boil. Anything to keep her hands busy and stop their trembling. As she turned round she found he had come up close behind her and his arms were around her.

'Well?'

She nodded. How could she deny it? He bent his head and as he kissed her his hunger grew. Both of them were carried away on the same surge of feeling. He lifted her up and carried her to the bedroom, even managing to kick the door shut before they were overwhelmed. The feel of his hands on her body, on her breasts, brought an even higher response and she was lost in it.

Later – she didn't know how much later – it was the telephone which brought them back to an awareness of the present. It rang once and then after a moment or so again, a longer peal this time. It was not the operator, she realised, but the connection with the house.

Merry moved away from Tom and climbed out of bed, pulling a dress over her nakedness before going through to answer. Tom turned on his back and smiled. It was as though Dr Macready would be able to see her lack of clothes down the line.

Dr Macready was saying that he and Kirsty would take Benjamin to visit his new school, if that was all right with her. 'I take it you won't be too disappointed to miss the outing? You still have Tom there? Well, tell him we'll see him some other time. I know you have a lot to talk about.'

Chapter Thirty-three

Ben Trent walked down the path which led through the field to the old, deserted village. He was dressed as a gentleman in a fine grey worsted suit and top hat. His jacket was single breasted with six buttons and the trousers were narrow above soft leather boots polished to a mirror shine. He swung a cane in his right hand, slashing automatically at the odd clump of nettles alongside the path.

'Hu-up! Hu-up!' The soft call of the farmer as he herded cows for milking caught his attention. 'Cush up!' the farmer called and the first cow trotted through the open gap from the field on Ben's right, soon followed by others. Then Vince Parkin appeared, waving his stick. Ben halted and waited for the cows to cross the path and turn of their own accord for the farm buildings further up.

'Now then,' said Vince, nodding his head in greeting and added 'sir,' as he took in the stranger's dress.

'Good afternoon, Mr Parkin,' Ben replied and slipped into the old greeting, 'Wot cheor?'

The farmer paused in his stride and stared hard. His mouth was already framing the question when he moved closer, incredulous.

'It's not, is it? Nay lad, you cannot be! Not Ben Trent? After all these years. We thought you were dead, man!'

Ben nodded and held out his hand. 'Yes, it's me, Mr Parkin. I'm back from the other side of the world.' They shook hands vigorously, both grinning broadly. 'By lad, I'm that pleased to see you,' Vince said. 'An' the wife will be an' all. Are you coming in to see her then?'

He was dying to ask a thousand questions about Ben's disappearance, why he'd gone, why he had deserted Merry, why ... but it was no good, the cows were crowding around the gate to the farmyard, lowing their complaints.

'Look, I have to see to the milking but will you call back at the farm? Are you going down to look at the old village?'

'I am, just for old time's sake. And I'll be pleased to call in. You were both so good to me when I was a lad.'

The farmer nodded and went on up the field after his cows while Ben walked on down to the stile and along by the old line to the double row of houses. It was astonishing to him that it looked the same as it had all those years ago. Well, perhaps there were more wild flowers and dead grass in amongst the stones and dust of the road, and more doors hanging drunkenly from their hinges. But there was still glass in some of the windows and still a drip from the stand pump on the end of the row near to the house where he and Merry had grown up. The sun was shining through between the trees on the bankside and the water sparkled as a beam hit it. He went inside his grandmother's house and up the ladder to the bedroom to where the few belongings he had left here were in a bundle in the corner. There was no reason for him to hide here at all now, for he was going to confront Miles Gallagher that very evening. But still Ben lingered. He walked to the window and looked out over the old road to the houses opposite, and felt a nostalgic sadness for the old days, hard though they had been.

Ben picked up his bundle after a few minutes and went out onto the road, closing the door after him. On impulse he went to the edge of the village, to the remains of Jane Pit, which were still visible. The wooden cap that had covered the shaft was rotten and there were only two walls still showing of the building beside it. The memorial was

280

across the road, almost invisible in the long, dank grass. He crossed over to it.

The stone was well weathered, the writing almost illegible. In fact the date of the disaster was illegible because someone, children perhaps, had scratched at it. But it had been like that when he was a boy here, he thought to himself. Thoughts of the old days were crowding in on him. He had worked in the gardens, done odd jobs for Mr Parkin, anything to turn a penny. He had worked no harder than Gran or Merry and yet they had barely scraped a living.

He was walking up the field to the farm when he finally admitted to himself that the woman he had thought his gran must have been his mother and it was a strong possibility that Miles Gallagher was his father. These last few weeks, even months, he had had the opportunity to watch both Miles Gallagher and his son Tom, and there was no escaping the fact that he bore a strong likeness to them both – to Tom in particular, but Tom was not so much older than he was himself.

Ben had discovered the true date of the disaster at Jane Pit from the Durham Miners' Union archives in Durham. He did not want to believe the conclusion the facts led him to but there was no escaping it. Could Farmer Parkin confirm some at least of this?

'Nay lad, I don't know anything about it,' Vince said as they sat drinking tea in the large farm kitchen. 'It's true, I saw the mine agent about the place a lot a few years ago but I mind my own business, like.' He did too, thought Ben. Vince never said anything about anyone, though he must have been surprised when he saw Gran with a baby. If he did, that is, for Vince and his wife rarely left the farm.

'Have some teacake,' she said now. 'I made it this morning, so it's nice and fresh.'

Ben was little further forward as he said his goodbyes and left the farm. He walked back to the stile that led to the lane where he had left his motor car and was soon driving

281

along to Canney Hill to visit Miles Gallagher. Or to confront him was more the term he should use. Bitterness welled up in him when he thought of the man who had treated him so badly, who had taken him away from Merry and who had almost killed him.

His palms were sweating as he parked his car on the road and walked up the drive, his heart pounding. 'I won't attack him,' he said softly to himself. 'He's my father.' He said it but he didn't believe it, not really. He paused for a moment at the foot of the steps before going up to the door and ringing the bell. After a minute the door was opened by a woman who was pulling on a pair of shabby gloves.

'Yes?' She asked before realising it was a gentleman and adding, 'sir?'

'I wish to see Mr Gallagher,' said Ben. He marvelled at how steady his voice was. But now the time had come to actually meet Gallagher he had steadied, his pulse slowed.

'I'm sorry, he's away to Winnipeg Colliery,' said Polly, for that was who the woman was. She had answered the summons to the front door dressed in her coat and hat for she was all ready to walk down to Winton Colliery to see her family, this being her afternoon off.

'Oh,' said Ben. He felt let down after he had been so keyed up. 'Thank you.' He turned away and walked back down the drive. He would just have to go to Winnipeg.

He drove into the town and along Etherley Lane to Newtoncap Bank. The road plunged steeply here and he had to drive very carefully to reach the fourteenth-century bridge that spanned the Wear at the bottom, then he was chugging up the other side. The 18 horse-power engine of the Napier took the steep hill beautifully and soon he was driving along to the Porritt house on a small rise outside the colliery village. Ben parked the car before the house and walked boldly up to the front door, grasping his cane firmly in his hand. By this time he was in complete control of himself. He rapped on the door with his cane, the sound reverberating inside and outside the house.

282

There was no answer though Ben could hear voices inside – a woman shouting hysterically, a man's lower range reply. But the voices were retreating; in a moment there was silence from inside. He waited a moment or two then went back down the steps and around the side of the house to the stables at the back. He was not about to give up now as he was determined to confront Miles Gallagher today and strode out purposefully, but came to a sudden halt at the scene outside the stables.

'You! Get off the place this minute or I'll have the law on you,' Miles shouted. For a moment Ben thought the order was meant for him but it wasn't, he realised, when he saw Miles had his back to him and was shouting at the stableman. John did not move. He had his arm around his mistress, supporting her. She had evidently suffered a fall for she was half fainting and her face was grazed and bruised. John held her up tenderly, ignoring Miles for the minute.

'Go and fetch the doctor,' he said to the manservant Albert, who was standing with the hysterical housemaid. She was wringing her hands and sobbing loudly, her mouth open slackly and the dribble joining the tears running down her face and chin.

'You do anything of the sort and you are dismissed as well as him,' Miles shouted grimly.

Bertha suddenly raised her head. 'You tried to kill me!' she screamed, gaining energy from her fury. 'You did! You did! Get the police, John, he'll pay for this, I swear he'll pay! Go on, I'm all right.'

Miles was beyond reason now, all his plans unravelling. Why had that interfering old pitman turned up just as he had knocked Bertha to the ground? Any other woman would have been killed outright – he'd given her a blow that would have felled an ox. Wasn't it supposed to be John's day off anyway? Well, he wouldn't let the old pitman frustrate his plans, he would be damned if he did.

'Hell's bells!' he shouted at Bertha. 'You ugly old witch!

283

Why didn't you die?' He went on and on, pouring out vitriol with Bertha paling at the viciousness of it.

'Watch your mouth,' said John, his voice low and menacing. For all his age he lifted Bertha in his arms, which were still hardened by his years at the coal face, and started towards the house. 'Howay, missus,' he said quietly, 'you need a lie down, pet.' Looking over his shoulder he shouted again to Albert who was dithering by the side of the maid.

'Hadaway and fetch the doctor and the polis when I tell you to!' The man scuttled off.

Miles suddenly went quiet. He was not going to wait here and have the police take hold of him, indeed he was not. He'd see all of them in hell first. No, he thought, his mind racing, he would get to the police first, tell them his stableman had gone stark staring mad. They would believe him before they believed an hysterical woman such as Bertha and the anarchic peasants who worked for him.

He rushed into the stable and came out leading his horse, Marcus II, which John had been saddling when the ruckus started. The ageing stallion was rolling his eyes and trembling, obviously upset by the shouting, but Miles jumped on his back and dug his heels in. It was then he saw Ben.

Ben had been standing at the corner of the house but now he stepped out in an effort to catch hold of the reins and stop the horse, but Miles pulled at the reins, yanking viciously at them, trying to get past. The poor horse whinnied in panic and reared so that Miles, his feet not even properly in the stirrups yet, flew off. He fell heavily against the brick corner of the house and slid to the ground, his eyes wide open and staring at Ben with an expression of horror and shock.

Ben had not had time to seize the reins and nor did he now, for Marcus was off, galloping round the house, down the drive and out on to the road. Ben was left gazing down at the man he had hated so long, the man he now knew to be his father. But Miles was quite dead, his head against the

284

bricks and a red stain slowly appearing on his collar. His head suddenly fell to one side and Ben jumped as Bertha began to scream.

It was a couple of hours before Ben managed to get away from Winnipeg Colliery. The village policeman had come with Albert leading Marcus. The horse was docile now and Albert led him round the opposite corner of the house and into the stable to avoid the body of his master.

Surprisingly, Bertha calmed down and gave the policeman an account of what had happened. 'My husband was angry, Officer,' she said. 'And his horse was startled when this gentleman appeared. Not that it was any fault of his. It was an accident.' John nodded his agreement with his mistress's story.

'What was your business here, sir?' asked the policeman.

'I lost my way, Officer,' said Ben, 'and called in to ask directions to Canney Hill. I am a visitor from South Africa.'

There were more questions and he had to wait until a more senior police officer came from the town, but after all it was an accident, an unfortunate accident.

Chapter Thirty-four

Tom and Merry had the precious afternoon to themselves and their love-making was urgent and all consuming. The ecstasy of Merry's feelings as she felt his hands on her breasts was almost too much to bear. Every nerve in her body responded to his touch after being so long denied. She had dreamed of this so many times since they were parted. And when it was over they lay together in each other's arms, drowsy and replete. She fell asleep and awoke in the same position, his arms around her, holding her almost as if he thought she might disappear.

Merry turned her head to gaze at him, his face smooth in sleep, his lips turned up slightly at the corners in a half smile. Oh, but he was so dear to her; waves of love swept over her. How could she have been away from him for so long? She marvelled at herself.

Tom opened his eyes and his arms tightened about her as he kissed her on the shoulder, the nape of her neck, her lips.

'I love you, Merry,' he whispered. 'I will never let you go again.' He echoed the very thoughts running through her own head.

They lay for a while, filled with contentment and satisfaction, and then Tom turned onto his back.

'We need to talk,' he said. So now, in the fulfilment of their love, they were talking as they had never talked together before.

'I have spoken to my father,' said Tom. They were sitting up against the pillows, he with his arm around her, Merry leaning on his shoulder.

'I'm so sorry you had to go through it all,' he went on. 'My father had no right to turn you away.'

Merry turned her head away, thinking of the time with Robbie Wright, the way Benjamin's early years had been so full of fear of his stepfather. She should not have put him through that; she was guilty too, she thought. All because she had been frightened of what the folk of the villages would say if she had a baby out of wedlock. Why hadn't she made more effort to get in touch with Tom? If only she had been stronger; if only she had trusted him more; if only she had taken her baby and left Robbie sooner – so many 'if onlys'.

'I don't want to make excuses for him. It's the way he is and nothing would change him in any case,' Tom was saying. 'I don't think he will ever alter his opinions.' He raised himself on his elbow and leaned over her with a serious expression. 'But we won't have to have much to do with him – we can go away. We don't even have to wait until you're free. This is the twentieth century and we need not stick to Victorian ideas.'

Tom paused, remembering the desolation he had felt when he discovered she had married Robbie Wright. He had had a need to get away from Winton and Eden Hope for he couldn't bear to see them together so he too had regrets but it was no good dwelling on them. 'The future is what matters,' he said.

'Yes,' said Merry. 'The past is over. So long as the three of us are together.' It was true, she realised. She didn't care what difficulties they had to face in the days to come; they would manage to get through them. But what would Benny think about having Tom as a father? She suddenly sat up straight.

'Benjamin! He's going to be home soon. I must get dressed. You too. He can't catch us like this.'

'Well, maybe he'll have to get used to it,' Tom said, smiling lazily, but he got out of bed and started to dress. They didn't even have time to straighten the bed when there was a perfunctory knock on the door and it was opened almost at once.

'Merry? Merry, are you there?'

Her brother Ben pushed open the bedroom door and pulled up short as he saw them both. The excited flush faded from his face as his glance took in the unmade bed and their state of undress.

'I'll wait in the other room,' he said stiffly and went out, closing the door after him. His thoughts were in a whirl as he tried to cope with yet another shock. When Merry, followed by Tom, came out he was standing by the window.

'As soon as Merry gets her divorce we will be married,' said Tom. 'I mean to do right by your sister.' Ben stood silently, watching him and then turned to Merry.

'He is my half-brother, for God's sake, and you are my sister, or as good as. You must realise that now, Merry so why?'

'I love him, Ben,' she said simply. 'Besides, I am not your sister, I am your niece. *You* know that. There is no reason—'

'But he has already let you down once when he left you on your own with a bairn on the way!' he cried.

'It wasn't his fault, he was ill, it was a mix-up, his father—' Her voice faltered, it was so hard to explain.

'In spite of what his father did to me.'

'Tom is not like his father,' Merry protested as Tom went to stand beside her and took her hand.

'What are you talking about, man?' he demanded. He had listened to the two of them and some of what they said made little sense to him.

Ben turned to the looking glass hanging over the fire-place. 'Come and stand here beside me,' he said to Tom who, after a glance at Merry, did so.

288

'We could almost have been twins, don't you think? But for the age difference, that is,' asked Ben, trying hard to keep the bitterness out of his voice. 'You are my half-brother, Tom. Your father raped my mother. And when he realised I was the result your father tried to hide the fact by sending me to a hell on the other side of the earth.' Ben marvelled at himself – he felt so in control that the rage, the search for vengeance were gone. Well, of course they were, he thought, Miles Gallagher was gone and he was free of him. Looking at Tom's image, he realised that indeed Tom was not like his father – he looked what he was, a kind, caring sort of man. Merry might just be all right with him. But oh, it would take a lot of getting used to.

'What can I say? I knew nothing of any of this,' said Tom. But his logical mind had already worked out an important fact. 'I am not related to Merry, am I? That is the important thing.'

'No, that's true.' Ben bit his lip as he looked at Tom. 'There's something else,' he said.

'Nothing is going to part us now,' Merry warned, coming forward and taking hold of Tom's arm. 'Don't try, Ben.'

'I'm not going to.' He glanced away for a moment, marshalling his thoughts. In all that had happened since, Ben had not yet told Tom of his father's death. Now it had to be said and the only way was to state the facts plainly.

'I have been to Winnipeg Colliery, Tom. I have to tell you that your father is dead. It was an accident.'

'What?'

Tom and Merry spoke together. Her grip tightened on his arm. 'Ben! You didn't—' She stopped as fear filled her.

'No, Merry, I didn't do it. It was an accident, as I said.' Ben told them what had happened as Tom led Merry to the sofa and sat down with her, their hands tightly clasped.

'I will have to go there straight away,' said Tom when he had finished. 'I don't understand how it happened, my father was still a competent rider.' He was silent for a minute or two. 'But if he had been rowing with Bertha – I know he had a terrible temper and he wasn't getting any younger.' He stopped and Ben realised he was just taking the news in and it was hitting him hard. Of course Tom had feelings for his father despite the man Miles had been.

'Are you all right?' Ben asked.

Tom nodded. 'Yes. It's just the shock, that's all. But I'd best be on my way.' He turned to Merry. 'I'll be back,' he promised her, 'if not tonight then tomorrow. We'll not be parted again.'

Merry watched out of the window as he drove away. As he turned the corner Benjamin came clattering up the stairs from Dr Macready's house.

'Mam? Mam, what's for tea? I'm starving. Oh, Mam, the school is grand, I can't wait to—' he said then saw Ben standing there. 'Uncle Ben!' he cried. 'Are you staying?'

'He's staying for a while,' said Merry. 'Now come into the kitchen and I'll make you a sandwich to put you off, as tea's not ready yet.' She cut bread, buttered it and spread strawberry jam on it; Benjamin sat down at the kitchen table with it and a glass of milk. 'Uncle Ben and I are just having a talk. You can tell me all about your new school when you've finished your sandwich,' she said and went back into the sitting room.

Ben was leaning forward in his chair, staring into the fire. He didn't look up when she went in.

'What are you going to do now, Ben?' Merry asked him.

'I've got a place in Durham now. I'll stay there a while. I think you and Benjamin should come with me. There will be less talk than if you live with Tom after all. Then when your divorce comes through you two can make it all legal, can't you? It will be better for Benjamin too.'

'I don't know,' said Merry. 'I'll talk to Tom. Then there's Benjamin's school and the Macreadys to think about. They have been so good to me.'

'Benjamin can still go to the Friends' School. And the

Macreadys will understand. Of course they will.'

Merry was silent, thinking about it. Of course Ben was right. 'I must go over to see them, Ben, and tell them what has happened. Will you stay with the lad?'

'Of course.'

Later, with Benjamin in bed, Merry, Tom and Ben sat around the fire, Tom and Merry close together on the sofa with their hands clasped, and Ben on the easy chair. The Macreadys had gone back to their own house having come through to hear Ben's account of the happenings of the day for themselves. And Merry had told them she intended to move to Durham.

'We'll miss you both, lass,' said Dr Macready 'But we didn't expect to keep you forever. You have your own life to lead.'

'We'll be back to see you,' said Merry. 'Of course we will.'

Now the couple had gone the little flat was quiet. Tom stared into the flames, his expression sad, and Merry squeezed his hand. He looked down at her and smiled.

'I did think of going back to South Africa when this is all settled. I have business interests there and friends too,' Ben said suddenly and the others looked at him.

'Oh Ben, I don't want to lose you again,' Merry said softly.

'Nor will you,' he replied. 'Now I think I will stay in the county, live the life of a gentleman for a while. I may even take up mining again. There are places over by the coast which show promising surveys. I may do tests, sinkings. Up to now it has been the limestone shelf that has prevented deep mining over there. But with modern ways, the coal can be won. I could build a model village—' He fell silent and stared into the red depths of the fire.

'Whatever you do you will always be a brother to me,' said Merry. They were both thinking of their childhood in the deserted village. It had been hard but there had been

291

some good times too. The bond between them would always be firm as steel.

'I must get back as I have a surgery in the morning,' said Tom, rising to his feet. Merry went with him to the door.

'We won't be parted for long,' he whispered. 'But I can't wait.' He kissed her and gave her a hug before reluctantly going out to his car. Merry watched him go, her heart full of love for him.

A few days later the postman brought the divorce papers which was quite a surprise as she hadn't expected them so soon. She opened them with some trepidation for she wasn't sure what Robbie was saying about her – she was worried he might cite adultery and what would that do to Tom? But no, desertion was what the papers said. Desertion, so it would all be straightforward, a weight lifted from her; she felt she could allow herself to be happy. She spent the rest of the day packing up her own and Benjamin's belongings for the move to Durham – not to Tom's house, not yet, but close, to Ben's where she and Tom could meet as often as his work allowed.

Next day there was a more unpleasant surprise. The *Auckland Chronicle* had got hold of the story and for a few days it was the talk of the district. Divorce was not unheard of in the mining villages but it was sufficiently rare as to provide plenty of gossip and speculation.

Merry surprised herself by how little she cared – the future was beckoning brightly and in a few days she was leaving.

'You will visit us, won't you?' she asked the Macreadys anxiously. 'I can't thank you enough for what you have done for us.'

'Try and keep us away,' said Kirsty as they watched Ben crank the engine before climbing into the driver's seat. They went down the drive and out onto the road.

'We'll come back though, Mam, won't we?' asked Benjamin. 'For visits?' He turned a solemn face to Merry.

We will, pet,' Merry promised. 'Indeed we will.' And his expression brightened.

They drove the fifteen or so miles to where his father was waiting for them. With an arm around both of them, Tom and his little family followed Ben into the house.

'Soon we will be in our own home,' said Tom.

'Yes,' Merry whispered. 'Soon.' Not yet but the day would come. And for now, well, they were together and nothing would part them ever again.